Praise for the New York Times *bestselling*
Wind River Mysteries

WINTER'S CHILD

"[A] vivid voice for the West." —*The Dallas Morning News*

"Coel's work has a maturity that comes from years of honing the writing craft . . . Her characters are not clichés, but real people who are imbued with the richness of their Indian heritage." —*The Denver Post*

"[A] tautly written, compelling mystery, grounded in and sympathetic to the Arapaho culture."
—*The Milwaukee Journal Sentinel*

"Outstanding . . . [A] superior series."
—*Booklist* (starred review)

"Compelling . . . Coel deftly inscribes Arapaho tradition and culture into the Western landscape, portraying both the grace and the squalor of reservation life."
—*Publishers Weekly*

"As always, Coel is excellent in painting a realistic, nonsentimental portrait of the Arapahos."
—*Daily Camera* (Boulder, CO)

"Hard to put down . . . Once again, authentic dialogue combines with historical fact to create an authentic, exciting read."
—*Examiner.com*

"[A] thrilling mystery . . . Enjoyable and intriguing."
—*Open Book Society*

WINTER'S CHILD

M ARGARET C OEL

BERKLEY PRIME CRIME
New York

BERKLEY PRIME CRIME
Published by Berkley
An imprint of Penguin Random House LLC
375 Hudson Street, New York, New York 10014

Copyright © 2016 by Margaret Coel
Penguin Random House supports copyright. Copyright fuels creativity, encourages
diverse voices, promotes free speech, and creates a vibrant culture. Thank you for buying
an authorized edition of this book and for complying with copyright laws by not
reproducing, scanning, or distributing any part of it in any form without permission.
You are supporting writers and allowing Penguin Random House to continue to
publish books for every reader.

BERKLEY is a registered trademark and BERKLEY PRIME CRIME and the B colophon
are trademarks of Penguin Random House LLC.

ISBN: 9780425280331

Berkley Prime Crime hardcover edition / September 2016
Berkley Prime Crime mass-market edition / September 2017

Printed in the United States of America
1 3 5 7 9 10 8 6 4 2

Cover art by Tony Greco & Associates Inc.
Cover design by Lesley Worrell

For my friend and mentor Virginia Sutter, who,
for many years, has guided me in the Arapaho Way.

ACKNOWLEDGMENTS

My heartfelt gratitude to the late Virginia Cole Trenholm, who first told me the story of Elizabeth "Lizzie" Fletcher Broken-horn, and to Jeff Broome, Ph.D., who generously shared with me his extensive research on Lizzie and her family, as well as his enthusiasm for Lizzie's story.

Many thanks to those who shared their expertise and took the time to advise me on various aspects of this novel, and to those who read parts or all of the manuscript and made superb suggestions that brought the story and characters into sharper focus: Karen Gilleland, Carl Schneider, Virginia Sutter, Jim Sutter, Sheila Carrigan, Bev Carrigan, Veronica Reed and, of course, my husband, George Coel.

It wasn't what I expected.
What a surprise
When it came to me.
And then I chose it.

—Margaret Coel

SNOW HAD FALLEN all day, dense cotton fluff that cocooned the brick bungalow in a white world and obscured the small sign: Vicky Holden, Attorney at Law. Now the snow dissolved into a white dusk as Vicky drove through the side streets of Lander, tires thumping over ruts and ridges. The heater kicked into gear, and warm air streamed into the frosty cold that gripped the Ford. She hunched over the steering wheel. She was late.

The monthly meeting of the Fremont County Bar Association would probably end early. Always a speaker, followed by a little socializing, catching up, exchanging gossip, which she suspected was the real purpose of the meetings; but with the blizzard, everyone would be eager to head home.

The call with Jim Peters, Fremont County prosecuting attorney, had lasted longer than she'd anticipated. She had almost given up hope of convincing him to allow her to turn

over her client, Vince White Hawk, to the sheriff at a prearranged time tomorrow. Five o'clock, say. Earlier, Peters had
said. Vince could take it into his head to disappear. She
hadn't argued, just kept insisting. The last thing she wanted
was the police at his mother's house, a SWAT team swarming
the place. Vince would panic and pull out whatever weapons
he had stashed away. Somebody would be shot, probably
Vince, and maybe an innocent bystander. And for what?
Attempted robbery at an ATM? Granted, the woman Vince
had threatened—he had not had a weapon on him, she had
pointed out, and Vince claimed he was only panhandling—
had been scared, thrown her purse at him, and bolted for her
car. Not so scared that she hadn't managed to get Vince's
license number as he tore out of the parking lot. Now he
faced a felony charge.

"Come on," Vicky had pleaded. "You have my word
Vince will turn himself in tomorrow afternoon." In return,
Peters would recommend to the court that Vince be released on bond and sent to rehab. Vince White Hawk needed
rehab.

Finally, a long, weary sigh had come over the line and
the prosecutor had agreed. But—always a warning—if she
failed to deliver, every cop in the county and on the reservation would be on Vince's trail. A hollow feeling had invaded her chest as she hung up. She had to find Vince and
convince him.

She had called Betty White Hawk, Vince's mother. Yes,
he was there, Betty said. Sleeping it off. The woman sounded
beaten down, as if the weight of worrying about her son had
pushed her into the ground.

"Tell him I've worked out an arrangement for him to turn
himself in. He'll be free on bond and sent to rehab. It's his
chance." She tried to disguise any hint of her own worry
that Vince would run. "I'll pick him up tomorrow afternoon."

* * *

NOW VICKY PULLED a slow turn onto Main Street, wishing she hadn't promised Clint Hopkins she'd attend the meeting when he called this afternoon. Clint had a one-man practice in Riverton devoted to family law, DUIs, and minor assaults, similar to her own practice, but Clint specialized in adoptions. If you had a difficult adoption case in Fremont County, Clint was the attorney. She had consulted with him herself on a couple of cases. It had surprised her that *he* wanted her to join him as cocounsel on a case. A complicated case, he'd said, involving an Arapaho couple on the rez.

"Complicated? Most adoptions on the rez tend to be pretty straightforward," she had told him. It wasn't unusual for grandparents, aunts, or uncles to step in and raise children abandoned by alcoholic or drug-addled parents. His request had caused her to draw in her breath, press the receiver against her ear, and concentrate hard.

"Nothing's straightforward about this case," Clint had said, a tight, anxious note in his voice. He hadn't wanted to discuss it on the phone, and they had made an appointment for ten o'clock in the morning. But he wanted her to have his notes before then. He would bring them to the meeting tonight. She would be there, wouldn't she? The whole conversation, with its sense of urgency and secrecy, had left her unsettled.

The vehicles in the parking lot that bordered the Sagebrush Motel and Restaurant looked as if a giant crane had dropped them at random angles. She circled twice before she slid to a stop and waited for a sedan with red beams of light sweeping over the snow to back out. She turned into the vacated space and, wrapping her scarf about her head and clutching her coat, made her way past the parked vehicles to the sidewalk. A narrow path had been cleared, leaving a sheaf of ice littered with blue deicing crystals that popped under her boots. Through the fogged plate glass window, she saw people milling about with bottles of beer and glasses of wine. Her breath floated ahead in the cold air.

Vicky let herself through the heavy front door into the aroma of beer, coffee, and grilled meat that drifted across the restaurant. People moved from group to group, mired in the buzz of conversation and the crack of laughter. No one looked familiar, and yet everyone looked familiar— faces she had seen in court, chatted with at other meetings, nodded to on the street. Other lawyers practicing in Lander or Riverton or in one of the other small towns flung about the county. But not friends, merely acquaintances moving around the same track she was on. She ducked into the coatroom on the right, hung her coat and scarf among the piles of coats already occupying the hooks, and went back into the reception. Nodding and smiling, she worked her way to the table propped under the window and was about to pour herself a glass of sparkling water.

"Allow me." A tall man materialized beside her and took the bottle. He wore a navy blue blazer over a white shirt open at the collar and blue jeans. A silver watchband studded with turquoise flashed beneath his cuff as he twisted off the cap and filled the glass almost to the brim.

"You must be the bartender," she said.

"Nowhere near as important, I'm afraid." He was smiling as he handed her the glass. "Rick Masterson. I would re-member if I had seen you in the audience."

"My apologies for coming late." She recognized the name. Rick Masterson, this evening's speaker. A lawyer from Cheyenne, known across Wyoming, Montana, Idaho, Utah, and Colorado for teaching other lawyers how to seat the most sympathetic juries for whatever case they were trying. "Rules for Reading Jurors" was the title of the speech on the flyer the bar association had e-mailed about the program. He was holding out his hand, and she slipped her hand into his. "I'm Vicky—"

"Holden, Arapaho lawyer. You practice in Lander."

"You know every lawyer in the state?"

"Pretty much in the Rocky Mountain region. It's my job." He was still smiling. "Hang on a moment," he said, backing away. Then he turned and plunged into the crowd.

Vicky sipped at the water and headed into the crowd herself, searching the faces for Clint Hopkins. A few people brushed past on their way toward the coats. The reception was starting to break up. Finally, she spotted the sandy-haired man with the quarter-sized circle of freckled scalp on the crown of his head seated at a table, bent in conversation with two other men. She veered diagonally in his direction.

Clint glanced around, then jumped to his feet with surprising agility for a man in his fifties with the stiff, bow-legged look of a rodeo rider. He had a slim build with narrow shoulders and a long, sun-blotched neck that stretched out of the collar of his plaid shirt. A bolo tie hung down the front. He looked more like a rancher than a lawyer. The weather lines at the edges of his eyes crinkled as he grasped her hand between both of his. "I had about given up."

She found herself apologizing: A conference call that ran late. His hands were rough and strong.

"You're here now." Clint released her and gave a little wave. The vertical worry line between his eyes set him apart from the other lawyers standing about, drinking beer, tossing their heads back in laughter. He lifted a briefcase from the floor and guided her to a corner near the doorway to the motel reception area. She could feel the slight tremble in the hand he placed on her back.

"We can talk over here." He threw a dismissive glance at the crowded room. "I appreciate your willingness to cocounsel," he said, slipping an envelope from inside the briefcase. He held the envelope close for a moment, as if he were reconsidering, then handed it to her.

"I can't make any promises until I know what the case is about." Vicky let her glance run around the room. "This place is filled with lawyers who have handled adoptions. It makes me wonder why you called me."

"This isn't about family members adopting a child whose parents can't raise her." He leaned in close and lowered his voice. "This is about an Arapaho couple and a white child."

Vicky sank against the wall, aware of the roughened plaster snagging her spine. White people wanting to adopt an Arapaho child from the Wind River Reservation—that she understood. A tribal matter. Only if tribal officials allowed the adoption would it proceed. Lawyers for the white people always portrayed them as good—saintly, even—Godfearing folks who would give the Arapaho child every advantage. One day the child would come to forget she was Arapaho, that she had ever been part of something bigger and richer than all the advantages. Or she would begin to wonder who she was, where she had come from, where she belonged.

Clint looked down at the envelope Vicky held in her hand. "Myra and Eldon Little Shield in Ethete. I assume you know them."

Vicky shook her head. Close to twelve thousand people lived on the reservation, nine thousand of them Arapaho. The rest Shoshone. She couldn't know all of them, but outsiders labored under the belief that every Arapaho knew every other Arapaho in the world.

Names were another matter. Names had history; names came trailing their own stories. Shadowed and contoured by people from the past: the old chiefs, the warriors, the medicine men. People had something to live up to, to aspire to, in names. Something glorious and admirable and never forgotten, passed down in stories of the Old Time. She had heard so many stories while sitting cross-legged around the fire in Grandfather's tipi when she was growing up—the tipi was where stories were passed down, not in the small frame house where her grandparents lived—that the people from the Old Time seemed real to her, as if they still walked the earth and might, at any moment, drop in for a visit. Their names were recognizable. If she had run into a couple named Little Shield in New York City, she would know they were Arapaho.

"Little Shield signed the Treaty of Fort Laramie." She lost him with that. She could tell by the distant look in his eyes, as if a snow cloud had passed between them. She pushed on: "An important treaty that made it possible for the people to come to the Wind River Reservation. He was much admired for his foresight."

"You're saying you don't know Eldon Little Shield or his wife."

Vicky shook her head. The crowd was dissipating. Every now and then a blast of cold air funneled into the room as the front door opened. The men Clint had been talking with at the table had left. She had the sense that they were alone, off in the corner.

Clint shifted his gaze to the envelope. "Read the notes. I'll fill you in on the rest tomorrow. I've been dealing with this case exclusively for a couple of weeks. Nothing about it is routine, and I worry about the consequences of pursuing the adoption." He looked up, eyes shining with the anxiety she had sensed during their phone conversation.

"Consequences?"

"You'll understand." He scanned the room. "Looks like the meeting's over. Come on. I'll walk you to your car."

Vicky slid the envelope into her bag as they crossed to the coatroom, where a few coats still clung to the hooks. Clint helped her with hers, then pulled on a dark, bulky jacket while she searched for her scarf. She found it draped under another coat, and she headed toward the entrance, Clint's boots clacking behind her. Through the window, the night was filled with snow.

She was aware of the pressure of Clint's hand on the small of her back, the briefcase swinging in his other hand. Great billowing flakes floated against the black sky and blanketed the trucks and cars in the parking lot. "I'm parked across the street," Clint said. "Where's your car?"

"Vicky!" A man shouted behind them just as she was about to gesture toward the Ford. They stopped in unison, she and Clint, and looked back. Coming through the front door and slamming it behind him was a man in a dark cowboy hat and a sheepskin jacket with the collar pulled up around his ears. She blinked against the snow that splashed her cheeks and eyes. The man started toward them, and through the glow of light in the window she saw that it was Rick Masterson. He held out a package.

She turned to Clint. "Go ahead. I'll see you tomorrow."

He divided his glance between her and the man hurrying through the snow and nodded. Wiping a gloved hand across his face, he turned, stepped off the curb between the dark hulks of parked vehicles and started across the street.

Vicky looked back at Rick Masterson. The package in his hand was the size of a book. "When I got back to give you this, you'd been whisked off into a corner by a very intent Clint Hopkins. I didn't like to interrupt, but I did want to give you this." He held out the brown package, an offering.

Vicky peeled back the bag far enough to read the top line of the title: *Rules for Reading Jurors*. "Thank you." She dusted off flakes of snow and folded the bag back into place. "I'm sure I'll be able to use it."

"Anytime you'd like to get together and talk about . . ." He stopped, lifted his face into the snow a moment as if a miraculous event were taking place around them. "I'd like to see you again. Dinner, lunch, whatever time you might have. I'm in the area consulting for a few days. How about it? You're not involved with anyone at the moment, are you?"

In the way he said it, the way he tilted his head and stared at her, daring her to disagree, she knew he had done his homework. *Check out the background on the juror* would be the first rule in the book.

She gave a little laugh, a brittle sound in the cold, like the spark of a match. "You don't leave anything to chance."

"Not if you want to win the case."

An engine roared behind them, like the sound of a diesel locomotive speeding down track. Vicky swung around, clutching the brown package against her chest. A truck was racing down the street, yellow headlights jumping through the haze of snow. In a blink, as if she had snapped a photo, she took in the entire scene: Clint Hopkins halfway across the street, a dark figure in the falling snow, briefcase in one gloved hand, silhouetted against the white night. The truck bore down, headlights jumping.

"Clint! Look out!" She was running into the street, the sound of her own voice surrounding her, cutting through the roar of the truck. "Clint! Clint!"

She was barely aware of Rick Masterson sprinting ahead, shouting around her. "Clint! Look out!" And the truck still coming, Clint frozen in place, stopped in time by the all-enveloping sound and the sheer incomprehensibility of it. Then he was flying over the hood, bouncing sideways, dropping onto the street like a limp bag of trash as the black truck sped past.

Vicky threw herself toward the dark, motionless figure, the bulky jacket pulled halfway off his shoulders, the plaid shirt ripped open. She was barely aware of Rick Masterson kneeling across from her. "Oh my God," she heard herself saying. "Oh my God."

Other people appeared from nowhere. Out of the parking

lot and the restaurant. Out of the darkened shops up and down the street. Someone shouted: "Did you see that? Ran him down like a dog."

Vicky was fumbling in her bag for her phone when she realized that Rick had his phone out. He shouted: "Ambulance on the way. Don't move him."

Something had changed, and she realized Rick had taken off his sheepskin coat and laid it over Clint. She set the tips of her fingers against Clint's neck. "I can't find a pulse." She sank back onto her heels. "Oh God. There is no pulse."

2

THE POLICE CARS and ambulance screamed in the distance, a wall of sound and a haze of blue and red lights coming through the snow. Clint was staring up at the sky, eyes wide in surprise, and Vicky reached over and closed his eyelids, the way Grandmother had closed the lids of her grandfather, lying inert on the narrow bed, a view of the tipi out in the yard framed in the window. Closed his lids, a sign that he had seen enough. There was nothing more to see.

She felt the pressure of Rick's hand on her arm, helping her to her feet, steadying her, and walking her across the street. "Was he a friend of yours?" he asked. When she didn't reply, he filled in the answer. "I'm sorry."

They stood at the curb and watched the vehicles pull up: three or four more police cars, a coroner's van, a couple SUVs. A growing crowd of officers in bulky blue jackets and plastic bags over their caps, others in parkas with knit caps pulled around their faces. Several officers had fanned out among the spectators, asking questions, jotting down notes on small pads they tried to shelter from the snow.

An officer stopped in front of them. "I saw it happen," Vicky told him before he'd asked. "The truck was waiting down the street. As soon as Clint started to cross, it pulled out and sped toward him."

"Did you get the license?"

"The license?" She heard the brittle sound of disbelief in her voice "It happened so fast. Clint was thrown over the cab. I ran toward him."

"You know the victim?"

"Clint Hopkins. A lawyer from Riverton."

"And you are?"

"Vicky Holden. I practice law here in Lander. We were at a meeting of the county bar association."

"You're saying the driver of the truck deliberately struck the victim?"

"It was deliberate."

The officer filled the small page in his notebook, turned to the next page, and smoothed away the flakes of snow. He fixed his eyes on Rick. "You?"

Rick gave his name and said he had just come out of the restaurant and stopped to talk to Ms. Holden when the accident occurred.

"So you believe it was an accident?"

Vicky felt as if the world had ground to a stop. But it wasn't the world that had stopped, she realized; it was she who had speeded up, shot forward on adrenaline. Is that what the other witnesses were telling the police? An accident? Had no one else seen what she'd seen? Not even the man who had been standing next to her?

She rounded on him. "Clint was murdered."

"The driver didn't see him in the snow."

"The truck came after him," she insisted. "It must have been waiting for him."

"Let the police figure it out, Vicky."

The officer spent another moment writing in the note-book, then started toward the bystanders a couple yards away.

Vicky felt Rick's arms around her, pulling her against the sheepskin coat that had covered Clint as he died, but the cold had already infiltrated her, turned her to ice. She realized she was crying, the tears like needles pricking her cheeks. Was she the only one who had witnessed a murder?

SHE WASN'T SURE how she had managed to drive home through the whiteout that had descended over Lander, tires bouncing through the snow, the radio blaring: Accident alert! Don't go out if you don't have to. And always moving ahead in the snow, the image of the dark figure in the middle of the street, the truck bearing down.

Inside the apartment, she dropped her bag on the counter that divided the small kitchen from the dining room and headed down the hall to the bedroom. She couldn't stop shivering. She stripped off her clothes and stood in the shower a long time before the shivering finally gave way to an occasional muscle spasm. She closed her eyes and lifted her face into the stream of hot water and tried to think back to the meeting. Clint Hopkins, alive, worried and anxious, caught up in an adoption case. Not a usual case, yet still a normal part of a lawyer's life. *Go ahead,* she had told him. *I will see you tomorrow.*

She toweled off, wrapped herself in a heavy robe, and went into the kitchen, steeled against the coldness that threatened to overwhelm her again. The dark figure had imprinted itself in her mind. She wondered if she could ever leave the image behind. Her black bag looked like a cat that had stretched itself over the counter. She could hear Clint's voice: *Read the notes. I'll fill you in on the rest tomorrow.*

She made herself a cup of tea, retrieved the sealed envelope from her bag, and settled into the corner of the window seat in the living room. The front of the envelope was blank. She managed to work it open and unfold two sheets of paper. Photocopies of what looked like pencil and pen jottings made at different times, as if Clint had jotted down thoughts as he'd delved into the case. She lay the pages side by side. A collection of notes was not what she had expected. She wondered why, if Clint wanted her to cocounsel, he hadn't given her a printed summary of the details. Nothing here other than random jottings, ideas that might have come to him at odd moments.

Scrawled across the top of the first page were the words: *Notes Little Shield Adoption.* The handwriting looked consistent, words neatly formed, lines running straight. But on the second page, the handwriting began to deteriorate. Scribbled words, difficult to make out. Lines bolted up and down, running into one another. She searched for the beginning of a sentence, but there were no capital letters, no punctuation marks. Another chill ran through her, and she took a long sip of tea. The random thoughts of a man in a hurry. An anxious man. A frightened man.

She read through the notes, teasing out the facts from the rambling asides and comments:

I don't know. Doesn't seem possible. Maybe. Look into this. Eldon and Myra Little Shield, Arapahos, Ethete. No appointment. Urgent matter. Agreed to see them. Desire to legally adopt five-year-old daughter, Mary Ann. White. Raised by LS's from infancy. Foundling. Left on front doorstep. Midwinter. Snow and cold. Woman ran away and got into truck. Truck sped off.

Did not call police. Felt sorry for woman, probably mother. Believed she would return for baby. Healthy, strong. Had been cared for. Own child dead at birth a

few weeks earlier. Waited for mother. Never returned.
Baby theirs.

Mary Ann five years old, starting school. Need legal
adoption. Based on desertion? Check with relatives,
friends. Newspaper articles. Internet. Police? No police.
LS's adamant. Must not lose child.

Vicky refolded the notes, slipped them back into the
envelope, and drew her knees to her chin, folding herself together. She stared out the window at the snow falling over
everything like a white shroud. There was nothing in the notes
to indicate the Little Shields had reported the abandoned baby
to the police, which could leave them in a vulnerable situation.
Certainly the police should have been notified.

ANNIE BOSEY, HER secretary, was already in the office when
Vicky arrived. Computer humming and coffee brewing,
fluorescent lights flickering overhead. The office had a
warm, welcoming feeling that reminded her of grandmother's kitchen after she and her cousins had been building
snowmen.

"Are you okay?" Annie, her usual solicitous self, came
around the desk in the reception area. "I heard about Clint
Hopkins. What a lousy night to be out."

"It was a hit-and-run." Vicky took off her coat and draped
it over the wooden coat tree. She wrapped her scarf on top.
"If it had been an accident, the driver would have stopped.
Right?" She'd reached that conclusion somewhere in the
night. An innocent driver would have stopped.

Roger Hurst, the other attorney in the two-person firm,
emerged from the back office, the same look of solicitation
stamped on his face. "Clint was a good man," he said. "He
handled the Mountain Man case, remember? Rip and Edith
Mountain Man adopted their grandson."

She gave a quick nod. People from the rez often found their way to Clint's office.

"Good lawyer. Thorough," Roger said.

"Too much, you ask me." Annie sank into her chair and swiveled back and forth, tapping a pen against her lips. "From what I heard, he delved into Rip's and Edith's backgrounds until he started finding things. So what if Rip did time in Rawlins when he was twenty-two for getting drunk and assaulting some guy? Who doesn't do stupid things when they're young? He'd lived a responsible life for thirty years. It was like Clint took on both roles, working for the couple and against them. Like his real client was the boy. What was best for the boy? Rip and Edith were afraid the judge would rule against the adoption, then what would have become of the boy?"

Always the dilemma, Vicky was thinking. The choice between the best and the available. They were not always the same thing. Clint had been dogged; Annie was right about that. He threw himself into adoption cases. He never gave up until he believed he knew what was best for the child. She squeezed her eyes shut at the image that had arisen unbidden, unwanted: the dark figure in the yellow headlights.

"What else do you know about Clint?" She looked at Annie. "Was he married?" For some reason, she believed he was married, but she had never met his wife.

Annie had started tapping the keyboard, looking straight at the screen. The printer on the table whirred into motion, and a sheet of paper popped off the top. "I figured you'd want to pay your condolences. Wife is Lacy. One child, a daughter at the University of Wyoming." She handed Vicky the sheet. "Address and telephone number are at the top."

"Thanks." Annie was good at anticipating her needs, Vicky thought, especially at times like this, when she wasn't sure she could anticipate them herself.

She had started for the beveled doors that closed off her office when Annie said, "There's something else."

Vicky swung back. Something else? She didn't want anything else, not today, not after last night.

"Betty White Hawk called. She said Vince went out last night and hasn't come home."

What had she expected? Betty had told her son he had to turn himself in today, and he had bolted. Vicky felt herself sagging against the glass doors. "Get her on the phone, please."

"You sure you feel like working today?" Roger took a step forward, as if he might catch her should she slump to the floor. "I can handle whatever you have going on."

"I'm fine," she called over her shoulder as she made her way to the desk. "Everything's just fine."

3

JAMES TWO HORSES was six feet tall with short black hair slicked back behind his ears, skin the color of cinnamon, thick wrists and knuckles surprisingly knobby for a man in his twenties. He had sown his wild oats, he once told Father John. Sown more than he could remember, since most of the time he had been drunk. Sober now and had been for five years, and for the last two of those years, he had felt the calling. Waking him from a deep sleep in the middle of the night, a quiet voice in the back of his mind: *Come follow Me.*

On two or three mornings each week for the last six months, James had shown up at St. Francis to serve Mass. Weighing the possibility of a vocation to the priesthood, he had explained. Seeking to experience what it might be like.

Father John O'Malley hung his cassock in the closet of the sacristy next to the altar while James arranged the Mass books, the stole, and the chalice in the cabinets. Father John was grateful for the help. For some time now, either he or

Bishop Harry had offered the early-morning Mass without a server to help set up the altar, bookmark the prayer books for the proper readings, and tidy up afterward. They alternated the weekday Masses, he and the bishop. Today had been his turn.

It was the fourth Tuesday in March, the Moon of Buffalo Dropping Their Calves, according to the Arapaho way of keeping time. A handful of parishioners had scattered themselves about the pews, the Old Faithfuls, he called them. No matter the weather, the blowing snow and icy roads, they propelled their old trucks to St. Francis Mission for early Mass. They were gone now. The silence in the church made its own sound.

He had offered his prayers this morning for the soul of Clint Hopkins, a white man hit by a truck last night in Lander, and for the family the man had left behind. James had told him about the accident while Father John was robing for Mass, pulling on the long white alb, the stole, the chasuble. "I hear he was a lawyer," James had gone on. "Adoption cases for the most part. He helped a number of Arapahos and Shoshones adopt kids. Witnesses saw the accident. Hard to see anything in the blizzard last night, you ask me. It's a wonder folks don't have the sense to stay home."

All of which, Father John gathered, James had learned from his sister, the night dispatcher at the Lander Police Department. Somehow, between last evening and seven o'clock this morning, the news had made its way across the moccasin telegraph.

Father John, pretty sure the telegraph hadn't missed any details, had asked if Clint Hopkins left a family. In his near decade at St. Francis Mission, he had come to regard the moccasin telegraph as nothing less than a miracle of technology.

"Wife and daughter," James had told him. "They must be in shock. The man went off to a meeting he'd probably gone to dozens of times. Everything the same. Sure, the weather was lousy, but he'd lived in the area all his life, so he probably thought he could handle whatever the storm handed out. He never came back."

"We'll pray for his family." So many deaths, and yet each one a shock, a disruption of nature, a realignment of the world.

With everything in its place in the sacristy, Father John followed James back through the small church built by the Arapahos more than a century ago. Faint odors of cold-stiffened leather and tobacco and perspiration hung in the air. He stopped to scoop up a wool scarf from the back pew before exiting through the front door, which James held open.

The mission was iridescent in the sunlight that had broken through the clouds and blazed like fire across the snow-covered grounds. Father John squinted into the brightness as he came down the front steps. The redbrick residence across Circle Drive, the old stucco school building that housed the Arapaho Museum, the yellow stucco administration building; all shining in the snow. He had been at St. Francis Mission on the Wind River Reservation nearly a decade, six years as pastor. Longer than Jesuit priests usually stayed in one parish. This was home.

James waited at the driver's door of his blue truck, the only vehicle still parked in Circle Drive. Red lights flickered in the tunnel of cottonwoods as the last parishioner drove toward Seventeen-Mile Road. Father John started to thank the man for helping out this morning, but James put up a black-gloved hand, palm out. "Got time for a sit-down soon?"

He always had time, Father John told him. He could see his breath in the brisk cold. He took his gloves out of his parka, pulled them on, and started down the snowy path across the center field to the residence. He turned back. "Give me a call first. Make sure I'm here." Things had a way of turning up at the mission. Emergencies, unexpected delays. The day was never his own. And this morning, his niece, Shannon O'Malley, the third of his brother Mike's six kids, was arriving. He had to pick her up at the Riverton airport.

Behind him he could hear the engine of James's pickup coughing to life and sputtering around the curve in Circle Drive out to the cottonwood tunnel. Walks-On, his golden retriever, came romping through the snow toward him, tossing snow with his nose and leaping on his three legs as if the snow were a disk he could snatch out of the air. Walks-On fell in beside him, and he patted the dog's head as they walked up the steps to the residence. He had shoveled the steps in the dark this morning before going over to the church, but a sheen of snow clung to the concrete.

He was thinking James would make an excellent pastor at St. Francis. It had always been a Jesuit mission, but there were fewer and fewer Jesuits, and the day could come when diocesan priests might have to take over. James would fit right in, one of the people. But years of seminary lay ahead. He was jumping ahead, he told himself. James was still pondering whether he even had a vocation to the priesthood.

Father John let himself into the front hall, draped his parka over a hook, and tossed his cowboy hat on the bench below. He tried to shake off the thought of another pastor at St. Francis Mission. But every now and then rumors reached him that the Provincial officials were reevaluating their commitments. There were times when he could feel the day when everything would change, closing in on him.

The dog skittered down the hallway, and Father John followed him into the kitchen. The odor of fresh coffee mingled with an unusual burned smell.

"Help yourself to the oatmeal." Bishop Harry Coughlin—in

his late seventies, round-faced and bald except for a stubborn fringe of gray hair that wrapped around his pink scalp—sat at the table, the *Gazette* opened beside his coffee mug. "Elena called. Her grandson's pickup was dead this morning. She'll be in as soon as they find someone to give them a jump. I made the coffee and oatmeal. I believe you will find them tasty."

Father John poured dry food into Walks-On's dish and set it on the floor. He took a bowl from the rack in the sink and ladled in some oatmeal, trying to avoid the brown, crispy chunks that clung to the bottom of the pan. The coffee he poured into his mug had the washed-out look of dirty rainwater. He smiled at the image of Bishop Coughlin, who had spent thirty years tending to the spiritual well-being of Catholics in Patna, India, puttering around the kitchen, preparing oatmeal and making coffee. Father John had never known Elena not to make it to work. If her grandson's car didn't start, there was every chance she would stride out cross-country through the snow. He set the bowl and mug on the table, took his cell out of his shirt pocket, and called the housekeeper's home. He told the young woman who answered—probably the wife of Elena's grandson—that he'd be glad to drive over and pick Elena up. "Oh, they got a jump and she's on the way, Father," the woman told him. "She was anxious about you and the bishop not having breakfast."

He slid the cell back into his pocket and sat down across from the bishop. "Elena's on the way," he said. In her seventies, maybe her eighties, he was thinking, but she would never admit it. She didn't even admit to being in her seventies.

"Anything wrong? Bad news was on your face when you came in."

Father John took a bite of the oatmeal. It had the taste of burnt toast. Picking up the coffee mug, he turned toward the bishop. "A lawyer from Riverton was hit by a truck last night in Lander. He didn't make it."

"The blizzard." The old man shook his head and looked away. "We all hang by a very thin thread, I'm afraid."

"Clint Hopkins. He handled some adoptions for people on the rez."

"Another friend lost. Did you know him?"

Father John shook his head. He wondered if it was Hopkins who helped his parishioners Jan and Mike Rivers adopt their niece last year. He made a mental note to give them a call, offer his condolences for the loss of a man they must have trusted.

"On a happier note, I'm looking forward to meeting your niece."

"So am I," Father John said. The last time he had seen Shannon, she was twelve years old. The woman stepping off the plane this morning would be someone else, a twenty-four-year-old doctoral student at the University of Chicago doing a dissertation on two sisters captured by Indians in the nineteenth century. There had been many white captives. Some had been rescued after a brief time, but others spent years with the tribes. Still others, like Cynthia Ann Parker, captured by the Comanches when she was a small child, had grown up with the tribes—become Indian—before being forcibly returned to their families. Those were the saddest cases of all, he thought after he'd read some of the stories. White women who no longer belonged in the white world, forced to live in a culture they didn't remember or understand.

Shannon had called a couple weeks ago. She was researching the lives of Amanda and Elizabeth Fletcher, captured in 1865 in a Cheyenne raid on their family's wagon train. Amanda had been rescued within months, but her two-year-old sister had had been traded to the Arapahos. She had lived out her life as an Arapaho. Lizzie Brokenhorn, as she was known on the reservation. "Think I could talk to one of Lizzie's descendants?" Shannon had wanted to know, and he had told her he would do his best.

He glanced at his watch, got to his feet, and carried his bowl with the half-eaten oatmeal and the mug still nearly full over to the sink. Bills to pay and calls to return, and only a couple hours before he had to leave for the airport. He thanked the bishop for a lovely breakfast.

"My pleasure." The old man was beaming. "I decided this morning to take up cooking. I believe I have a natural talent, and it's so relaxing and rewarding to make a meal for someone else. Yes, I do believe I'll take up cooking."

RIVERTON REGIONAL AIRPORT occupied a high plateau north-west of town. The wide, empty spaces of the reservation stretched into the distances with the Wind River Range rising into the Western sky. The music of *Il Trovatore* blared from the CD player on the center of the seat. A white world this morning, seamless and bright in the midmorning sun. Father John bumped through the snowy ruts that criss-crossed the parking lot in front of the terminal, parked close to the main entrance, and turned off the CD player. In the distance he could hear the low roar of a jet, but the sky remained as clear as newly washed glass.

A few people stood around the polished vinyl floor next to the gate that accommodated the passengers. Father John walked over to the wall of windows that gave out over the runway and the great openness beyond. The plane was coming in low from the south, a metallic twinkling in the blue sky. He watched it glide, until finally it was on the ground, coming down the runway, braking gradually. It stopped outside the windows.

He had been wondering if he would know her; she'd been

so young the last time he saw her. A child still, with light, reddish hair and blue eyes, teasing and mischievous. She had liked to play games, and he remembered long stretches at the dining room table playing Monopoly and gin rummy and poker. Shannon O'Malley played deliberately, her freckled forehead wrinkled in concentration, but she jumped to her feet, shouted, and high-fived everyone in the house when she won.

A line of passengers started down the metal steps, but there was Shannon, standing on the landing, looking around. He would have known her anywhere, even on the crowded streets of Manhattan. Tall and slim with masses of curly hair that caught the sunlight in waves. And so like her mother that, for a fleeting moment, Father John felt something grip his heart. Then down the steps she came, hopping, half running, a backpack bouncing on her shoulders. The same exuberance she had shown after bankrupting him in Monopoly.

Dodging around the other passengers, glancing about the airport, she came through the gate. "Uncle John!" she called as he made his way toward her. "It's so great to see you." She was in his arms, hugging his neck, kissing his cheek. "You haven't changed at all."

He held her for a moment, then set his hands on her shoulders and took a step back, wanting to take her in. This daughter of Eileen and Mike—part of him, his own family. She was laughing and smiling, pinpricks of light in her blue eyes. She had her mother's creamy complexion and delicate nose. But the way she stood, the deep blue of her eyes, and the frankness in her expression were her father's. "You're beautiful," he said.

She tossed her head, laughed, and waved away the compliment. "I'll bet I'm the only girl you can tell that to."

"Pretty much."

He reached for her backpack, but she shrugged away. "I'm used to it," she said. "It's part of me, like a large hump I carry around."

"Any other luggage?"

She shook her head. "I travel light. You can move faster that way."

4

"I'VE FOUND SOMEONE for you to interview," Father John said. They drove off the plateau onto the straightaway that led into town, through the traffic light, a few cars and pickups in the two lanes. "Di tale amor" was playing softly. Snow alongside the road had melted into streams that splashed the windshield. The wipers in the old Toyota pickup operated on a hit-and-miss basis, and he had to lean sideways to see through a cleared space.

"*Il Trovatore*," Shannon said.

"You like opera?" He glanced over at the girl in the passenger seat, one elbow braced on the window frame, the backpack on her lap. She seemed at ease, almost at home, as if she knew the road well and had driven it many times.

"Doesn't everyone?" She gave him a wide smile. "I never doubted you'd find someone for me to interview. You've been on the reservation so long, you must know everybody. One of Lizzie's grandchildren, I hope."

"Wilbur Horn, a great-grandson."

Shannon let out a yelp. "Fantastic. How old is he?" Gloved fingers strummed the straps of the backpack. He could almost smell the excitement emanating from her.

"Probably in his sixties. Hale and hearty."

"The closest I can get, I'm sure. Lizzie had five children who would be centenarians now. Wilbur sounds perfect." When he looked over again, she was smiling. "It's a good place to start. People send you on, you know. Wilbur could remember other family members who might have different stories"

It was true, Father John was thinking. It had taken only a couple phone calls before he found that Wilbur Horn, one of his own parishioners, was descended from Lizzie Brokenhorn. He had gone out to Wilbur's ranch and over a cup of coffee explained that his niece was writing her dissertation on his great-grandmother and her sister. Stories were private, Father John knew; they belonged in families, defined families, gave them understanding, courage, and strength. They weren't for students who could never grasp—feel—the importance. They weren't meant to be scattered to the winds as if they were nothing.

"You say she's your brother's child." Father John had nodded. In the Arapaho Way, his brother's child was also his child. Wilbur had nodded with him, a silent agreement struck.

Now Father John smiled at the exuberance in Shannon's voice and the truth of what she said: "I never know where the road will lead, but I know it will lead to something I couldn't have anticipated or even imagined from reading the old records." She shifted toward him and plucked at the straps of the backpack again as if she were playing a melody on a guitar. "The history books, the old records and archives, only tell part of the story."

Father John met her smile for a moment. Her blue eyes

crinkled in the bright sunlight. "And sometimes the records are wrong." How many times since he had been with the Arapahos had he come face-to-face with the way that stories passed down by people who had lived through the massacres and the terror in the Old Time contradicted the official reports accepted by historians? If it was written down, it must be true, historians believed.

"They do tell us a lot, of course," she said. "You can't ignore them."

"Of course not." Not if you want to get your doctorate.

"They give you the outline of what happened. A good starting point. Take the women I'm concentrating on. Amanda Mary Fletcher, Lizzie's sister, in a Cheyenne camp for seven months. Elizabeth Fletcher, never rescued. Lived her life as an Arapaho."

Shannon was still leaning toward him. He could feel the intensity of her concentration. "What I'm looking for, Uncle John, is the outside of history, the details and feelings never written down. What happened to these women? How did they live out their lives? I've interviewed five of Amanda's descendants. What was it like for her when she returned home? Did she continue as if nothing had happened? Just a little blip in her life journey? Questions like that. And what about Lizzie? Changed from being white to Indian in a matter of minutes. What did that mean? How did that determine the woman she became?"

"I'm proud of you," Father John said. She was going after the lost parts of history. Going for the whole, or as much as she could find. Not just the accepted truth. She was doing what he should have done twenty-five years ago, back at Boston College, when he'd been studying to become a history professor. Before his own life took a path he hadn't anticipated. After graduation, he had joined the Jesuits, the Society of Jesus, and eventually taught history in a Jesuit prep school, doing research for a doctorate. All those records and archives to plow through, and the loneliness and the terrible thirst that had taken him over. The crash had come hard.

He turned right and drove south toward the reservation. Set-back storefronts and snow-gripped parking lots started to give way to warehouses, liquor package stores, and the edges of trailer camps. A passing semi splashed snow and gray slush over the windshield, blinding him for a moment until the wipers surged into action. It had led him here, all of it, to an Indian reservation in the middle of Wyoming.

Shannon was saying something about starting with the records, and he tried to concentrate. She was so much further ahead than he had been at her age. So much wiser. "Take Elizabeth Fletcher," she said. "The records tell us all about how Jasper and Mary Ann Fletcher set out from Illinois in 1865 for the California gold fields with their five children. They had joined a train of seventy-five wagons on the North Platte River trail through Indian country, all of their belongings piled inside two wagons."

She went silent a moment, gazing out the window as if she could see the family and the wagons. After a moment, she went on: "Jasper made a big mistake. Instead of staying with the large train, he pulled ahead. Northwest of what is now Cheyenne, he stopped the wagons so the kids could wade in the river, cool off, and have a little lunch. That was when a band of Indians led by the Cheyenne chief Sand Hill attacked. Wounded Jasper, left him for dead, and killed Mary Ann. The three young sons ran back for the wagon train. The Indians were busy ransacking the family's wagons, so they let the boys go. But they took Amanda Mary, who was seventeen, and her baby sister, Elizabeth, who was two years old. Tied their feet and arms, threw them on horses, and rode away before the large train could arrive. For the next thirty-five years, Amanda Mary feared her sister had been killed, but she never stopped looking for her.

In the early 1900s she learned that Elizabeth was living on the Wind River Reservation. So that's it, the story outline. I'm here to fill in the blanks."

"How far along are you?" Father John turned right into the reservation. Empty white spaces stretched around them, broken here and there by blocklike houses and ponies nodding in corrals. The melting snow had turned Seventeen-Mile Road into a creek. The sun shimmered on the hood of the Toyota pickup.

Out of the corner of his eye, he saw Shannon shrug. "Two weeks in Michigan and Iowa interviewing Amanda's descendants. A variety of stories, little glimpses of truth in each one, I suspect. The problem is, her story changed over the years. She was a prolific writer, not shy about recounting the horrors of her experience with the Cheyennes. At the time she was rescued by a white trader, she said the Cheyennes had treated her well and that Sand Hill's wife had been good to her. As the years went by, she began filing claims against the government for her family's losses. Anyway, with each filing, the amount of losses grew and so did the horrific sufferings she claimed to have undergone."

"You don't believe the claims."

"You said it: records can be wrong."

"What did her descendants say?"

"They were all over the map. A couple of great-granddaughters recited all the horrible things that had happened to her: beatings, starvation, struggles to keep warm, lack of sleep, being treated like a slave. Pretty terrible, and straight out of the reports Amanda had filed with the government, which made me wonder if the great-granddaughters really had heard any stories at all. Other descendants—further removed, I grant you; great-greats—claimed their parents and grandparents had heard Mary describe her captivity as filled with hard work. But all the Indian women worked, and she had to work alongside them. In times when food was scarce, everybody went hungry. Most of their buffalo-hide tipis had been destroyed at the Sand Creek Massacre the year before, and their canvas tipis barely kept out the cold."

"So you have to make sense out of it." Framed against the blue sky ahead was the large blue and white billboard with the words *St. Francis Mission* splashed across it.

"Our job as historians, right?" She let out a long sigh. "What Amanda wrote makes it harder to zero in on the truth."

"You're saying what she wrote could be unreliable?"

"Historical records." She shrugged again and shook her head.

Father John slowed for the left turn onto the road that ran through a tunnel of cottonwoods. Globules of snow dropped off the branches and splattered the windshield. The rear wheels shimmied on the slush.

"So this is the mission." Shannon sat forward, craning toward the windshield as he drove out of the tunnel and onto Circle Drive. "Let me guess. Your office is over there." She nodded in the direction of the administration building, yellow stucco and two stories high, easily the largest building on the reservation, a ghost from the past. "The church over there, just like your Christmas cards. Seems as if the steeple floats in the sky. The gray stone building must be the old school you turned into the Arapaho Museum."

Father John took a left into the alley that ran between the church and the administration building. Past Eagle Hall, where the social activities took place. Boy Scouts, Girl Scouts, Sunday-morning donuts and coffee, the women's social committee, the Ladies Altar Society, the Men's Club, Alcoholics Anonymous, the New Moms group.

Shannon had shifted herself partway around and was staring out the back window. "That redbrick house over there must be where you live. I don't see the baseball diamond."

"Behind the redbrick house," he said. Lost in the snow, he was thinking. A wide-open field of snow.

"And I will be staying in the guesthouse." She was bubbling on, all of it a new adventure. "Your e-mail said you've put up a lot of famous people in the guesthouse. Name one."

"Everybody who stays there has a claim to fame." He slid to a stop near the front stoop.

"Because they stayed there?"

"Something like that." He got out and started through the wet, melting snow to the passenger side, but Shannon O'Malley was already off her seat. She slammed the door behind her and gripped the backpack to her chest.

"Let me help you." He reached for the backpack again, and this time she let him take it. She spun around. "I feel like I know this place. Every year I confiscated your Christmas card and tacked it up in my room over my desk. It was the first thing I saw every morning. After a while I had five or six, all lined up in a neat row. Each one with a different photo, and all those photos formed a big picture of the mission. I took my collection with me when I left for college, and every Christmas I added the next card. Tacked up in a whole series of dorm rooms and apartments with a lot of roommates and"—she swallowed—"boyfriends wanting to know where those cards came from. Africa? The Serengeti? Some other exotic place? Oh, you'd be surprised by the exotic places they suggested. I guess that's what the Christmas cards meant to me, a grand adventure in an exotic place. You were my hero because you got away. I mean, nobody else I knew when I was a kid ever got away."

Father John pushed the front door open, gestured her inside, and wondered what he had gotten away from. Family? Home? What he had found again, here. He set the backpack down on the worn sofa, which sloped sideways, and its pushed-up springs bit into your thighs when you sat down. Better than no sofa at all, he reckoned, and none of the guests ever complained. "This is it," he said. "I've stocked the kitchen with some essentials: coffee, cereal, milk, fruit, sandwich meat and bread, in case you get hungry while you're working."

Shannon brushed past him into the alcove that served as a kitchen. She thumped the top of the old oak table. "Perfect place to set up my laptop. It's sure quiet here." She rolled her head around, as if she expected to detect noise somewhere. "I'm not used to so much quiet."

"You get used to it." It was one of the best things about being here, the infinite quiet. "Bedroom's in back, extra blankets in the closet. Make yourself at home and let me know if you need anything at all."

Father John turned toward the door, then looked back. "Lunch at the residence promptly at noon; dinner promptly at six. I'll drive over and get you."

"No. No. No. I love to walk in the snow."

"See you in a little while."

"Oh, Uncle John," she called as he stepped outside and started to close the door. "Are you always prompt?"

He glanced back. Her eyes were dancing with mischief. How had she figured out that, despite his best intentions and promises to change, he seldom made it to meals on time? Something always intervened. He and Elena had reached what he thought of as a good working arrangement: he promised to be on time, and she pretended to believe him. "I'm afraid I'll have to take the Fifth Amendment," he said, pulling the door shut behind him.

5

VICKY MADE HER way through the white faces in the Hopkinses' living room. A comfortable, lived-in room with overstuffed sofa and chairs, small tables piled with magazines, and a bookcase crammed with books. Mullion windows framed broken pictures of the snow-heavy trees in the front yard and the cars passing in the street throwing up fountains of snow and slush. She didn't recognize any of the faces—Clint's colleagues, family, friends. She was an interloper, an intruder on private grief.

"I'm a colleague," she told the woman with the not-unfriendly face and the taut look of someone who spent hours in a gym. She had light hair with dozens of colors in it that brushed the shoulders of her light blue dress.

"Oh, you must be Vicky Holden." She peered at Vicky with wide blue eyes behind small wireless glasses that gave her the mock-studious look of a seventh grader.

Vicky recognized the high-pitched, childlike voice of Clint's secretary. "Are you Evie?"

At this, the woman—she looked like she was in her mid-twenties—produced a tissue and began dabbing her eyes. The glasses jumped upward, riding along her nose at a precarious angle. She adjusted them and bit into her lower lip. "I've been with Clint since I was seventeen, just out of high school. I needed a job bad, with my dad out of work and Mom sick and my two brothers still in high school. Clint was struggling to get his practice going. 'I don't know if I can pay you,' he told me. 'I don't even know if I'll have any clients.' Well, it was better than nothing, which was what I had. I found out later that Lacy has plenty of money, so money wasn't a problem. Plus, Clint was good at what he did." She went back to dabbing the tissue at her eyes, the glasses stuttering about. "Lacy will be glad you came by." She swiped her eyes a last time and adjusted her glasses.

Vicky followed the woman through the gauntlet of white faces. She could feel the laser heat of eyes on her back. Did they all know? How Clint had gone to the meeting in a blizzard to meet her? How he had started across the street alone? She had tossed about all night, half-asleep, half-awake, going over and over those last minutes. If she had crossed with Clint, would the truck have roared out of the snow?

"Lacy, Vicky Holden is here." The secretary leaned over a small woman with sandy hair and red-rimmed eyes who sat, shoulders hunched, on an armchair. "The Arapaho lawyer from Lander," she said, stepping back and beckoning Vicky forward.

A hush dropped over the living room like the quiet fullness of a rodeo stadium when a bronco rider flies into the air, just before he hits the hard-packed earth. There was a faint sound of water running from a faucet somewhere. The coffee smell was so strong, Vicky could almost taste it. A woman sitting next to Lacy got to her feet and Vicky took the chair. She leaned sideways, but Lacy was staring across the room at something only she could see with a distant look in her expression, as if the people milling about had vanished.

"I came to tell you how sorry I am about Clint," Vicky said.

Lacy did not respond. Still staring off into space, a private movie in her head. A moment passed before a girl who looked about nineteen, with long dark hair and lively eyes, stepped over to the armchair. "I'm Julie," she said, looking at Vicky. "We've had a terrible shock." Her mother's hand lay in her own like a dried leaf as the girl leaned forward. "This is one of Dad's colleagues, Mom."

Something inside Lacy seemed to switch on, and she made a slow, robotic turn toward Vicky. "Thoughtful of you." She spoke in a whisper. "I don't know why Clint went to the meeting last night. Do you? It was a terrible night. No one should have been out."

"I'm afraid he wanted to give me some papers about a case he wanted me to cocounsel. We had arranged to meet this morning . . ." Vicky stopped. This was not a road she had intended to start down. At this very moment, Clint Hopkins should have been seated in her office. They should have been discussing the efforts of a couple named Myra and Eldon Little Shield to adopt their little girl. Instead she was seated in Clint's living room across from his shell-shocked wife.

She hurried on, making a futile effort to cover up what she could see in Lacy's eyes: an acknowledgment of what should have been. "Clint wanted me to read through his notes before we met."

Lacy was shaking her head. "Yes, of course. It was an adoption case. I begged him not to go out, but he said it was important. All the adoptions were important. Every child was Julie looking for a good home. He took every case personally. Carried it around like precious baggage. Brought it home, dropped it in the middle of the living room, carried it to the dinner table, took it to bed. Every case, the most important in the world. Naturally, if he wanted to talk to you about a case, he would go out in a blizzard. He would have gone to hell and back for some kid because that kid was always Julie."

She was sucking in rapid gulps of air, moisture blossoming at the corners of her eyes. "Did you see what happened?"

Vicky nodded. "We had walked out of the restaurant together. Clint started across the street where he had parked his car. I saw the . . ." She hesitated, picking through the minefield of words. "I saw what happened."

"You saw him die?"

"There was nothing anyone could do; it happened so fast. I ran over and knelt beside him." Vicky could feel the tears pressing in her eyes. "I'm so very sorry. I didn't get the license plate number."

"The driver didn't even stop." Julie sat down on the armrest, pulled her mother close, and kissed the top of her head.

Vicky didn't say anything. The driver. A man who had wanted to run down someone. A murderer. "I'm sorry," she said again. "If I can help you in any way . . ." She left the thought hanging between her and the two women huddled together. What a flimsy gesture. What could she ever do to lessen the pain and the horror? She felt light-headed as she got to her feet and started for the door.

The living room was more crowded now. People jammed together in little groups, sipping coffee from foam cups, glancing over at Lacy and Julie and shaking their heads. "Do you have a minute?" Vicky realized that Evie had fallen in beside her and was guiding her toward a side door.

"We can talk in here," the woman said, depositing her in a small room with the look and feel and smell of a study. A masculine study, where Clint Hopkins had sat at the desk, file folders upright in a metal rack and a laptop computer, open as if Clint had just stepped away.

"Do you really believe it?" Evie closed the door against the hum of conversation and the odor of coffee.

"Believe what?"

"It was an accident."

"I don't know."

The woman turned partway toward the window and looked out, clasping and unclasping her hands. The blue dress clung to the curves of her hips and calves. "It's just that . . ." She faced Vicky again. Her glasses looked smudged and cloudy with moisture. "I've been worried about Clint. He spent the past two weeks working on the Little Shield case. He wanted you to come in with him. I've never seen him so obsessed. Oh, Clint was always obsessed with whatever case he was working on, but this was different. I could see it taking a toll."

"Did he say what was he worried about?"

Evie shook her head. "He was never one to blab about a case, but he talked to various people and did research on the internet. The more information he collected, the more uptight he became. When I heard what happened last night, I got a sickening feeling. What if he'd stumbled onto something he wasn't supposed to know?"

"Have you told the police?"

She dropped her head into both hands for a moment, then looked up. She straightened the little wireless glasses. "All I have is a strange feeling. I guess I'm just looking for a rational explanation, and the truth is, there isn't any. All Clint cared about was getting little Mary Ann legally adopted by the people who loved her. The last thing he would want is for me to start stirring up trouble. If I went to the police with my crazy feeling, they'd open an investigation. I can't do that to the Little Shields." She held out a hand as if she were soliciting alms. "I went into the office this morning to contact a few of his associates. Make sure the file drawers were locked, the computers locked. I canceled his appointments. Tidying up, I guess, because I didn't know what else to do. The phone was ringing off the hook. Eldon called the minute he heard about Clint. I could tell by his voice how upset he was. He trusted Clint. He wanted to know what they should do now, so I told him Clint wanted you to co-counsel the case. I suggested he call you."

Vicky remained quiet a moment. If her instincts were right—if the secretary's instincts were right—she could be stepping into whatever had gotten Clint killed. If he was murdered, he must have been apprehensive about what he'd uncovered. Still, he had gone forward because of a little girl.

"Clint gave me some notes to read over," she said. "There's nothing in them he hadn't mentioned when we spoke."

The secretary drew in her bottom lip again, a habit, Vicky thought. It made her look like a child, except for the pencil lines that formed on her forehead. "I'm afraid he was somewhat paranoid. Kept very sparse notes and put very little on the computer—you know, in case somebody hacked it. He kept everything in his head, and he was very thorough. I hope you can help the Little Shields."

"I can talk to them. I don't know if I can help."

Evie looked startled, as if Vicky had thrown out an idea she hadn't considered. "Clint was sure you would know how to handle the case."

"If I take it on, I'll need his records."

"I told you: he didn't keep records. Everything is in his notes."

"There was nothing helpful in the notes."

"Well, Clint was thorough but concise. I'm sure he would have filled you in on the details when he came to your office." She took a moment before she went on: "I can check his computer, but I don't expect to find anything else."

"Perhaps some other case Clint was working on that might have worried him?"

Evie shook her head. "He spent all of his time recently on the Little Shield case. He interviewed a lot of people."

"And didn't make notes?"

This stopped the woman, as if a brick wall had descended. "Like I said, I can check his computer in case he left something else."

"I'll speak with the Little Shields," Vicky said. "I can't agree to anything until I hear what they have to say."

Evie nodded. "They're good people, and little Mary Ann has a happy home."

Vicky left the woman standing in the small office surrounded by the items that had belonged to Clint, the space permeated by his presence. She made her way across the living room, visitors shifting about, new visitors coming through the front door, which closed with a sharp thwack.

She let herself outside and, hurrying down the sidewalk to the Ford parked at the curb, checked her text messages. One message from Annie: "Vince's mother called."

Vicky slid onto the driver's seat and started the engine. Cold air blasted out of the vents. She pulled her coat around her, found Betty White Hawk's number, and pressed the call key. Five rings on a cell phone somewhere on the reservation, then a voice said: "Hi, this is Betty."

Vicky was waiting for the familiar *leave a message* when the voice went on: "Vicky? I've been waiting for you to call."

"Have you heard from Vince?" Vicky checked her watch. Still several hours before the time she had promised to deliver Vince to the sheriff.

"Not yet, but I've left messages all over the rez. He's got a lot of no-good friends, but they'll tell him to call me. I have to give them that—they don't want a lot of cops creeping around their places looking for him." The faint sound of hope broke through the weariness in the voice. "Soon's he sobers up, I'm sure he'll call and tell me where he is."

"Call me as soon as you hear anything." Vicky was about to end the call when she said, "If you talk to Vince, it might be best not to mention that I will come by to pick him up wherever he is."

"I got it." The voice was faint with apprehension.

Vicky pulled into the lane, turned onto Federal, and drove south toward Lander. She was coming around the bend past Hudson when the cell rang. Annie again. "You just got a call from Eldon Little Shield. He wants to see you right away. I told him you'd work him in this morning."

Clint Hopkins wasn't dead twenty-four hours yet, and the Little Shields wanted to talk to another lawyer. "That's fine," she told Annie before she hit the end key. It was the way it was. No matter the horror of what had happened, the Little Shields wanted to adopt their little girl, and nothing would prevent them from trying.

6

THEY MIGHT HAVE been any family on the reservation. At the powwows, tribal meetings, celebrations at Blue Sky Hall, dozens of get-togethers. A serious look about them: responsible, involved. Good people, Vicky would have said if anyone asked, the best of her people. The man in a parka, blue jeans, boots. The woman in a red flower-print dress, coat hanging off her shoulders. A little girl, about five years old, with hair the color of sunshine and eyes like blue ice.

"Eldon Little Shield." The man advanced across the office, hand extended, a warrior leading the way into unknown territory, his wife and child a couple of steps behind. He was tall, a little paunch above a silver buffalo belt buckle, a cowboy hat clasped against one thigh. He tossed a backward nod. "This here is my wife, Myra. And this is our daughter, Mary Ann." He reached over and placed a protective hand on the child's head.

Vicky came around the desk and shook the man's hand first, the palm roughened and wind-seared. His wife's palm was softer, the grip surprisingly strong and resolute. "Hello, Mary Ann," she said, leaning down toward the pretty little girl, who lifted a hand and gave a little wave.

Vicky gestured toward the chairs in front of her desk, then took her own seat and waited for the family to settle in. Mary Ann had a small bag, beaded and quilled, which she spread on her lap. She removed a pad and pencil and set about drawing something.

"Clint's secretary mentioned you might call," Vicky said. An awkward beginning, an awkward circumstance.

Myra Little Shield pulled a tissue from the woven bag on her lap and began dabbing at the corners of her eyes. She glanced over at the child, who looked up and gave her mother a reassuring smile, then went back to her drawing. The smile seemed to fortify Myra, who straightened herself against the chair and drew in a long breath. Thirtyish, black hair brushing her shoulders, no makeup or lipstick, and a take-me-as-I-am look about her. She was attractive, with traces of the kind of beauty that had propelled a number of young Arapaho women to the Miss Indian America crown. She gave Vicky a weak smile, squeezed the tissue in the fist she dropped on top of her bag, and turned toward her husband. Waiting. It was his place to lead the way.

Eldon took his time. Vicky could almost see the thoughts shadowing his face. Sun splashed the window behind the couple, and a column of sunlight illuminated the dust in the air. Finally Eldon said, "We were shocked when we heard about Clint. Never expected anything like that to happen. Talked to him yesterday, and he said he was going to meet with another lawyer. That lawyer being you, from what Clint's secretary told us. He sounded a little, I don't know"—he shrugged—"serious."

"Did he say why he wanted to bring me in on the case?"

The man gave another shrug, then gripped the armrests hard, knuckles popping white in his brown hands, like a cowboy steadying himself on the fence before the bronco hurtles out of the gate onto the rodeo grounds. He glanced down at the little girl, then back at Vicky. "This isn't the time . . ."

Vicky came around the desk and smiled down at the child. "Mary Ann, would you like to keep Annie company in the outer office?"

"Who's Annie?" The little girl made several pencil swipes on the pad before she looked up, blue eyes filled with innocence and wonder in a heart-shaped face. There was a little dimple in her chin. Her fingernails were rosy pink.

"My secretary. You met her when you came in. You could show her your drawings. She would like that very much."

The little girl gave her father, then her mother, a sideways glance. They both nodded, and she jumped up and started for the outer office. Vicky went with her. "Mary Ann has some drawings to show you," she told Annie as the child sidled in next to Annie's chair and opened her pad.

Vicky closed the beveled glass doors behind her and went back to her desk. The Little Shields had angled their chairs toward the doors so they could keep an eye on Mary Ann and—more important, Vicky realized—so Mary Ann could keep an eye on them.

"Clint wasn't one to talk about his business," Eldon said. "Went about doing what he had to do."

"Never wanted to give us reason to get discouraged." Myra's eyes locked on her husband as if they were the same person. His turn to speak, then hers; one story.

"Fact is," Eldon went on, "Clint believed in our case. It was obvious we were Mary Ann's parents. We raised her from the time she was no bigger than a puppy. We been worried sick some nosy social worker could show up on our doorstep and take Mary Ann away, despite the fact we take good care of her. I've got a steady job at the body shop in Riverton going on eight years now, and Myra works part-time at an insurance company. We see that Mary Ann has everything she needs. We talked to Father John at the mission. He's the one said we need legal papers saying she's ours so nobody can take her away. You can bring him in on this, if you want. He knows all about our case."

"Why don't we start at the beginning?" Vicky said. Of course they had gone to Father John O'Malley. He was the man her people turned to for advice and consolation and help. "Tell me how you came to have custody of Mary Ann."

Eldon swallowed several times, his Adam's apple bobbing. "Five years ago last week, March twentieth—what we call Mary Ann's birthday, 'cause that's when she was born to us—there was a knock on the front door. It was pretty late. We were just about to go to bed, and we sure weren't expecting company."

"I remember being scared." Myra squared herself to the desk and kept her eyes on Vicky. "I sensed something wasn't right. It was snowing hard, and nobody should've been out. I told Eldon not to answer." She glanced at her husband. "Thank God he ignored me and opened the door. I was right behind him, and I saw a woman running toward a pickup parked out by the road. Her boots made holes in the snow, like postholes. She had on a black coat that came down to her knees. I remember the way her long black hair swung from beneath the knit cap pulled low over her ears. Like a black shadow running through the snow. Eldon shouted, 'What do you want?' but she jumped inside and the pickup took off. Bounced down the road, taillights swirling in the snow, like whoever was driving couldn't get away fast enough. I was so busy watching the pickup I didn't notice the box until Eldon said, 'What's this?' I looked down and saw the kind of brown carton you get at the grocery store.

Stuffed with a pink blanket and the blanket was moving. We didn't say anything. We stood there like rocks."

Eldon shook his head and smiled off into the distance. "It was like we were dreaming. Something moving inside the blanket? I thought it was a small animal. Maybe a puppy or a kitten. Well, we had a couple dogs and some cats that lived in the barn. We sure didn't need any more."

"But the pink blanket," Myra said. "I knew it was a baby. I lifted the box and took it inside. It was so cold out, and the blanket sparkled with snow. I could barely pull the blanket back, I was shaking so hard. A thousand thoughts went through my mind. How can this be? She was beautiful." Myra stopped and drew in a long, shuddering breath. Her eyes were shiny. She seemed to make an effort to steady herself before going on: "A tiny pink face, just a wisp of hair, little clenched fists. She looked at me with the biggest blue eyes you ever saw, and it was like she knew I was going to be her mother."

Eldon reached over and patted his wife's hand. "It was like a miracle," he said. "Our little girl died at birth only five weeks before, and here was this perfect baby whose mother was giving her away."

He looked sideways at his wife, who nodded, lips clenched. "I picked her up, our precious little baby, and held her close, and it was like . . ." The tears started as she mimicked rocking the baby back and forth. "Our own baby had come back to us. I remember saying her name: Mary Ann. 'Mary Ann,' I said, over and over, and that became her name."

Eldon waited a moment before he said: "I figured the mother must be in a terrible situation to leave her baby like that. I told Myra she was sure to come back. If not right away, she'd come back for her baby when she got herself into a better situation. I could see that Myra was"—he patted his wife's hand again—"falling in love, and after what we had been through, losing our own baby, I didn't want her to have any more grief. I tried to warn her . . ."

"It didn't do any good." Myra flashed a sideways smile toward her husband. "I was already in love. All I wanted to do was take care of her. I felt she was mine, that for some reason the mother wanted me and Eldon to raise her as our own. She was white, but that didn't make any difference. We were going to be her parents. We still had everything ready for our own baby: crib, clothes, diapers, formula, all in her own bedroom. We had closed the door because I couldn't bear to look at it. All we had to do was open the door. Eldon had found a rocker at a secondhand store and painted it red, and I had made a bright, cheery cushion. I took Mary Ann into the bedroom and cuddled her in the rocker and I . . . I let her nurse. She had been breastfed, because she knew how to nurse. It was a miracle the way my milk started to come back. Not right away. I had to give her formula for a couple of days, but I kept offering my breast, and after a few days, I had enough milk for two babies."

For an instant, the memories flooded back: her own babies tugging at her breast. Vicky swallowed hard and said, "Did you ever hear from the mother? Did you try to make contact?"

"Not a word." Eldon gave a quick, dismissive shake of his head. "She abandoned her child, and that was that. As for trying to make contact, we had no idea who she might be."

"Indian," Myra said.

"Why do you suppose so? The child is white."

"Half-breed, we decided," Eldon said. "Father was probably white. I figure that's why the mother gave her up, because her daddy didn't want a half-breed kid. I guess the mother wanted him more than she wanted her own baby. It happens."

Oh, yes, it happens, Vicky was thinking. A parade of

clients, usually grandparents or aunties and uncles seated in the same chairs the Little Shields occupied, explaining how they had been left with a child, sometimes two or three children, because their daughter or sister or niece or even a close friend had run off with some man she couldn't live without, no matter the price.

"If you think the mother was Indian . . ."

"The way she ran away, the black hair, the pickup truck," Myra said. "Everything about her said Indian."

"You didn't see her face."

The couple shook heads in unison. "We knew," Myra said.

"I'm surprised she didn't leave the child with relatives. Is it possible one of you is a relative?" When neither spoke, she said, "Why didn't you call the police?"

They seemed to be struck dumb by the question, as if it were unfathomable. Finally Eldon said, "The police? We didn't even think about it. We called Myra's cousin over at social services and told her about the baby. She got us papers that said we could keep her while they investigated. The papers were notarized. Said we had temporary custody. We thought everything was okay, and we just took care of our baby."

"She was our baby," Myra said, "come to us out of no-where. I couldn't bear the thought of losing her. We told folks she was our foster child, and nobody said anything. Then my cousin had a stroke and died, and we never heard any more about an investigation. I guess she knew we needed a baby. Pretty soon it was natural for there to be three of us. Everywhere we went, powwows, Sun Dance, people knew Mary Ann was ours."

"What has changed?" The case had fallen through the cracks. It should have been settled five years ago. From the outer office came the muted sound of the phone ringing. Both Myra and Eldon swiveled toward the beveled glass doors. Mary Ann was still at Annie's side, pushing the pencil over her pad. Annie picked up the phone.

The couple looked back at each other, regathering their thoughts. "We've changed," Eldon said after a moment. "We want the legal papers that say we are her parents and no one can take her away. We have to register her for school. They're going to want her birth certificate."

Myra pulled at the tissue in her hands. "Mary Ann worries. She looks in the mirror and sees she doesn't look like Mommy and Daddy. She wants to know who she is, where she came from, and we're afraid to tell her the truth about being left on our doorstep because there'll be an investigation for sure. We tell her she is our child and we couldn't love her more if I had given birth to her. She needs to know she is legally ours."

"We found Clint on the internet," Eldon said. "His Web site said he had experience with adoption cases."

Vicky nodded. The adoption should have been easy, a clear case of abandonment. Nothing Clint couldn't have handled himself. "Did Clint mention finding anything that might have stopped the case from going forward?"

Myra was shaking her head, but her husband stared into the center of the room, a somber look about him. "When we hired him, he said the fastest way to finalize the adoption was to prove abandonment. It should be easy, given the facts, but the judge would want to make sure we had done everything to find the birth mother. Clint put two ads in the *Gazette*, asking if anybody knew about an infant abandoned five years ago. We gave him a list of our relatives and friends that knew we'd been caring for Mary Ann. He went out and talked to people. Last time I asked him how things were going, he said he would get back to us. Like I said, he called the day he died. He didn't sound upbeat, like usual. Now he's gone."

Vicky could picture the notes Clint had given her, the

tight, hurried handwriting, the tension growing page by page. Newspapers. Interviews. The usual ways to obtain information that would support the clients' claim. "I'll need a copy of the list you gave Clint," she said.

A sheet of paper materialized from the woven bag on Myra's lap. She scooted forward and handed the paper across the desk. "Does this mean you have to start all over? We were hoping to have the adoption finalized by now."

Vicky glanced down the sheet. A number of Little Shields scattered among other familiar names on the rez. No one she knew, but she supposed that, at one time or another, she had crossed paths with most of them. "I'll see if I can find out if Clint ran into any obstacles." She glanced up and tried for a smile of encouragement. "I'll be in touch."

It took a moment before the Little Shields seemed to realize the appointment was over. Myra crunched the woven bag, then swung the strap over one shoulder and got to her feet; Eldon gripped the armrests and propelled himself upward into the sunlit motes of dust. They started toward the beveled glass doors.

Vicky walked them out. She watched Myra bundle Mary Ann into a pink coat, pull a blue hat over her hair, and help her with her mittens. Then the family was out the door into the glare of sunshine and snow, Mary Ann between her parents, holding their hands. A peaceful family picture, yet she could still feel the turmoil and anxiety in Myra and Eldon Little Shield.

She went back to her desk, another image crowding into her mind: the dark figure in the falling snow, the headlights snapping on, the truck roaring down. What is it you learned that you had to die for?

"Vicky?" Annie stood in the doorway. "Are you all right?"

She was not all right; she was thinking, but she tried for a reassuring smile.

"Rick Masterson wants you to call him." Annie walked over and placed the message on the desk.

She had turned back when Vicky said, "See if you can reach Clint Hopkins's secretary and set up a time when we can meet at Clint's office. The sooner, the better."

7

SHANNON O'MALLEY WAS like her mother, kicking up white clouds as she came down the alley, the same air of confidence and assurance Father John remembered in Eileen, as if she would soon make the world turn her way. He went to meet her. "You're early," he said, falling in beside her. She was tall next to him, filled with energy, sunlight shimmering in her reddish hair. Elena wouldn't serve lunch for ten minutes. This could be the first time, he realized, that he was on time for a meal. "All settled in?"

"Doesn't take long to unpack a backpack." She glanced up at him. "Can't wait to transcribe my notes and start writing." She tossed her head about. "You didn't tell me about the buffalo herd on the other side of the fence."

Ah, the buffalo. The rancher next to the mission had raised buffalo for decades. Quiet animals, grazing in the pasture in the summer and fall, nibbling on bales of hay the rancher tossed out. If you stood close enough to the fence, you could sometimes hear a buffalo snorting, but most of the time he forgot the herd was there. "What did you think?"

"I landed in the Wild West. Wyatt Earp and Doc Holliday could show up at any minute. Any gunfights lately?"

"Not lately." You never knew. You never knew. "Did you see the church?"

She stopped walking and turned toward the white stucco church across the alley. "Looks interesting."

"Come on, we'll have a look."

"Do we have time?"

"It's a small church." Father John ushered her up the frosty concrete steps that sparkled in the sun. Opening the heavy oak door, he nodded her into the vestibule. It was chilly inside. The furnace he had adjusted this morning and the sun splashing through the stained glass windows were not enough to banish last night's frigid temperatures.

Shannon started down the center aisle, taking in the windows on one side, then the other. "The geometric symbols are Arapaho," he said, staying with her. "Horizontal lines for the roads we must travel. Rectangles for the buffalo that give their lives so the people can live. Tipis for the people and the villages." Dozens of different symbols; he was still learning the meanings.

Shannon nodded and walked over to the small tipi the women had made from tanned deerskins, the finest skins. Geometric symbols painted in red, blue, black, and yellow decorated the outside. "The tabernacle," he said.

"And that's the altar?" She nodded toward the large drum next to the tabernacle, then twirled about, taking it all in again before she began walking back down the aisle. "It's beautiful," she said when they were outside. "Like a church in a fairy tale."

"Fairy tale?" He walked her across Circle Drive, over the hardened ridges of tire tracks, and through the snow-mounded field, following the footprints he and the bishop had left that morning.

"Where Cinderella marries Prince Charming. Nice, if you believe in fairy tales."

"And you don't?"

"Come on, Uncle John." She stopped in her tracks and was looking up at him. "No one in my generation believes in fairy tales. *Ever after* just doesn't happen. It never did, really. Your generation was the last to cling to that belief. My generation, we take things as they are. Don't expect the impossible. People change and grow, and they need to move on. What works for a while doesn't work forever."

She was looking away now, out across the mission grounds and the open, snowy plains where the buffalo herd grazed, and he caught the shadow of disappointment in her expression. She covered it up quickly—she was a good actress, like her mother. He had never been certain where he stood with Eileen. Always off-balance.

"Anyway, David and I . . ."

"David?"

She took a moment, as if this was a road she wasn't sure she wanted to start down. "I guess you'd call him my boyfriend. We've been together three years now. We live together. We knew it wasn't forever, and that was okay. It's been great, but now it's time to move on. He'll finish his Ph.D. in religious studies this spring and take a position at the University of North Carolina."

They started up the shoveled sidewalk to the residence. "You could write your dissertation anywhere," Father John said.

"Maybe for your generation things were that simple, Uncle John, but we accept that everything has an end."

They took the steps side by side, and he pushed open the front door. No, things were never simple, he wanted to say.

Twenty-five years ago, he had come to that same point, where it was time to move on.

"I'm just saying we don't pretend to believe in *happily ever after.* We're okay with the present." She was pulling off her jacket, and he took it from her and hung it on a hook. He set his own jacket on the bench and placed his cowboy hat on top. Maybe that was the real difference in their generations: the ability to move on without regret. With gratitude, even. But in the smile she gave him, he detected the smallest flicker of sadness and disappointment, which disappeared as quickly as it had flared up.

"If you ever want to talk," he said, but Walks-On came clicking down the hallway, and Shannon swung toward him.

"And who might you be?" She leaned over and ran a slender hand over the dog's coat. "My, you're a handsome fellow. What happened to your hind leg?"

"He lost it on Seventeen-Mile Road when he was a puppy." The conversation about fairy tales and going forward without regret—oh, yes, without any regret that this niece of his would ever admit to—was over.

"Let me guess. You found him and brought him home."

"After a trip to the vet's. He pretty much patrols the mission, keeps us in line."

"Of course you would have a dog. I can't imagine you without a dog."

Walks-On had pivoted about. Looking back to make sure his two charges were in line, he headed down the hallway to the kitchen. The air was filled with smells of tomato soup and grilled cheese, the lunch his mother used to make, Father John was thinking, on frosty winter days.

"Shannon." He kept his voice low, a few feet behind her. "If there is anything you would like to talk over . . ."

"There isn't." She glanced back and flashed the same knowing smile he had found so annoying and attractive in her mother.

"Welcome." Bishop Harry, wrapped in a white apron, pushed himself off the edge of the counter and plunged toward Shannon, hand extended. "A pretty Irish lass, I see. I'm the pastor's assistant."

"Bishop Harry Coughlin," Father John said. "I may be the pastor, but he's the bishop. This is Elena, our housekeeper."

Elena stood at the table, holding several plates. She nodded in Shannon's direction and went about placing the plates on the table. The Arapaho Way, Father John knew. She would hold back until she decided what type of character Shannon had, whether her heart was good. There was no sense in giving yourself to a bad heart. As soon as she decided Shannon had a good heart, Elena would take her in and love her like an orphaned child.

"We've prepared a sumptuous lunch in your honor." The bishop waved at the stove, where grilled cheese sandwiches browned in the frying pan. Father John glanced over at Elena, who looked up and rolled her eyes. "I am pleased to say I am learning to prepare new dishes today. Cooking is not hard if one applies himself. Do sit down." The bishop made a courtly gesture of pulling a chair from the table. "Make yourself at home, because this is your home for as long as you like."

Shannon smiled and shrugged and thanked the old man, then settled herself on the chair. Father John took his usual chair across the table. "I hope the cooks will join us," he said.

"Yes, yes. Naturally." The bishop scooped the sandwiches onto a platter, which he set in the middle of the table, while Elena moved over to the stove and began ladling soup into bowls. One by one, the bishop delivered the bowls. Finally he dropped onto the chair next to Shannon. Fingers of steam curled above the thick red soup.

Elena took her usual place across from the bishop. "Eat

up," she said, scooting her chair into the table. Since Father John had been on the reservation, Arapahos had been placing food in front of him and telling him to eat up. Just like in the Old Time, he knew, when no one was sent away from an Arapaho village hungry. You never knew, heading onto the plains, when you might find food again.

Shannon had dipped her spoon into the soup when Bishop Harry said, "Let us pray." Father John bowed his head, conscious of a sense of contentment flooding over him. Shannon O'Malley, not much more than a girl, carrying with her a connection to his family, to his own past, and to an essential part of himself that, he realized, he sometimes forgot to remember. He had settled in here, at a remote mission on a remote Indian reservation that many of his classmates in the Jesuit seminary, bound for teaching positions at Georgetown or Marquette or some other university, would have considered the dead end of a career, where priests like Bishop Harry Coughlin went to recuperate from the frailties of old age.

"We thank you, Lord, for blessing us with the presence of Shannon O'Malley, and for allowing us to share this meal together."

"Amen," Elena said. "Dig in."

Shannon took a sip of soup and told Elena how delicious it was. "I would love to know how to make it."

"One cooking student is all I can manage at the moment." Elena stirred her own soup and stared at the bishop.

"A very fine teacher you are, I may add," the bishop said. "I had no idea toasted cheese sandwiches could require so much effort. Why, you must watch them like a hawk or one may burn."

"Or two." Elena reached over and pushed the plate of sandwiches in Shannon's direction. A first step, Father John was thinking, in accepting her.

The bishop helped himself to a sandwich and shoved the

plate toward Father John. "I understand you are researching the lives of white sisters held captive by the Plains Indians."

"There were a number of captives between 1860 and 1880." Shannon's voice sparkled with excitement as she moved into familiar territory. "I'm interested in how those who survived viewed their captivity. In what way did it influence or change their lives? I'm especially interested in Elizabeth Fletcher, who was never rescued. She lived here on the reservation."

"Lizzie Brokenhorn." Elena spoke softly, as if the name had triggered a memory.

Shannon gave a smile of acknowledgment, which Elena ignored. "She lived as an Arapaho. Married an Arapaho man when she was only fifteen."

"John Brokenhorn," Elena said.

Father John could feel the excitement building in his niece as she shifted sideways toward the housekeeper. He could almost read the questions popping in her eyes. He stared so hard at her that finally she glanced his way, and in her glance he saw that she had some comprehension of what he was trying to convey. Be patient. Wait. Elena was still making up her mind about Shannon's heart.

"I wonder if it was hard for her to leave her own family and culture behind and live in a completely different world. Oh, I know she was practically a baby when she was captured, but still, a part of her must have known she was different from the people she thought of as her family. Like a blood memory that stayed with her, shadowed her. I can't help but think there were times when it was hard for her."

This seemed to do it. A young white woman's sympathy for an Arapaho captive. Father John watched the lines in Elena's face soften into a smile. She reached over and touched Shannon's hand. "My grandmother was a friend of hers."

Shannon sat upright, questions jumping in her eyes, and Father John shot her another look. Elena had offered a small gift of information. She would offer more if she wished, and all the questions Shannon might come up with wouldn't pry another piece of information out of the housekeeper if she didn't want to provide it.

"My grandfather's ranch was next to Brokenhorn's," Elena said after a moment. "They had been scouts for General Crook when he was chasing the Sioux around, so they went back a long ways." Elena nodded as if to punctuate the friendship. "Only natural the women were friends, too. Grandmother tended to Lizzie when she gave birth, and Lizzie did the same for her. Giving birth was women's work. The men went down to the river, smoked pipes, and waited. Grandmother and Lizzie raised their kids together. Kids went back and forth from house to house. Felt at home wherever they went. Always a mother to feed them, put them to bed when they were tired, make sure they were doing okay."

Elena lifted her head and stared at the ceiling as though an old black-and-white movie were playing there. "It was a hard time when the people first came to the reservation," she said, still watching the ceiling. "Government had already sent the Shoshones here, and they weren't looking to share the rez with Arapahos. We had no place to live. All our lands gone. The hunting grounds, the villages, all gone. Everywhere we went, the people were hunted down. Soldiers, white posses, ranchers, homesteaders. Open season on Indians back then. Shoshones say Chief Washakie's heart was so big he couldn't turn us away."

Elena lowered her eyes and turned toward Shannon. "Hope you'll get it right when you tell your story."

"I want to very much. I'll do my best."

Elena patted Shannon's hand again. "Remember that Lizzie was Arapaho. She lived Arapaho. Grandmother said Lizzie hated the way she looked. She rubbed dirt on her face and arms to make them dark. She washed her hair in mud to turn it black, but she still had light skin and hair as golden red as wild grass in August. But no one thought of her as anything but Arapaho."

The bishop had finished eating. He stacked his soup bowl on top of the empty sandwich plate. "I'm thinking she must have been a remarkable woman to make the best of what life had dealt her."

"Oh, more than that." Elena shook her head at the obstinacy of the white people at her table. Her table, Father John knew. Her kitchen, her house to keep, and her white priests to marshal about. "Grandmother said Lizzie loved her husband, and he loved her. He got scared the government agents would take her away after it dawned on them she was white, so he found a place in the mountains that was real hard to get to. No roads. You had to go cross-country on horseback. He built a shack. Of course, Indians weren't supposed to go anywhere without the agent's permission. Darn near needed permission to go to the outhouse. But Brokenhorn swore he would do whatever was necessary to protect Lizzie. Sure enough, the agent started snooping around, asking questions, so Brokenhorn took his family to the mountains. Grandfather kept denying Brokenhorn had gone anywhere. Just off helping neighbors round up cattle. After a while, the agent stopped coming around, and grandfather went up in the mountains and told Brokenhorn it was all clear. Before winter set in, Brokenhorn, Lizzie, and the five kids came back. Grandmother said she was sure glad to see Lizzie again. The house next door had seemed lonely without them."

Elena got to her feet and began clearing the table, and Father John understood this was the end of her story. He stood up and took his dishes over to the sink. "Thank you, Elena." He waved a hand to indicate both the lunch and the story, everything that had taken place in the kitchen.

"Yes. Thank you very much." Shannon cleared her dishes and went back for the bishop's.

"A very delicious lunch." The old man lumbered to his

feet. The white apron still hung from his neck and was looped about his waist. "A most interesting story and, I must say, a most enlightening cooking lesson. At what time shall we start preparing dinner?"

Elena threw a glance over her shoulder at Father John. There were layers of meaning in her glance. He could write a whole sermon on how we are made holy by the way we claim our place in the world and do our work the best we can. Another glance from Elena, and he decided he would have a talk with the bishop.

He motioned Shannon ahead and followed her down the hall, Walks-On between them. The dog had an uncanny sense for adventure, and he didn't want to miss out. Most days he climbed into the pickup and accompanied Father John on rounds of visits to the elders and the sick and those needing someone to stop by for a chat and a cup of coffee.

But not this afternoon. Father John didn't know if Wilbur Horn would welcome a visit from a dog. He helped Shannon with her jacket and pulled on his own jacket before he leaned down and patted the dog's head. "You have to take care of Elena and the bishop today," he said. Then he opened the door for Shannon, followed her out into the bright, cold air, and set his cowboy hat on his head.

Shannon hurried ahead down the snowy path. "I have to get my laptop," she called over her shoulder.

"You won't need it."

"To make notes during the interview." She stopped in the middle of Circle Drive, shadows of impatience on her face. Did she have to explain the obvious?

He placed an arm around her shoulders and steered her along the drive to the passenger side of the old pickup. "You can make notes when you get back."

He closed the door behind her and gave her a smile through the windshield as he walked around to the driver's side. "So that was the look you were shooting at me over the table," she said as he jiggled the key in the ignition and tried to coax the engine into life. "I recognized the O'Malley look. Dad used it on us kids when we asked too many questions. It was his way of saying, 'Stop talking and you might learn something.'"

Father John laughed. The pickup jumped ahead as if it knew the way through the tunnel of cottonwoods out to Seventeen-Mile Road. In his mind was a flash of memory: his own father shooting the O'Malley look across the table to Mike and him.

"I get the way it works around here," Shannon said. "Ask no questions and pray for answers. Write it down later."

A cottonwood branch scratched at the top of the pickup, and a pile of snow slid down the windshield. He flipped on the wipers and tried to keep the pickup steady through the tunnel. Then he turned left onto Seventeen-Mile Road and glanced over at Shannon. "That's about it," he said.

8

WILBUR HORN STOOD at the edge of the driveway, gloved hand waving them forward. Across the barrow ditch and along the two-track that marked the driveway. The old pickup shuddered and jumped over the ice-hardened snow. "Lizzie's great-grandson?" High notes of excitement rang in Shannon's voice.

Father John glanced over and smiled. For an instant he was back in grad school at Boston College, researching some obscure event in American history, and with a turn of a page or an idle remark, he'd be plunged backward in time, as if the past itself had reached out and grabbed him. He could still feel the excitement.

She gripped the door handle with one hand, bracing herself against the dashboard with the other and nodding, excitement shooting off her like fireworks. He stopped at the end of the driveway in a clear spot Wilbur had waved to. Then the man yanked the door open. He might have been a doorman at a hotel. "Nice to see you, Father." He had a wide grin and black eyes that sparkled with light in the shade of his cowboy hat. His denim jacket was lined with fur that poked out around the collar. "This your niece?"

"Shannon O'Malley," Father John said, but Wilbur was already advancing toward Shannon, who had let herself out on the passenger side.

"Sure a lot prettier than you." Wilbur smiled at Father John while he pumped Shannon's hand. "Well, let's not waste good daylight. Come on inside." He dipped his head in the direction of the rectangular house with yellow siding and a three-step stoop at the front door, like most of the houses on the rez. Inside, two bedrooms, bath, living room, kitchen. Larger than the log cabins and tiny shacks that, for nearly a hundred years, the government had considered satisfactory houses for Indians.

Wilbur led the way across the hardened snow and up the steps. He pushed open the door and gestured them inside. The house was warm, suffused with smells of freshly brewed coffee and sizzling oil. "I put on a pot of coffee." Wilbur took a few steps across the living room toward the kitchen. "Belle made fry bread before she went to work this morning. She's going to stop by on her lunch break." He motioned them through the arched doorway, tilting his head in the direction of a round table and four wooden chairs in the corner of the kitchen. Shannon took one of the chairs, and Father John sat next to her. When he had spoken with Belle Horn at a powwow last summer, she told him she had just taken a job as the nursing supervisor at the health clinic.

"Belle's got a bug about all this history stuff." Wilbur was bustling about the counter, pouring mugs of coffee, setting them on the table. "You'd think she was the one descended from Lizzie and Brokenhorn. She was always telling stories to the kids about their great-great-grandmother, the white captive. You like fry bread?"

Shannon nodded, and Father John caught the flash of curiosity and amusement in her eyes. Indian reservation, fry bread, the descendant of Lizzie Fletcher Brokenhorn. Exactly what she would have imagined. This girl had a big imagination and, he was learning, a big appetite for life.

"Bread's nice and warm." Wilbur lifted a plate stacked with fry bread from the oven and set it in the center of the table. The chunks of bread were rounded and irregular, like biscuits. Then, a stack of small plates, paper napkins, a bottle of honey, and a plate of butter and a knife appeared on the table. "Belle's proud of her fry bread. Used to watch her grandmother make it in a pot of hot oil on the campfire. Help yourselves." Wilbur dropped onto the chair next to the window. "She'll expect a good review." He nodded toward the vacant chair, as if Belle were about to materialize.

"I'm not sure how to do this." Shannon took a chunk of bread, set it on a plate, and studied it as if she might unlock its mystery.

"Butter first." Wilbur pulled a piece of bread apart, lathered on a slab of butter. "Honey next." He held the bottle of honey over his plate and let the golden liquid drizzle over the bread. "Then, good eating."

Shannon followed along. She took a bite of the honeyed, buttered bread and sat back, a look of contentment flowing over her like water. "Oh my gosh," she said. "Nothing like this in Boston."

Father John helped himself and bit into the warm bread. Fry bread always came with the memory of the first time he'd eaten it: a brush shade at the Sun Dance, temperatures hovering around a hundred degrees, a little breeze stirring the cottonwood branches that covered the ceiling and three walls, the Fast Pony family gathered around, proud of the family's fry bread recipe—no one could make it like Grandmother—waiting for his confirmation. Like Shannon, he had realized how much he had been missing. Odd how such memories crowded him lately. He had an urgent sense that he should capture every experience, keep it safe so that he wouldn't forget.

Then came the whoosh of the front door opening. A stream of cold air shot through the kitchen, and the door clacked shut. Belle Horn, younger than her husband by a few years, clutching a brown bag of groceries, walked into the kitchen, and Father John got to his feet. "Good to see you," he said as the woman set the bag on the counter. She turned and took his hand. A handsome woman, on the stout side with a strong grip, broad shoulders, and shoulder-length black hair streaked with gray.

"No way was I going to miss this." She let go of his hand and turned to Shannon. "I'm Belle, the better half."

Shannon started to get up, but Belle placed a hand on her shoulder. "Don't let me interrupt. Keep on talking about whatever you were discussing."

"I was just about to ask how our guest likes the rez." Wilbur kept his eyes on Shannon, took another bite of bread, and washed it down with coffee. Now would come the polite preliminaries, before the conversation moved to the topic that Shannon, Father John knew, was eager to talk about.

Belle pulled a carton of milk out of the bag and set it in the refrigerator in a slow, relaxed motion. She hadn't missed anything important. Then she hung her coat on the back of the vacant chair, sat down, and helped herself to the fry bread, switching her gaze between her husband and Shannon.

Father John tried to give Shannon another look. He hadn't warned her about the polite preliminaries, but she was sipping at her coffee, eating her fry bread. Nodding and smiling at Wilbur Horn. She liked the rez fine. Wide spaces that go on forever. She'd never seen so much space and so few people. "Beautiful," she said, and Wilbur and Belle grinned.

Oh, this niece of his had an instinct for fitting right in, picking up the reins, and riding along.

Shannon looked over at Belle. "The fry bread is delicious. Thank you for making it."

Belle smiled and shrugged. After all, it was what she did, saw to it that guests were fed, like any other woman on the rez.

After a few minutes on weather, the snow expected tonight, Wilbur said, "I understand you're writing a report on my great-grandparents."

Great-grandparents. Shannon glanced over at Father John, something new in her eyes. They were a pair, weren't they? Part of each other's lives, Lizzie and John Brokenhorn.

"Yes." She turned back to Wilbur and told him she was researching the lives of Lizzie and her sister, Amanda, both captured by the Plains Indians. "I'm looking for the details. Personal stories that make the women human and help us to understand them."

"History books get things wrong," Wilbur said. "They make out how bad things went for captives, like all Indians were barbarians. Sure, some of the white women had it tough, especially when the warriors went on the rampage after that terrible massacre in Colorado."

Silence dropped over the kitchen. Shannon kept her eyes on the last piece of bread on her plate, then looked over at Father John. He had read about the Sand Creek Massacre in 1864, the massacre that drove the Arapahos and Cheyennes from their Colorado homelands. "It was a terrible time," he said.

"I'm not saying the Cheyennes didn't mistreat white captives."

"Plenty of white men mistreated Indian women," Belle said.

Wilbur leaned forward. "History books lump all the

tribes together. Arapahos traded for white captives. They returned them or kept them with the people. Those old Arapahos knew it was a good thing to have new people and fresh blood. Good to strengthen the tribe. You see Arapahos with blond hair and blue eyes on the rez today. They come down from whites, some of them captives. Like my family. Blue eyes here." He lifted a hand to his eyes. "I'm proud I came down from Lizzie Brokenhorn. I got cousins with hair the color of pink sand, like hers. We're all proud."

"I'm not sure how Lizzie came to the Arapahos," Shannon said. A comment, not a question. His niece was a quick study.

Wilbur sipped at his coffee. Finally he said, "She wasn't captured by Arapahos, like the history books say. My father did his own research. Talked to some of the elders that went back to the time of Sand Creek. Lizzie was captured the next summer, in 1865. There were some Arapaho warriors riding with Cheyennes that day, but it was a Cheyenne attack. After Sand Creek, there was no peace. Cheyennes had been raiding on the North Platte that summer, and Arapahos joined them."

"Lizzie never would have been captured if her father had used common sense." Belle shook her head and pulled apart a piece of bread. "Tell them what your dad found out."

"Jasper Fletcher, Lizzie's father, decided to move his family from Illinois to California so he could find gold and get rich. He and Mary Ann had five kids. Jasper had joined a large wagon train that no Indians with any sense were gonna attack. He should've stayed with the train, but he decided to pull ahead. Stop along the river, have lunch. That's when the Cheyenne Chief Sand Hill and his warriors rode down on them. Killed Mary Ann and wounded Jasper. The boys got away. The Indians took Amanda Mary and Lizzie and rode off."

"Seven months later"—Belle was shaking her head—"a trader found Amanda Mary in a Cheyenne camp and ransomed her. But there was no sign of Lizzie."

"My father told me the old Indians he talked to said that Cut Nose, another Cheyenne warrior, gave Lizzie to his wife as their new daughter. She was a real pretty little thing, with blue eyes and light-colored hair. Cut Nose called her Little Silver Hair. He always treated her kindly, and his wife kept her dressed in fine clothing. She grew up speaking Cheyenne."

Shannon sipped at her coffee. Holding the cup in both hands, she said, "I didn't realize she grew up Cheyenne."

"Cheyenne, until Brokenhorn and some other Arapahos went to Cut Nose's camp to trade. Great-grandfather always said the minute he laid eyes on Lizzie, he knew she would be his wife. At first Cut Nose refused. There weren't enough ponies or robes or glass beads or tobacco to make Cut Nose give her up." Wilbur shook his head and smiled to himself, a faraway look in his eyes, as if he could see the Cheyenne warrior standing firm, refusing to trade his daughter. "Brokenhorn didn't give up. He kept coming back to Cut Nose's camp. He trailed a half dozen ponies packed with pots and pans and food he'd gotten trading with other bands. Everything he owned, he brought to Cut Nose. It still didn't persuade him."

Belle tilted her head back and laughed at the ceiling as though she were reliving the bargaining herself. "The one who persuaded Cut Nose was Lizzie," she said. "Brokenhorn had taken the opportunity to talk to her alone. Followed her to the creek when she went for water, waited for her in the brush when she went to pick berries. They fell in love. Finally, Lizzie convinced her father to let her marry Brokenhorn, and Cut Nose himself presided over the wedding. There was a big feast, and afterward, Brokenhorn and Lizzie went to Brokenhorn's village. Her father gave her the ponies

Brokenhorn had given him because Cut Nose did not want his daughter to come to the Arapahos as a beggar. She rode into the village as a proud and much-loved Cheyenne woman. She was fifteen when she became Arapaho. After that, she was called Kellsto Time."

"White folks always want to know, were they happy?" Wilbur clasped his hands on the table and leaned forward. "Like that's all that matters. My father told me that great-grandfather always looked after Lizzie. They were traditionals, stayed close to the old ways. In the summers, Brokenhorn pledged the Sun Dance and Lizzie cooked for the dancers. Even after the government outlawed the Sun Dance and threatened people with prison if they took part, Brokenhorn and Lizzie and the other traditionals went into the mountains, where the government agent couldn't find them, and held the Sun Dance anyway. That's the kind of people they were. After she married Great-grandfather, she never spoke another word of Cheyenne. She took pride in being Arapaho."

The coffeepot made a rhythmic blipping noise in the quiet that dropped over the kitchen. Wilbur had told the story he intended to tell; there was nothing else. "Thank you," Father John said.

"Oh yes." Shannon jumped in. "Thank you so much."

Belle shifted sideways toward her husband. "You suppose your relation Daisy might talk to them?"

Wilbur drew in his lips and shrugged. He took a moment before he said, "That old lady makes it her business to keep track of family history. Spends most her time off visiting her grandkids. Not sure you can catch her."

Belle had turned toward Shannon. "Daisy's a granddaughter. She thinks she's an expert on the Old Time. She likes telling stories."

"Self-proclaimed expert." Wilbur started to his feet. "Doesn't think anyone else has a right to poke into family history. I'll give her a call and see if she's around. You might want to see if you can talk to another old granddaughter. Theresa Horn is pretty sharp sometimes, and other times not so much. Give her grandson, Thomas, a call and see if the old lady will talk to you."

Father John stood up and pushed his chair into the table, catching Shannon's eyes as he did so. That was the way research went, just as Shannon had said. You start somewhere and are sent somewhere else. You never know where you might go. He thanked Wilbur and Belle, and Shannon joined in. Praising the delicious fry bread, the generous gift of information, the Arapaho hospitality.

THROUGH THE TUNNEL of cottonwoods shimmering in snow, Father John spotted the dark maroon truck in front of the administration building. He turned onto Circle Drive and pulled up alongside the truck.

"Looks like you have company." Shannon had talked nonstop on the drive back to the mission, recalling everything Wilbur had said, exclaiming over the emptiness of the reservation, the small houses, the abandoned cars and trucks and appliances in the yards, laundry stiff as cement on the lines.

"How did you get used to this place?" she had asked at one point.

He wanted to say it had been easy. It seemed easy now, but ten years ago, fresh out of rehab for the second or third time, frightened that this was his last chance, an Indian reservation nobody had ever heard of—at least no one he knew—in the middle of nowhere. The truth was, it had been hard.

"I like it here," he said. Then he told her that James Two Horses, a parishioner, had stopped by to fix his Wi-Fi.

"A parishioner? I'd like to meet him."

Father John got out and started around the pickup toward the passenger side, but Shannon had already jumped out. She bounced ahead of him up the steps and into the administration building.

9

"HEY, FATHER. YOU have Wi-Fi again." James leaned into the corridor from the doorway to the bishop's office. "Just saying my good-byes," he said, walking toward them. "This must be the niece I've heard so much about. You're uncle's pretty proud of you." He took Shannon's hand; a large brown hand enclosing the small whiteness.

"I can't imagine why." Shannon tossed a glance over one shoulder toward Father John. "I mean, he's the historian. I'm just getting started."

"Well, getting started can be the hardest thing to do."

Shannon left her hand in James's, and for an instant Father John felt as if he had stumbled on a live wire with electricity shooting around. Finally, Shannon withdrew her hand. "You fix computers?" She tilted her head back, staring up at the Arapaho.

"Pretty much keep the computers up and running for the school districts in the area." James hadn't taken his eyes from her. Was this the way it happened? Father John had forgotten, or maybe he had decided not to remember. Eileen walking across campus, red hair blowing back in the breeze, and everything about her perfect somehow. He had known before they had spoken a word to each other that she was the woman he wanted to marry.

Some memories were better left forgotten. He had been called elsewhere. In the middle of the night. And he had broken off their engagement and answered the call, and two months later—he was still settling in at the seminary—Eileen had married his brother, Mike. And here was one of their six kids, this beautiful young woman, as close as he would ever come to having a child of his own.

He had many children. He tried to grab on to the idea. A whole reservation full of children. He was a father in a different sense. God help me. Let these memories pass.

James was saying something about installing a different router. No problem. He had a whole closet full of routers the school district had discarded. This one worked just fine.

"I'm in your debt."

"How about dinner one of these days? I hear Elena's a great cook."

"She has a good assistant." Bishop Harry made his way down the corridor. "And her assistant hereby invites you to dinner anytime."

James was still watching Shannon. And this from a man who believed he had a calling to the priesthood. Odd how the calling to the priesthood went, Father John was thinking. It didn't always encompass everything.

"I was thinking you and I could go out to dinner this evening." James said.

Shannon hadn't stopped smiling. "I think I'd like that a lot."

"Good. I'll look forward to hearing about your research on Lizzie Brokenhorn."

"You've heard of her?"

"Hard to find anybody on the rez who hasn't. White woman with blue-eyed, blond-haired Arapaho descendants."

"I'd love to hear your stories."

"I'm not a descendant." James looked up at the ceiling and laughed. "At least as far as I know. See you later." He edged past them.

"Six o'clock," Shannon said just before the door closed. She was still smiling when she turned back.

"Let me show you where we hang out." Making an effort now to break the spell that had dropped over the corridor, Father John gestured toward the doorway to his office on the right.

"May I issue a formal invitation to visit my abode at the end of the corridor?" The bishop made a little bow and started back toward his office.

Shannon moved past Father John. She took a moment, surveying his office, the desk and chair, the worn visitors' chairs scattered about, as if a strong wind had blown them onto the brown rug with the path worn down the middle, the bookcases along the back wall, crammed with books that stood upright and fell against one another, the CD player on the top shelf, the little metal table with the coffeepot and jars of creamer and sugar.

She turned on her heels. "I assume he isn't married."

"The bishop?"

Shannon rolled her eyes at his attempt at humor, like one of his students in the Jesuit prep school where he had taught American history.

"If you mean James, he's been busy getting an education and starting a career, I suspect." It was on the tip of his tongue, the fact that James Two Horses was considering the priesthood, but he didn't say anything. James would have to tell her.

"There's more to see." He gestured her back into the corridor and around the corner into the side hallway. A small kitchen. Bath. And over there, the mission archives. She was welcome to use them. "Lizzie was a traditional," he said, "but even traditionals sometimes came to the mission. They prayed both ways, the old way and the way the early missionaries taught."

Shannon smiled up at him. Light flickered in her eyes. Another place to do research. The reservation, a treasure trove of the past.

She took a minute, new thoughts flitting through her expression. "He seems very nice." She hesitated, then pushed on. "Centered. Yes, that is how I would describe him. Centered. I mean, he looks like he knows himself and what he wants."

Maybe not, Father John was thinking. James, struggling with what he wanted. It was not an easy struggle.

"Let me show you the rest of it." Father John retraced his steps past the bath and kitchen and headed across the corridor, the tap-tap of Shannon's boots following him. He opened the door into a storage closet—a hoarding place, really—where generations of Jesuits had dropped old, broken equipment, used-up lightbulbs, stacks of newspapers and magazines they no doubt intended to read someday, three-legged chairs and cracked tables, and more junk than he had wanted to wade into, but he had waded into it anyway. Now it was a small office. Desk, chair, filing cabinet, and crooked-neck lamp that flooded the room with light.

"You're welcome to work here"—he stood back and ushered Shannon inside—"anytime you'd like to be in the center of things, rather than off by yourself in the guesthouse."

"Parishioners dropping in all the time? Phone ringing? A buzz of activity?"

"Pretty much."

"I think I'd love it." She stepped back into the corridor and eyed the door. "I'd better start recording my notes while the interview is still fresh."

"First, the bishop's abode."

"Oh yes." She laughed, and her laugh was like music, he thought. It was her mother's laugh. She headed down the hall and disappeared through the last doorway.

Father John followed and poked his head around the door frame. Shannon was examining the laptop, the easy chair, the braided rug the bishop had resurrected from the storage closet, the wall poster of Arapaho dancers whirling about at a powwow, a blur of bright reds, blues, and yellows. A cozy office Bishop Harry had made his own. But then, the bishop could probably make anyplace his own. Wasn't that part of the calling? To go wherever you were sent, and make the place your own?

"Very comfy," Shannon said with the bishop beaming under her approval. She was used to charming her way, Father John was thinking.

"I look forward to more of your home cooking." She pushed the edge of her coat sleeve back and checked her watch again, and then she was through the doorway, leaning back. "Just not this evening. Sorry."

Bishop Harry let out a bark of laughter. "I'd say she's got the number of a couple of bachelors."

"She's like her mother." Father John perched on the seat of the wooden chair in front of the bishop's desk.

"Oh yes. I believe you've mentioned her. Eileen, wasn't it? She married your brother after you went to the seminary. I assume it has been a happy marriage."

Father John took a moment before he said, "I hope so." He pushed on, as if the topic were unimportant, a thing of the past not worth considering. "There's something I would like to talk to you about."

The bishop lifted a hand and pulled it toward his chest; he might have been waving the words forward. "About Shannon?"

"James," Father John said. Odd how Bishop Harry had

jumped ahead. Perhaps the topic would eventually be about Shannon. "Has he mentioned he believes he might have a calling to the priesthood?"

"I gathered as much." The bishop shifted about, settling himself against the back of his chair. "Serving Mass almost every morning before going off to work. Yes, it makes sense he is grappling with a possible change in his life."

"I believe you could be a great help to him. I'm sure you've counseled many young men thinking about entering the priesthood."

"As have you, John. I can see how the man looks up to you. You're his ideal priest."

"I hope that isn't the case." Father John heard the sound of his own laughter, forced and choked. "You have far more experience and the wisdom that comes with it."

Bishop Harry tipied his fingers under his chin and swiveled toward the window. The sun had disappeared behind a sky as flat and gray as a sheet of metal. The bare cottonwoods looked like streaks of brown painted on the exterior of Eagle Hall.

He swiveled back. "I would have to pull out my notes and read through them, refresh myself about some of the issues James may be grappling with. It has been a long time since I went down that path myself, and the times were different then. There's been a lot of research on how to counsel young men considering the priesthood since my day. I would have to read the most recent literature. Quite a project, I would say." The old man's eyes had come alive. "Of course, if you believe I could be of help, I will be glad to offer James my services."

"Thank you." Father John got to his feet and started toward the corridor.

"By the way, you had a call this afternoon."

He stepped back, took the small piece of paper the bishop handed across the desk, and read the message scribbled down the middle: *3 p.m. Father Jameson. Please return call as soon as possible.*

"Father Jameson in the provincial's office?" He looked over at the bishop, waiting for confirmation, snatching at time—a little more time here at St. Francis. "Did he say what it was about?" He knew what it was about: the call that had always been coming, down through the weeks and months and the years at the mission.

The bishop shook his head. "Very businesslike, Father Jameson. Said an important meeting had been scheduled. One of my seminary students thirty years ago when I was teaching theology . . ." He shook his head. "Well, one never knows what the Holy Spirit has in mind."

Father John stuffed the message into the pocket of his jeans and glanced at his watch. "I have to go out again," he said. "Should be back in an hour or so."

"Something else has occurred to me," the bishop said as Father John started into the corridor. He swung back. The old man was rocking in his chair, hands clasped over his chest. "It strikes me this new project of counseling James will take quite a bit of my time. I may have to give up other projects, like my cooking lessons." He gave Father John a wide, knowing smile. "But you knew that, didn't you?"

10

HER NAME WAS Dolly. At least that's what Vince told his mother. Dolly was all she knew, Betty said, when Vicky had tried to push for some other identification. Dolly lived in an apartment on the northeast side of Riverton—that two-story building with brown shingles on the outside walls, like they had run out of bricks or concrete blocks and just kept putting on shingles.

Vicky knew the building. Friendly to Indians; a number of Arapahos lived there, moving in and out, piling in with friends for a time. Dolly lived on the ground floor, first door on the left, a fact that Betty White Hawk remembered from the time Vince had called and said he was sick and she had picked him up there.

"How do you know he's there?" Vicky had asked. She could still feel the raw irritation she had felt after Vince threw her hard-won deal with the prosecuting attorney out the window and took off.

"Jason Eagle—you know him?" Betty hurried on, not waiting for an answer. "He didn't want to tell me. You know, boozers don't snitch, sort of a code, cover each other's tracks. I convinced him you were the only hope Vince had for staying out of Rawlins. Nobody wants to get sent down there. The county jail looks like a resort compared to prison, so Jason stalled and tried to make me believe he'd call me back. I said, 'Jason, I know too much about you. Tell me where Vince went.' The minute he said, 'Dolly's place,' I thought, jeez, I should've figured he'd go running to his ex-girlfriend. I called over there and Dolly picked up. Took ten minutes to get her to admit Vince was sleeping it off in the bedroom."

That had been thirty minutes ago. Vince White Hawk was like a shadow that crossed time zones, disappeared in the blink of an eye. Vicky had thrown on her coat, grabbed her bag, and, on the way out the door, told Annie to have Roger handle her afternoon appointments—there were two: Mo Standing Bull seeking workmen's compensation for injuries at the loading dock where he worked, and Mara Whiteman, facing a third DUI charge. Roger was perfectly capable of explaining options and consequences and suggesting possible steps.

And Vince could already be gone. Vicky tightened her grip on the steering wheel and pressed down on the gas pedal, pushing the Ford as fast as she dared, past the pine trees drooping under pillows of snow, past the bungalows that resembled her own office, to Main Street. She followed the wide curve out of town, through Hudson and north onto Highway 789.

On instinct now. She had a sense of where the brown-shingled apartment building was located, but not the exact address. God, she could be driving up and down side streets for fifteen minutes before she happened across it, and Vince would melt away.

She wondered why she cared. She had done her best to help this twenty-two-year-old, despite the message drummed into her at the law firm in Denver where she had worked after graduating from law school: save your energy and time—the firm's precious, expensive time—for appreciative clients who work with you, not against you. And wasn't that exactly what Adam Lone Eagle had said when they practiced together in Lander? Holden and Lone Eagle, specializing in natural resources law, important matters. Losers don't deserve you, Adam used to say. Which she supposed made logical sense, in Adam's world. But weren't they the reason she had gone to law school? The losers, the people who *couldn't* help themselves? They had gone separate ways: She, back to what Adam always called "little cases," and he, to a large natural-resources law firm in Denver.

Up ahead, on the corner, she spotted the brown-shingled building. The street was unplowed, thick with snow, crust-hardened and slushy at the same time. She steered the Ford alongside the curb, got out, and hurried up the sidewalk to the door. She rapped twice, hard, and leaned in close, listening for footsteps, the scrape of a chair. Nothing. She glanced about. No sign of Vince's tan pickup on either side of the street. She could feel her heart hammering. The friend would have called Dolly, who would have told Vince, and Vince would have taken off.

She removed her glove and knocked again, and this time, the thin wooden door jumped beneath her fist. "Vince," she called. "I know you're here." That was a laugh. There was no reason in the world to believe he was still there. "It's Vicky Holden. Open up."

She heard it then, a slow shushing noise, like wind blowing through a tiny crack. The door slid open the width of a chain lock, and part of a face appeared, a single eye, a Cyclops, blinking at her. "Dolly? I'm Vince's lawyer. I have to talk to him."

The door slammed shut. There was the rattling, disengaging noise of the chain breaking loose, then the door opened wider. Filling up the narrow space was a young woman, slender, bent forward, as fragile-looking as a twig that might snap in two. Blond, with eyes like pewter, flat and opaque. It took Vicky by surprise, the blond hair and white face and arms that hung from a tee shirt with ragged edges where the sleeves had been. She had expected Dolly to be Indian. Arapaho. This was an apartment building where Arapahos lived.

"He's not here." The woman could have been anywhere between eighteen and forty, vacant-looking, with sunken eyes above sharp cheekbones and the sucked-in look of a woman who no longer had back teeth. Meth did that to people.

Vicky could almost taste the defeat rolling off the woman. "Are you Dolly?"

She hunched her shoulders and gave a slow, obsequious nod. Yes, she was Dolly.

"Where is he?" Vicky tried to push past the sadness of it, the loss of a life.

Signs of a struggle worked through Dolly's expression: the desire of an addict to please warring against the desire to protect a man she might love, who might even love her. "I'm trying to help him," Vicky said. God, Vince could be miles away, heading to some obscure house on the rez where no one would think to look for him. He could hide out for days. Sooner or later, it was bound to happen—one of his buddies would give him up and the cops would show up and Vince would fight or run or try to do both, and he could be shot.

"I can't help him if I don't know where he is. Look . . ." Vicky leaned in closer. There was the acrid smell of some half-dead thing about the woman.

The pewter eyes blinked against the moisture welling at the corners. "I promised not to tell anybody."

"If you care about Vince, help me to help him."

That seemed to convince her. The signs of struggle disappeared; the pale face hardened in a new resolve: She would have to help Vince because, yes, he loved her. She was sure he loved her. She said, "You just missed him."

"I need to know where I can find him."

"He left to get some more booze. He needed a drink real bad, and I didn't have nothing left."

"Is he coming back?"

She gave a weak smile and shook her head. "Like I said, I didn't have nothing around. He'll go drink somewhere else 'til he gets enough of it and is sick as a dog, then he'll come back around. He always does."

"Where did he go for the booze?"

She lifted her thin shoulders. "He was pretty thirsty."

The nearest liquor store, Vicky was thinking. She tried to picture where that would be. On Federal, a few blocks away. She thanked Dolly and hurried down the sidewalk, barely aware of the door cracking shut behind her. Vince had a good ten or fifteen minutes on her.

Vicky spotted him as she turned into the parking lot in front of the liquor store. Stooped forward like an old man, wearing a dark sweatshirt, clutching a brown bag to his chest. The door swung shut behind him as he started weaving toward the tan pickup at the curb.

She drove down the rows of parked vehicles and braked in front of Vince, who jumped sideways, surprise and fear stamped on his face. She jumped out, walked around, and stood between him and the driver's side of the pickup. "We had an appointment," she said.

He tossed his head back and forth, as if there might be someplace to run, fright and desperation in his eyes. "I got other things to do."

"We have to talk. Let me buy you a cup of coffee." Vicky set her hand on the man's arm. Pulling him forward, guiding him along the snow-patched sidewalk, past the liquor store, the barber shop, the knitting store to the coffee shop. She could feel the trembling deep inside him. And something else: the hard metal of a gun beneath his jacket.

"This is no good." He yanked himself free.

"It's important, Vince. You can use a cup of coffee." She held the door open and gestured him inside. The booth next to the door was empty, used napkins and cups with traces of coffee in the bottoms piled in the center. The next booth had been cleared, but it was a good three feet farther into the shop, an extra moment in which he could swing around and run back outside.

She handed him into the red plastic seat and sat down on the other side of the table. "The sheriff is expecting us," she said.

"Well, I changed my mind." Vince was still holding the brown bag close to his chest, leaning over it so that the top of the bag crumpled under his chin. "No way am I going there."

"It's your only chance."

The waitress appeared and scooped the dirty cups and napkins onto a tray, then waited, as if words weren't necessary for the obvious.

Vicky leaned toward Vince. "Do you want something to eat?"

He threw her a dismissive look. Food wasn't what he wanted. She couldn't decide where he was in the cycle of alcoholic addiction: Coming off a bender? Going into a bender? Not yet sick enough to have been drinking for a while, she realized. Vince was still getting started.

"Two coffees." Vicky waited until the waitress had turned on her heel and disappeared into the back of the shop, then she said, "I've worked out the best deal possible." She kept her voice low, confidential. "Now is not the time to walk away."

"I don't want nothing to do with the law."

"You don't have a choice." My God, what was he thinking? The whole legal system would just ignore an attempted robbery charge? "You tried to steal a woman's grocery money at the ATM outside the supermarket. You're all over the video. You were there, you did it, and the prosecuting attorney can't overlook it."

"Jeez, Vicky. You're supposed to be my lawyer. I told you what happened. I just asked if she had any extra change 'cause I was . . ." He bit on his lower lip a moment. "I was bad thirsty. I needed a bottle."

"A good story." Vince White Hawk could charm snakes. He could conjure any scenario he wanted. "The prosecuting attorney has watched the video and so have I. You were aggressive and threatening. The woman threw her purse at you and ran for her life."

Vicky leaned back. The waitress was at the table again, delivering cups of coffee, a metal pitcher of milk, a bowl of sugar packets. She rummaged in the pockets of her apron and pulled out two spoons, which she dropped next to the cups.

"Look . . ." Vicky said, moving forward against the edge of the table when the waitress had left. "You turn yourself in, and Peters will consider lowering the charges from attempted robbery to a misdemeanor." She was thinking she would have to find a way to get the gun before she took him in. "It's your choice whether you do time in Rawlins," she went on, "or in the county jail with a rehab program thrown in. We have to be at the sheriff's office this afternoon, the sooner the better. Not tomorrow after you've finished off the bottles."

He was shaking his head, and Vicky realized he had been shaking his head the whole time, denying, refusing. "I'm telling you, there's no way I'm giving myself up."

"What is it? You were willing to go along with the deal. What's changed?"

"I got plans." Vince tried to lift his coffee cup, then set it down, hands shaking. Brown liquid sloshed over the top and ran in rivulets along the table. She knew what had changed. Vince had been desperate for booze. So desperate last week he had tried to rob a woman at an ATM. There was no money for booze, so he had agreed to the deal. Since then he had somehow come into money to buy the three bottles in the brown bag. And he had a gun.

"I'm laying low on the rez until I can get out of here. So far away the cops'll never find me." He bent his head over the bag and slurped at the coffee.

"Listen to me, Vince. They will find you. They will find you at whatever drinking house you hide out in. One of your buddies will snitch on you to get some kind of a deal for himself. Every cop in the county will be looking for you. You'll never make it out of here." She took a moment, watching for any sign that what she'd said had sunk in. "Where did you get the money?"

Vince slurped at the coffee, his eyes on the table.

"The money for the booze. The money to leave here. Gas. Food. Motels. Booze. Where did you get the money?"

"You're crazy." He had started shaking, as if the trembling she had felt earlier had worked its way to the surface and spread over him like a rash.

"Your mother's worried sick." Vicky tried a different tack. "She wants you to take the deal."

"You don't get it. Everything's different." Vince went back to his coffee. "There's no more deal."

"I can take you to the prosecuting attorney's office and he can explain your options."

Vince pulled himself upright, still shaking. "I got my pickup here," he said, as if that were the most important matter.

"I'll arrange to have your pickup taken to your mother's."

He didn't protest. She had worn him down, she was thinking. He really didn't have any options. She glanced around for the waitress, but there was no one at the counter. The shop was empty. Then the waitress sauntered out from the back, as if she had been summoned, and took up her place behind the cash register.

Vicky dug several bills out of her wallet. "Wait here." She slid out of the booth, walked over to the counter and plopped down the bills. She told the frozen-faced waitress to keep the change, then turned back.

The booth was empty, the door still swinging shut. Through the plate glass window, she watched Vince weave toward the pickup, holding on to the brown bag as if it were a wall that held him upright. She stopped herself from running after him. She couldn't stop him.

She watched him fall into the pickup, then lean out so far to pull the door shut that, for a moment, she expected him to tumble onto the pavement. There was a burst of black exhaust as the pickup backed up, then shot forward toward the street. A cop will stop him, she thought. God, let a cop stop him before he kills somebody.

11

STEEL-GRAY CLOUDS MASSED over the mountains and crept across the reservation and into town. Snowflakes dotted the windshield. Vicky fiddled with the temperature controls until the heater whirred into life and warm air burst from the vents. In the short time she and Vince had been in the coffee shop, the temperature had plunged ten degrees. Another storm on the way, with fresh snow piling on the corrugated surfaces of last night's storm.

She reached inside her bag on the passenger seat, found her cell, and ran a finger over Betty White Hawk's number. A phone rang somewhere on the rez, long beeps that melted into Betty's voice: "Hi. Can't take your call right now. Leave a message."

Vicky swiped disconnect. The time at the top of the phone was 3:48. Betty was a custodian at St. Francis Elementary School on the road to the mission, twenty minutes away. She might still be at work. Vicky could swing by the school, give Betty the bad news that her son would probably hole up in a drinking house tonight and drink himself senseless. But there was always the chance he could regain his senses tomorrow and agree to give himself up before the cops called out the SWAT team.

Except that the deal with the prosecuting attorney would be off the table. The deadline was almost an hour away. With any luck, she could talk to Betty and get ahold of Jim Peters before he left for the day. She would have to convince him to extend the deal.

She drove past the warehouses, liquor stores, and trailer parks that led out of town, then took the turn into the reservation. The snow was getting heavier. Always a surprise, how fast the weather could change. Touches of spring one moment, a blizzard the next. All part of life on the plains, and probably the reason her people had become experts at adapting. You had to know how to adapt, change your plans in the space of a heartbeat, hunker down in the storms and make new plans. And wait. Survival required adaptation and patience.

Rising into the gray sky was the blue billboard with white letters that spelled out *St. Francis Mission*. The rear tires skidded on the slippery new snow as she slowed for the turn onto the mission grounds. Familiar, all of it. The cottonwoods, bare and silent with snow tracing the branches, marshaled on either side of the road. She hadn't seen John O'Malley in several months. She laughed at the idea of not remembering the last time she had seen him. Of course she remembered. The exact day, the sun moving west, a red ball of fire gathering energy for the plunge over the mountains and the wind plucking the sleeves of his plaid shirt. She tried to blink back the memory because memories never meant anything, except that she missed their time working together for her people. She would not blink away the memory of those times.

Just before the road bumped into Circle Drive, which wound through the mission grounds, she turned right onto the road to the school. The low brick building with the two-story entrance shaped like a tipi lifted into the sweep of gray clouds overhead. A few pickups and cars stood about the parking lot next to the school. She slowed down and scanned the side of the road for the driveway, a narrow spread of gravel and snow that crossed the barrow ditch. She swung right, took a diagonal route across the parking lot to the front of the school, and parked at the sign that read Buses Only.

Inside the entrance, the tipi poles rose high overhead around glass panes that shimmered in the fading light. The school had the shocked, left-behind feeling of a deserted building, the life and energy having moved elsewhere without warning. Faint smells of wet wool and used crayons and mud-caked boots floated down the wide corridor that led to the classrooms. At the mouth of the corridor was a glass-enclosed office under bright ceiling lights. The door in the back opened and a round-faced woman with black, silver-streaked hair walked over to the counter that divided the office from the corridor. She slid back a glass window. "Help you?" she called.

"I'm Vicky Holden. I'd like a brief word with Betty White Hawk."

The woman was shaking her head, silver streaks in her hair catching the ceiling lights. "Betty's on duty. She'll finish her shift soon." She stole a glance at her watch. "You'll have to wait outside."

"I'm her lawyer, and I need to speak to her now."

Lawyer. The word tumbled across the woman's expression. Well, one never knew. A custodian with a lawyer.

"It will only take a moment."

The woman pushed a clipboard across the threshold of

the window. "Sign in here. Technically, I shouldn't allow this, but if Betty's in some kind of trouble . . ."

"She isn't." Vicky signed her name and added the time: 4:13. "Where can I find her?"

"She usually finishes up in first grade. Three doors down on the left."

Vicky thanked the woman and started along the green vinyl that gleamed like polished marble. The roar of a motor flooded the corridor. She followed the noise to the third door. Inside, Betty White Hawk hunched over a machine that crawled along the floor, its giant brush reaching under desks and chairs. The noise expanded inside the classroom like wind funneled through a canyon. Vicky maneuvered around a desk and waved. It took a moment before Betty located the switch and turned off the machine. She stood up straight, fingers tightened around the handle as if she were ready to meet bad news head-on with the machine for strength. "Where's Vince?"

"I don't know." Vicky leaned back against the edge of a desk, grateful for the solid support. "I found him at a liquor store in Riverton. For a few minutes I thought he would come with me to turn himself in, but . . ."

Betty waved away the rest of it. "Vince can make you believe anything. He can change the temperature, the time of day, the day itself, all by making you believe it's different. You know what's funny? He can make you think you got the facts all botched up. I swear"—she was shaking her head, half laughing, half crying—"my son should go to Hollywood and get in the movies. He'd be the best. He's handsome enough, don't you think?" She was crying now, shoulders shaking, knuckles turning white on the handle. "Everything going for him, except the booze. He can't lay off the booze. He's gone somewhere to drink, right?"

Vicky waited a moment to allow the reality to claim its

own place, fill up the vacancy in the room. "There's one thing I don't understand."

Betty let out a harrumph. "Only one?" She found a tissue in the pocket of her blue jeans and mopped at the moisture on her cheeks. "Sometimes I think I don't understand anything about my son. I've been thinking he's been two or three different people, depending on what he wants you to believe. Vince was twelve when his daddy died, but he figured out he had to be two people. The boy and the man in the house. He had to take care of things, and I . . ." She was crying again, blotting the corners of her eyes. "I encouraged him. He was like a headstrong pony, and I gave him his way. So there he was, fifteen and already drinking like his daddy. He made me believe he could do anything, even quit drinking if he wanted. I've been praying for him to want that."

"Where did he get the money to go on a bender?"

"What?" Betty's eyes opened in wide circles. She went back to gripping the handle.

"It takes money to drink. He had three bottles in a brown bag when I found him. Last week he tried to rob a woman for money to buy booze. What has he been up to? Did he rob somebody else?" God, it was possible. Staged a robbery, and this time got away with it.

Betty looked as if she had been jolted by a live wire. Then she studied the floor for half a minute before she glanced up, shaking her head. "I gave him money yesterday . . ."

"You gave him money?"

"Five dollars. Not enough . . ." She let her voice trail off. "He was flat broke, and he needed gas money to meet up with some friends. He promised he'd give himself up today, so I figured, what difference did it make if he had a little fun before he went to jail?"

She gripped the handle, knuckles popping out like rocks, then turned sideways and stared at the rows of crayoned stick-figure drawings tacked to the wall.

"What is it?"

Betty stayed quiet a long moment. Finally, she looked back. "It's nothing."

But it was something, Vicky knew. Something different and new had invaded the space between them, like a physical presence she could sense but not see.

"Tell me, Betty. How did he get the money? What are you afraid of?"

The woman's fingers moved toward the switch. "Vince is a good boy," she said. "He didn't do anything. Got drunk sometimes, and tried to panhandle that woman, but that was because he needed another drink real bad. He never would have hurt her. Vince wouldn't hurt anyone."

"Then what are you afraid of?"

"I don't know what you're talking about." An index finger moved up and down on the switch.

"Listen to me. I'm trying to help your son. He has a chance if he turns himself in. If there is anything you can tell me . . ."

"I already told you what I know."

"Who did he go out with last night?"

"What?" A dull, opaque look clouded the woman's eyes.

"What friends? He could be with them now."

Betty bit her lip. "How would I know? Vince has lots of friends."

"You knew who to call this morning. You found out Vince had gone to his old girlfriend's place."

"Yeah. Well, I got lucky." She had bitten her lip so hard that a tiny trickle of blood started down the crease alongside her chin. "Besides, chances are none of his other friends are snitches. So what does it matter who they are?"

"I can't help Vince if you won't help me." This was becoming her mantra, she thought. Help me to help a client who doesn't want my help.

Betty was shaking her head. She stared at the ceiling and

ran her finger over the switch. "He'll be okay. He knows what he's doing. He's always had what you call a sixth sense about what's best for him."

"Don't you understand? The police will come for him with guns. Anything could happen." And would happen, she was thinking. "I need to find your son."

Betty stared into some distant space beyond the desks and the tacked-up papers as if she were considering the possibilities. After a moment, she blinked and brought her eyes back to Vicky. "This is all a mistake. Vince must think he's going to be railroaded into prison 'cause he stopped a white woman and asked for a little help. It's no reason to put a man in prison. He's desperate. He knows what he's got to do."

Vicky took a moment before she said, "There's something else. I think Vince is carrying a gun."

Betty dropped her eyes and studied the vinyl floor, flecked with brush strokes and lines of wax. She gave a little shrug. There was effort in the way she brought her eyes back to Vicky's. "Ridiculous. Why would Vince carry a gun?"

"Does he own one?"

"He never pulled a gun on that woman at the ATM."

"No, but he's carrying a gun now. Level with me, Betty, or I can't help him." Vicky waited, hoping the woman would say something that made sense. Her son was on the run, and he was carrying a gun, which made it all the more dangerous for the cops to try to arrest him. Betty White Hawk was making excuses, denying facts.

The woman flipped on the switch, and the noise rose to a high, whining pitch. The conversation was over.

Vicky took her time. Turning around, walking toward the door, waiting for the noise to stop and Betty White Hawk to call her back. The noise followed her down the corridor and into the tipi. The glass in the high, pointed ceiling had turned dark with the oncoming dusk.

She sat in the Ford several minutes, replaying every conversation with Betty. Two days ago, Betty had come to the office and begged her to help her son. She had seemed to understand the importance of the deal Vicky had struck with the prosecuting attorney. This morning, Betty had called to say that Vince had disappeared. Then, another call: he was at Dolly's. Always cooperative. At what point had her attitude changed?

The money. The truth of it jumped out at her like a rattlesnake. Vince had gotten his hands on some money, maybe a lot of money. Enough to purchase bottles of whiskey. Enough to make him think he didn't need a deal. Enough to take off, light out of there.

That was what had frightened his mother—the thought of what Vince might have done to get the money.

Vicky fished the mobile out of her bag and tapped in the prosecuting attorney's number. It took a moment to get past the secretary to Jim Peters himself. "I'm going to need more time," she told him. "A couple of days."

"Any more fairy tales?" Peters made no effort to conceal the disdain in his voice. "I take it your client skipped."

"Vince is a sick man. He's drinking, and he's incapable of making a rational decision until he sobers up."

The line went quiet for several seconds; nothing but the faint sound of breathing. "You got a one-day extension," Peters said finally. "Then we're coming for him."

The call ended before she could say anything. She stared out the windshield. The day was moving into evening, shadows lengthening. The voice rang in her head: *we're coming for him.*

Finally, she made herself check her messages. One message, from Rick Masterson. "Dinner tonight?"

12

THE FALLING SNOW diminished the buildings that crouched against the darkness on Main Street. The sidewalks were empty, snow piled everywhere. An eerie orange glow hovered over the streetlamps. Vicky gripped the steering wheel hard as she drove along the stretch where Clint Hopkins had been struck, forcing herself to focus straight ahead, avoiding the place where she had left Clint and turned back to Rick. The dark figure was still there, looming before her.

She drove onto the next block and parked in front of the restaurant. The dining room on the other side of the foggy plate glass windows was nearly empty, a few customers scattered at the tables, a waitress moving listlessly about. A sheen of ice shimmered on the sidewalk. Warm air wrapped around her like a blanket the instant she stepped inside. A man in a white shirt hurried over. "One?" he said, examining a seating chart on top of the podium.

Vicky started to say she was meeting someone when Rick

Masterson materialized out of the dining room. "She's with me," he said.

"Oh yes." The man started to pick up a menu, but Rick waved it away. He helped her out of her coat and hung it on the rack. His hand was firm and confident against her back as he guided her through the dining area to a table next to the window.

"I'm glad you called," he said when they had sat down. "I've been wondering how you're doing. Last night was pretty tough."

Vicky spread a red napkin on her lap and studied the menu. How should she be doing? Was there a protocol, a way of behaving, after witnessing a death?

She glanced up at the man on the other side of the table. "I went to see Clint's wife and daughter this morning." She hesitated. "It made the whole thing real. Until then it was like a nightmare. I'm not sure which is worse. Reality or nightmare."

"Do you care for a drink?"

"No thanks." Is this what alcoholics like Vince were in search of? A place between nightmare and reality?

A waitress had appeared: black hair pulled into a ponytail, orange-red lips, blue-black eyebrows, and a notepad in one palm. They ordered ravioli, lasagna, garden salads. One glass of red house wine.

"How about you?" Vicky asked when the waitress had walked away.

"Trying to stay busy to keep the images out of my mind."

"Clint starting across the street in the snow." Vicky left the rest of it unspoken: headlights and the truck out of nowhere. The words would only bring the image into clearer focus.

Rick was nodding. His eyes were gray, almost silver, and they caught the light the way a piece of metal catches light. He had a broad forehead and a prominent chin with laugh lines carved into the sides of his mouth. Flecks of gray shone in his sandy hair. It struck her that he was handsome.

He started to say something, then sat back and waited while the waitress delivered the plates of food, all of it crowding the tabletop. She added two waters, the glass of red wine. When she left, Rick lifted the wine and said, "To happier times."

He took a sip, set the glass down, and leaned forward. "It's been a hard day. Everywhere I went, people wanted to talk about Clint. It was like a shock wave had hit town, and people were reeling, trying to make sense of it."

Vicky took a bite of the ravioli. Hot and spicy, and she realized how hungry she was. She hadn't stopped to eat all day. She took another bite and thought about how different her day had been. Except for Clint's wife and secretary and the Little Shields, nobody else had mentioned the man's death. Not Vince White Hawk. Not his mother. As if it had happened in another time zone, somewhere far away and unimportant.

"There are a lot of theories about Clint," Rick said. He worked at the lasagna a moment before he sat back again and gazed at her. "He was a damned good lawyer. Every other lawyer I talked to today mentioned how good he was, especially at adoption cases. Nobody wanted to be on the opposing side of Clint Hopkins. He was dogged and thorough. Kept all the details in his head, but no one could cross him up. Interesting way to practice law. Almost as if he feared someone looking over his shoulder."

Vicky nodded. She pushed the plate of ravioli away and started on the salad. "I know he had a good reputation."

"Not in everything."

She looked up. "What are you saying?"

"You know how it is. Someone dies a sudden death, and people start to remember things they had forgotten, or chosen not to remember. A couple of lawyers brought up Clint's secretary, Evie Moran. Evidently she's a big part of his success. Started working for him when she was still in high school and never left."

The words fell like stones between them. Vicky stared at the man for a couple of seconds. "What are you implying?"

Rick spread both hands on the table. "I'm not implying anything. No one made any outright accusations . . ."

"That there was something more between them than a professional relationship."

Rick shook his head. "I gathered he meant the world to her. He was her life. And he depended on her."

Vicky sat back. She reached for her water and took a couple of sips, trying to organize the thoughts tumbling through her mind. "Someone could have had a motive to arrange for Clint's death."

Rick blinked at her, as if she had pulled a rabbit out of a hat and were holding it up for display. "It was an accident. The driver didn't see him in the snow. Clint was like a shadow."

"Why didn't the driver stop?" Vicky felt a surge of annoyance. It was no accident. It was as obvious as the white tablecloth, the half-eaten ravioli and lasagna, the traces of wine in the glass. "If Clint was having personal problems . . ."

"I didn't say that."

"An inappropriate relationship with his secretary that he refused to give up. Maybe his wife found out. Either woman might have been desperate, not thinking straight."

"Listen to me, Vicky. You are not thinking straight. We don't know anything inappropriate was going on. Do you really believe either his wife or his secretary could have"—he paused and searched the ceiling for the exact words—"arranged for his death?"

"It happens." Vicky rolled her napkin and tossed it onto the table.

"The driver didn't see him. It was an accident. A terrible accident. The driver was frightened, so he drove away. He might not have realized he'd hit someone. He could come forward as soon as he gets the nerve, and we'll know the truth."

"You were there, Rick. Walking beside me. We saw the same thing." God, it was so obvious. "The truck waited down the street until Clint came out of the restaurant, carrying a stupid briefcase. Who carries a briefcase to a dinner meeting? The driver spotted him, cranked up the engine, and pulled out into the street. Going for him, the dark, shadowy figure in the snow."

"Don't make it something that it wasn't, Vicky. It's terrible enough."

Vicky got to her feet, barely aware of Rick standing up beside her, the soothing tone of his voice: "Wait. Hold on." As if he were trying to reason with a balky child. "Don't run off."

She found some bills in her bag and tossed them on the table. "I know what I saw." It was still in front of her, and Rick Masterson wanted her to believe she had seen something else. That she was delusional, imagining things, coming up with plausible explanations, not thinking straight.

"Don't tell me I didn't see what I saw." She threw the comment over her shoulder as she started for the door.

13

TEN THIRTY, AND still no sign of Shannon and James. Father John felt like a parent, pacing the floor, listening for an engine on Circle Drive. The mission grounds were shrouded in falling snow, the streetlights shimmering gold against the black sky.

He forced himself back into his chair and stared at his laptop screen. James Two Horses had shown up just before six o'clock, a loud roar that swung into the curb in front of the residence and cut off. Then he was at the front door, knocking softly, as if he could conceal his excitement and determination. Shannon had walked over from the guest-house and was standing in the entry. She hadn't even removed her coat and scarf. She opened the door and James had burst in.

"Hope I'm on time."

Well, yes, he was. From the kitchen came sounds of dishes and pots and pans clanking together and the noise of running

water. Father John was about to suggest that Shannon and
James have dinner there. Elena always made plenty of food,
in case someone dropped by. It was the Arapaho Way.

"A good hamburger place has opened up in town," James
said, all of his attention focused on Shannon. "Are you up
for hamburgers?"

Shannon assured him that she was and began snapping
together the front of her coat, which she had just unsnapped.
He supposed he shouldn't be surprised. He had seen the look
that passed between them earlier outside his office. They
had gone off, a young woman with things still unsettled with
her boyfriend back home and a young man who might have
a vocation to the priesthood. One never knew, could never
predict. Human beings, always full of contradictions and
surprises.

Was that how he had be been almost thirty years ago?
Picking up Eileen at her apartment for a bite to eat at the
local hamburger joint, or was it that mom-and-pop Italian
place they'd liked, where no one spoke English and they had
to guess about the menu, which made it fun, exciting. All
the time, the voice playing like a melody in the back of his
head: *Whom Shall I Send?*

Now he tried to concentrate on the list of Web sites he
had pulled up. He had started with Elizabeth Fletcher, which
produced an overview of the surprise Indian attack on Jasper
Fletcher's wagons on a sunny, blue-sky day in Wyoming.
Jasper had come from England, where he and his brothers
owned coal mines, which put him in a higher social status,
he believed, than the other men on their way to the California gold fields who had nothing except dreams and scrawny
women and children. They built fires out of timber scav-
enged on the plains, roasted hanks of deer, if they were
lucky, or rabbit. Content to stay alive.

It was better to pull ahead, distance themselves from the
rabble. Until the Indians had ridden out of the sagebrush

and the hot dust. When it was over, Jasper lay wounded, his
wife dead. Their young sons had made a run for it, and the
Indians had let them go, too busy tearing into the wagons
for food and clothing and pots and utensils. When they rode
off, they took the girls, Amanda Mary and Elizabeth.

Father John skimmed the rest of the site: how Amanda
Mary was rescued seven months later, how Elizabeth grew
up, became an Arapaho, married John Brokenhorn, and
lived on the Wind River Reservation.

Nothing that Shannon called "outside of history," such
as how Lizzie had felt about her life. He had closed the site,
typed in *Lizzie Brokenhorn*, and another list materialized.
The noise of an engine gearing down came from outside.
His senses went on alert, a thousand tiny antennae sprouting
on his skin. The noise faded into the distance. A truck out
on Seventeen-Mile Road.

Past eleven o'clock now. How long did it take to eat a
hamburger? Stop it, he told himself. He trusted James Two
Horses. Trusted the man with his niece.

He scanned the Web sites, looking for something different, personal. Halfway down the page he read: *Lizzie Brokenhorn on the reservation*. He clicked on the link and
waited for the text to sort itself onto the page. It was a short
newspaper article, a feature story on how a white woman
had lived as an Arapaho for almost fifty years. How she had
had five children who'd grown to adulthood.

He moved to the second page. Here was something: The
photo of a crumbling shack on the plains, the panorama of
the foothills in the background and splotches of sunshine
on the barren ground. He enlarged the photo and read the
caption: "The cabin built by John Brokenhorn for his wife
and family."

He sat back, taking it in. He had passed the shack a
thousand times, out on Blue Sky Highway, falling down and
forgotten, a barbed wire fence running next to the road. So

this was where Lizzie and John Brokenhorn had lived. He'd had no idea of the history attached to a shack that resembled nothing more than a pile of logs. But why wouldn't the shack have a story? There were stories all over the reservation; the past was everywhere.

This time the noise of an engine was coming closer, growing louder through the tunnel of cottonwoods. He got up and peered out the window, wondering what Shannon would make of his attempt to stand in for her father, waiting for her to come home. He laughed out loud. She was twenty-four years old, an adult, hardly in need of her father—or, for that matter, her uncle—telling her what to do. He watched the thin stream of headlights bounce through the snow and turn onto Circle Drive.

He went back to the computer, relief washing over him, and pressed the print button. The old printer on the bookshelf whirred into life. He grabbed the photo of the old cabin as soon as the printer spit it out, then checked the window again, expecting to see James's pickup turning into the alley between the church and the administration building.

A sedan, light colored and splotched with snow, was wobbling and slipping around the drive, heading toward the residence. He felt as if an icy hand had clutched his heart. What was this? What bad news at this time of night? What had happened to Shannon?

He watched a woman—slight-looking, bundled in an outsized jacket, scarf looped around her neck, a dark hat pulled low over her forehead, head bent against the snow—start up the sidewalk.

Father John opened the door as Betty White Hawk was about to knock, a fist lifted like that of a boxer. Gratitude and something else—worry, despair—crossed her face. "Oh, thank God, you're still up. I didn't know where else to go."

"Come in." He pulled the door back. She lunged inside, bringing with her the frosty cold and pellets of snow that flew around her. He helped her with the jacket, draped it over the hook above the bench, and motioned her into the study.

"What's going on?"

"It's Vince."

He could have guessed as much. A talented athlete, Vince had played shortstop for the St. Francis Eagles. Smart kid, doing well in school, looking at a promising future. Then alcohol and most likely drugs, and a tough crowd, had taken over. He had dropped out of school, out of his life. This wasn't the first time Betty had come to the mission gripped by desperation.

"Can I get you something? Coffee?" He pulled an armchair closer to his desk.

Betty White Hawk sank down and shook her head, the frivolity of sipping coffee absurd, out of the question. He walked around the desk and sat down. "Talk to me," he said.

"He's in trouble, and I don't know where to find him."

"You mean for attempted robbery?" Last week the *Gazette* had reported that Vince White Hawk was wanted for trying to rob a woman at an ATM in Riverton. The article said the police were looking for him.

Betty nodded. The despair sat on her thin shoulders like a heavy cape. She was still fairly young, early forties, he guessed. Raising her son on her own, sitting in the bleachers and cheering him on, bringing cupcakes for the team. She had once been pretty. She looked faded and worn now, as if a gauzy veil had fallen over her face.

"Vicky made a deal with the prosecuting attorney," she said. "She was supposed to bring in Vince today and the charges would have been lowered to a misdemeanor. He was supposed to plead guilty and get sent to rehab. God, he needs to go into rehab. He agreed to everything yesterday."

"What happened?"

"What you expect." She shrugged and drew in a long,

noisy breath that she held on to as if it were her last. "He went drinking last night. I guess I can't blame him. The thirst overpowers him; he can't help it. One last drink—that's all he wanted."

Father John was quiet. There was more; he could almost see the words bunching in her throat. He had learned from years of counseling and listening to confessions to wait and allow the words to find their own way.

It took a moment before Betty said, "He got some money, so he thinks he can do what he wants. Nobody telling him what to do. No court sending him into rehab. No white people controlling his life. He took off."

"Where did he get the money?" Another robbery attempt, Father John was thinking, one that was successful. He was aware of the cold draft creeping through the windows.

Betty blinked hard and shook her head. "He went out last night and never came home. I called some of his friends and found out he'd gone to an old girlfriend's place in Riverton, so I called Vicky. She went and found him. She told me he had a wad of money on him. Instead of going to the prosecutor's office with her, he took off. I don't know what he's been up to. I don't know who he's been hanging out with. He could have some new friends I don't know about. All I know is, the cops are coming for him and . . ." She closed her eyes against whatever images had materialized. "Somebody's going to die. I'm afraid Vince is going to die." There was an ominous tone in the woman's voice, as if she had seen the future.

"What else haven't you told me?" he said.

"He's carrying a gun. I knew he got an old revolver in a trade last year. Said it was for target practice. Far as I knew, he kept it in a box in his closet. I checked the box. It was empty. Vicky says he had the gun on him. That's how I know he's made up his mind nobody's going to arrest him. He's making a plan. He's going to leave here and go somewhere else. Denver or Los Angeles. Somewhere nobody knows about an arrest warrant for attempted robbery." She drew in another long breath. "I've been calling everybody I can think of. Nobody's seen him. I'm at my wits' end. I don't know what do."

"Is there anything he might have said about his new friends? Anything that might suggest who they are?"

"No. No. No." Betty curled her hands into fists and rubbed at her eyes, then dropped both fists into her lap and stared at him. "I figure he got the money from them. God knows what they've been up to."

"Where could he have met them?"

She gave a shout of laughter that resembled a sob. "Anywhere. Everywhere. No shortage of lowlifes around, especially when you're hooked on alcohol or drugs."

"At a bar? Did Vince go to bars?"

Her head snapped backward. "A bar, yes. That's where he met them. One of the guys I talked to this morning said the last time he'd seen Vince was a couple weeks ago at a bar. What did he say? The Buffalo something . . ."

"Bar and Lounge."

"Yeah." She reached out with both hands, as if she could grab a lifeline. "Vince never said anything about going to a bar, but . . ." She dropped her hands, fists curled, back into her lap. "He never told me what he was up to. I didn't ask. I didn't want to know."

She jumped to her feet as if a bolt of electricity had hit her. "Somebody at the bar might know where Vince is."

Father John got to his feet and stole a glance at his watch. Eleven fifteen. The bar would probably be open. "I'll go with you," he said.

HE DROVE THE old Toyota, bumping and slipping over the snow, Betty in the passenger seat, her breath a small cloud on the side window. Something different about her now, some twinge of hope running through her. She had pulled on gloves and she clapped her hands, making a soft, swishy noise. The pickup plunged into the tunnel of cottonwoods, the branches sagging under the new snow.

Yellow headlights turned off Seventeen-Mile Road and came toward them. Father John slowed and moved to the edge of the road to make room for the pickup: James giving a little salute in the driver's seat, Shannon beside him, waving.

Father John felt his muscles relax. Of course she was safe.

14

RIVERTON LOOKED DESERTED. A few pickups crawling through the snow, streetlights casting a dim glow over the buildings that huddled in the shadows. Father John slowed on Federal and hunched toward the windshield, searching for the Buffalo Bar and Lounge. "On the corner ahead," Betty said, but when it wasn't there, she told him to try the next block. The woman wasn't any more accustomed to visiting the local bars than he was.

There were a number of bars, you realized, when you started looking for one. Each bar an oasis of light and activity with music thumping into the night past the clapboard and shingled walls, the plate glass windows singed with frost.

Buffalo Bar and Lounge pulsated in white letters on a sign ahead. The bar itself was a dark brick affair with traces of light escaping around the front door and shimmering in the window. Father John turned in to the lot next to the bar and pulled into a vacant space. The headlights washed over the words *Owner Parking* printed on the curb.

Betty was already out of the pickup. Stomping toward the front door, head bent in the falling snow. He followed her inside. The heavy wooden door rattled and creaked shut behind them. A warm fug of steam mixed with smells of beer and spicy barbecue filled the place. The wide mirror behind the bar reflected the half circles of light that dangled over the tables. A dozen customers lounged about the tables and hung on to the bar. Country music thumped through a loudspeaker.

Betty stood frozen in place, glancing about, taking it in. This was where Vince found new friends, friends who had helped him get a wad of money and the chance to escape.

"He's not here."

Father John wondered how she could be so sure. It was hard to distinguish one patron from another. The same cowboy hats, long-sleeved shirts, blue jeans, and boots. The wide shoulders, tapered backs, and slim waists of men who worked outdoors. The off-shoulder blouses and swishing skirts and cowboy hats of the few women.

Aware of the heads lifting over mugs of beer, the eyes following them, he took Betty's arm and steered her around the tables to the bar. Cowboys had claimed either end of the bar, but the middle was vacant, and that was where he led her. The bartender was a big man, as big as a bouncer, with an apron tied around his waist and a methodical manner about him as he swished glasses in a sink full of soapy water. He looked over, not breaking the back-and-forth rhythm. "Dining room's closed."

"We'll have something at the bar."

"Yeah?" This seemed to take him by surprise. "Hold on a sec."

Betty turned sideways and stared at him with wide, frightened eyes. "All I want is to find Vince."

"What'll it be?" The bartender had moved toward them. He swiped a wet cloth over the bar.

"Two coffees."

"Make mine a Coke." Betty seemed to have caught on that what they needed was information, and information came at a price.

"Irish coffee? Bourbon and Coke?"

"Just plain," Father John said.

The man shrugged, stepped away, and went about pumping Coke out of a nozzle and into a glass. Then he poured a mug of coffee and set them both down. "Never seen you in here before." He put his hands on his waist, elbows crooked outward, and waited.

"Father O'Malley from the mission." Father John nodded at the jar of creamer on the bar and the bartender slid it toward him. "This is Betty White Hawk. She's looking for her son, Vince."

The man was shaking his head. "Look," he said, as if he'd seen the picture and didn't like it, "customers come here for a little R and R, you know what I mean? Maybe they don't like folks knowing where they are." He turned to Betty. "Sorry, ma'am, but that goes for mothers."

Father John stirred some cream into the coffee and took a sip. "You know Vince?"

"I just said—"

"He could be in trouble. There might be somebody here who could help us find him. We know he liked to come here." It might be true, he was thinking. "I hear he has friends here. Any of them around?" He turned and glanced about the tables, as if one of Vince's new friends might step forward and identify himself.

"What kind of trouble?"

"Nothing that involves the bar."

"He tried to rob somebody, I heard."

"His lawyer's taken care of that."

Betty was sipping the Coke. She set the glass down. "He can be a hothead. I'm trying to keep him from getting into trouble."

The bartender studied her for a moment, as if a different picture had started to form. The ATM robbery attempt had been taken care of; there wasn't any new trouble. Just the effort to keep Vince away from trouble.

"Tell you the truth, we never had more than a few words. Another Indian from the rez. They're all the same, pretty much stick to themselves. Have a couple beers, ignore everybody else just like the cowboys ignore them." He shrugged. "I don't need any cowboy-Indian trouble. So Vince comes in once in a while . . ."

"Was he here last night?"

"I don't want any trouble."

Father John gave him a nod of understanding.

"Came in early. Ordered a beer, carried it over to a table and had a powwow with another Indian. Only guy I saw him talking to last night. I seen them having a couple drinks together a few times."

"Who was it?" Hope flared in Betty's voice.

"Ask him yourself." He gestured with his chin toward a table over on the side where a thin, bent Indian sat alone, cowboy hat pushed back, empty beer glasses lined up in front. He was working on another beer.

Father John thanked the man, laid a few bills on the bar, and started after Betty, who was already halfway across the dining room, shoulders back, like a runner at the finish line. She stopped at the table as if she had hit an invisible wall and stared down at the soiled, rain-marked brim of the Indian's cowboy hat.

Father John moved in close, slid out a chair, and motioned Betty to sit down. He took the chair between her and the Indian, who was looking at Betty as if she had sprung, genielike, from an empty bottle.

"Don't recall inviting you."

"Sorry to bother you." Father John set both hands, palms down, on the table. He had no intention of leaving, and neither did Betty, a fact the Indian must have comprehended, because he gave a little nod and went back to looking over Betty, who was trembling, face flushed.

After a moment, the Indian shifted sideways. He had a jagged scar that ran across his cheek. "I seen you at the mission," he said. "Who's this?" He tossed his head in Betty's direction.

"You know me." Betty was leaning forward, fists clenched into small balls on the table. "You can't have my son. Tell me where he is, or I swear . . ." She let the rest of it hang like smoke over the table.

"Vince?" The Indian held a steady gaze. He might have been in a poker game.

"White Hawk." There was something between them, Father John was thinking, something out of the past that nipped at the present. But that was true with a lot of families on the rez. Old animosities and conflicts, sometimes going so far back nobody remembered what they were about.

"Are you a friend of his?"

"Might've had a few beers with him." The Indian lifted and dropped his shoulders, as if he were used to shrugging away uncomfortable moments. And yet there was something forced in the gesture, as if he were hiding a deep nervousness.

"What about last night?" Betty leaned even closer. Her breasts pressed into the edge of the table.

"What about it?"

"We're trying to find him," Father John said. "Any idea of where he might have gone? Friends he might be with?"

"He never ran his social calendar by me." The Indian gave another shrug. "So we had some beers a couple times. Don't make me his keeper."

Father John leaned back. "You used to come to the mission?"

"Long time ago."

"Your people still come? Let's see, that would be the Yellow Horses?" He was guessing. The Indian hadn't given his name. The fastest way to find out which family an Arapaho belonged to was to place him in the wrong family.

The Indian sensed the trap. A wily hunter. "Yellow Horses? Never associated with the likes."

"I remember everything," Betty said, keeping her eyes on the man. She leaned in closer. "Vince is all I've got. For God's sake, tell me where he is or . . ." She clamped her lips over the rest of it.

The Indian drew back, bringing the glass of beer with him. "Or what? You gonna cough up a lot of stuff nobody cares about anymore? Can't help you."

Father John took a moment. Whatever lay between the White Hawks and this man was raw and unsettled. "Anyone else," he said, glancing around, "who might have had a few beers with Vince?"

The Indian gave another shrug, finished the last of his beer, and lifted an arm into the air. "Far as I know, Vince tended to his own business. Good idea, I'd say."

The bartender had sauntered over, an unhurried, end-of-the-night air about him. He wiped his hands down the sides of his apron. "About to close," he said.

The Indian looked up sideways, brown neck muscles stretched out of the collar of his Western shirt. He had a long, narrow face with a hooked nose, as sharp as a blade. "Another beer."

"Haven't you had enough, Lou?"

Lou. Father John had it now. Lou Bearing. Lou and his wife—what was her name? Debbie—had come to Mass a few times when he had first come to St. Francis more than ten years ago. He hadn't seen them since, as if they had disappeared, taken a different path. It happened. Most of his parishioners retained their traditional Indian beliefs. Attended the Sun Dance every summer, went to the sweat lodges and healing ceremonies. The ancient ceremonies that connected them to the ancestors. They still came to the mission. Mass and confessions, baptism and confirmation, funerals. Arapahos were the most spiritual people he had ever been with. Pray and pray and pray some more, he had heard the elders say. Pray in every way.

It was possible that Lou and Debbie had decided to leave off with the mission and keep to the Arapaho ceremonies. Or leave off with all forms of worship. The moderns, the skeptics, those who didn't need any spiritual help because they didn't believe.

He wondered what it had been.

"Just bring me a beer," Bearing said. "I don't need a lecture."

"What about you?" The bartender glanced around the table, but let his gaze linger on Betty. The flush of hope had dissipated, and the pale, worn-out look had returned, making her seem older, tired out.

She waved away the question, and Father John said, "Nothing for me." They were done here, he was thinking as the bartender walked away. Lou Bearing had told them everything he intended to, which was very little. It was what he left unsaid that counted. He knew Vince White Hawk. He drank with him. They'd been drinking together last evening and on other occasions before Vince had miraculously come into a wad of money and started carrying a gun. He had been the only one Vince had talked to in the bar, which suggested that last evening's meeting had been set up, prearranged.

And there was more. Father John had the sense that the man was covering up something.

Father John stood up. Across the table, Betty pushed

herself to her feet. She looked unsteady, holding on to the back of the chair. He took hold of her arm and started to turn toward the door, then stepped back. Out of the corner of his eye, he caught the massive figure of the bartender carrying a mug of beer. He leaned close to Bearing. "Whatever trouble Vince is in might implicate you. If you know anything that could help find him, I suggest you help yourself by telling me."

The Indian watched the mug appear on the table, then brought it to his lips. A foamy white mustache smeared the top of his lip when he set the mug down. "You threatening me?"

Father John rapped his knuckles on the table. "If you decide to help, you know where to find me."

"WHAT IS IT?" They were outside in the pickup, the engine sputtering and trying to catch. "Why do you hate him?"

Betty sat hunched over beside him, her breath raspy. She kept her eyes down. "It happened a long time ago. Like he said, nobody cares." Then she looked up at him with so much alarm and pain in her eyes that he leaned closer.

"Betty," he said, "what is it?"

She was shaking her head. "He's going to kill my son."

15

THE DOOR WITH *Clint Hopkins, Esq.* etched in the pebble-glass window was locked. Vicky tried the knob a second time, then knocked. A moment passed before a shadow moved across the glass and the door swung open. Evie leaned into the edge. Behind the small wireless glasses, she had the flushed red-rimmed eyes of someone who had been crying hard.

"Sorry about locking you out." She didn't look sorry. She looked sad and helpless as she gestured Vicky inside

Vicky walked past, taking in the front office at a glance. Desk swept clean, surface polished to a glow. A pair of upholstered visitor's chairs that looked as if they had been vacuumed. Filing cabinet with drawers closed—probably locked—and a small trophy on top with the figure of a golfer. Bookcases against one wall, books neatly stacked around a plant in a pottery bowl and a large, clear vase. The office of a man who was no longer there.

She turned around and realized the young woman was still leaning against the edge of the door. "Are you all right?" Evie Moran, the beautiful secretary Clint had hired out of high school and never let go. And Evie had not wished to leave. It could be true, the gossip. It always struck Vicky how secretive and tight-lipped lawyers could be about a case, and how schoolgirl gossipy they were about one another.

"It's been so hard," the young woman said. And she *was* young, Vicky was thinking. Maybe even younger than she had guessed yesterday, but yesterday the secretary had been in shock, drawn and pale. "I mean, Clint was . . ." She stopped and bit into her lower lip. The word she had been about to utter seemed to float in the air between them. *Everything.*

She hurried on: "Crazy people do crazy things. They get hurt, so they strike out, hurt everybody else."

"What are you trying to tell me?" God, she could have hit on the truth. Last night in the restaurant with Rick, she had jumped to the conclusion that Clint's wife might have had motive to arrange his death. A wild conclusion, plucked out of her own exhaustion and shock.

"You said you didn't think it was an accident." Evie was still clinging to the door. "That means somebody killed him."

"We don't know for sure." Vicky could feel the weight of the truth in Evie's words. "I believe the police think it was an accident. The investigation—"

"The hell with the investigation." Evie slammed the door, sending little shock waves through the carpeted floor. "They can miss the truth by a mile."

"What do you think happened?"

"Somebody wanted him dead and hired a killer. It happens, you know."

Vicky waited a moment before she said, "Who would want him dead?"

"I'm not saying." The young woman shrugged and rolled her eyes. "I don't want to be next. I've got to think of myself."

"Are you referring to his law practice or to his personal life?"

Evie had been advancing into the room. She tripped forward, then caught herself. "How would I know about his personal life? I don't care what gossip you've heard. I was his secretary."

Vicky absorbed this for a moment. Evie had heard the gossip. Legal secretaries talk to one another. "Do you think," she said, trying to change direction, "someone believes you know whatever Clint knew?"

Evie gave another shrug and sank into a chair. Vacuum streaks ruffled the gray carpet at her feet. "All I know is I'm out of here as soon as I can get away. I've been tidying up, putting things in order. It's the last thing I can do for Clint. He and a lawyer in Casper had an arrangement to close up each other's practices, if something . . ." She squeezed her eyes shut against the moisture clouding her glasses. "Shouldn't take long to close down. Adoption cases? Not exactly big ticket. A lot of cases Clint took pro bono. He didn't care about money. He fell for any kid with a hardship story. All he wanted was to get kids into safe, permanent homes."

"I'm not following." Vicky perched on the other chair and swiveled in a half circle to face the woman. "Why are you anxious to get away?"

"Maybe he stumbled onto something he shouldn't know. He was always on the internet. Somebody might think I know what he found." The woman tilted her head back and laughed. "He kept things locked in the vault, the vault being his head. He was paranoid about people breaking in or hacking his records."

Dead end. There was nothing there, Vicky was thinking.

No sign that Evie Moran believed Clint's wife was behind his death. She could see herself in the restaurant last night, arguing with Rick Masterson over what they had seen, grasping at the gossip and jumping to the conclusion that Lacy Hopkins could have been responsible.

She blinked back that train of thought. She had seen the black truck smash into Clint, toss him over the hood, and no explanations could change that.

"Did you find anything that might be helpful in the Little Shield case?"

Evie looked at her as if she were trying to place her, recall why she was sitting across the office asking questions. Finally, comprehension spread across her face. She jumped to her feet, walked around the desk, and yanked open a drawer, then thrust a folder toward Vicky.

"Clint's calendar for the last couple weeks," Evie said. "People he interviewed on the Little Shield case. I checked his desk in his study to see if he had brought any work home. Funny, when you think about it. He trusted the doors on his house more than the doors here. I found this folder in the top drawer."

Vicky took the folder. Most likely Clint had intended to bring it to her office. He would have explained the details missing from his notes. Without his explanation, she didn't expect any notations on his calendar to make much sense.

The folder contained two sheets, each representing a week, with the days across the top of each sheet. Monday. Tuesday. Wednesday . . . Lines of tight black writing filled the space beneath each day, the letters as upright as posts. There were various names, followed by comments and memoranda.

She slipped the sheets back into the folder. "Did you make a copy?"

"That is the copy," Evie said.

"If you come across anything else . . ."

The young woman held up a hand, palm out. "I know Clint." She swallowed hard. "There won't be anything else."

ALL LEGAL NOTES are alike: a collection of terse facts. And the notes Clint had jotted on the calendar were the same, except they were more terse and less informative than Vicky had expected.

She lay the calendar pages on her desk, then began marking the names on each page with a yellow highlighter. A dull splash of daylight filled the window. From the outer office came the muffled sound of tapping, then the sound of the phone ringing. Through the beveled glass doors, Vicky saw the distorted figure of Annie reaching for the phone.

Vicky took the list of contacts Myra Little Shield had left with her and started comparing the names on the list with the names on the calendar. They lined up chronologically. A methodical man, Clint. He had started with the top and proceeded through the list. The buzzer sounded, and she pressed the button. "Betty White Hawk on line one," Annie said.

Vicky lifted the receiver, her gaze still on the pages. "Have you heard from Vince?"

She understood by the silence that the answer was no. A long moment passed before Betty said, "Last night I ran into a man that knows him. I think he knows where Vince is hiding out."

Vicky waited, and finally the voice went on, low and precise, as controlled and deliberate as the upright letters of Clint Hopkins's handwriting. "I remembered Vince saying something about a bar, so we went to the Buffalo Bar and Lounge. We met up with Lou Bearing."

"We?"

"Father John."

John O'Malley. Vicky gripped the phone while the

woman went on talking, the words blurring together with no logic or meaning. It had been a long time since she and John had worked together, a long time since anyone had needed both a priest and a lawyer, the excuse that brought them together. At times she had imagined making up an excuse, inventing a client. What a laugh. He would see through it immediately.

"Do you know him?"

"Father John?" Vicky tried to refocus her attention.

"Lou Bearing."

The name was familiar. Vicky glanced down the names on the calendar. She had just run yellow smudges through the name Lou Bearing, listed three different times. Odd, she realized now. Clint had x-ed out three days between the first two mentions of Bearing's name and the last. Also odd: The name was not on Myra Little Shield's list. "What did he tell you?"

"Nothing. He didn't tell us anything. But the bartender said Vince and Lou had a couple beers together the night before last. And he'd seen them drinking together before that. You ever get that feeling when you know, you just know, somebody's lying?"

"Who is Lou Bearing? What did Father John say?"

"I don't know. I don't know anymore." There was an edge of hysteria in her voice. "I keep seeing cops at a crummy house somewhere and Vince going crazy. He won't let them take him." She had started crying, loud sobs that bolted down the line. "He's gonna get himself killed."

"Listen to me," Vicky said. "I'll see if I can locate Lou Bearing. It's not too late. I can still bring Vince in today if I can find him."

"Oh my God. You have to find him, Vicky. Please find him."

Vicky was about to say she couldn't make any promises, she would do her best—a mouthful of platitudes that she realized were unnecessary. The line was dead.

She went back to comparing the Little Shields' list with the calendar entries. Clint had visited each person once, yet he had interviewed Lou Bearing three times. Twice on succeeding days, followed by three days that were x-ed out. The third visit was the day he had died. Next to the name, the spaces were blank.

She read through the calendar again. Alongside all the other names he'd written the same terse words. *Confirm. Will swear. Good parents. Child happy.*

She sat back. What else would these contacts say, except that Eldon and Myra Little Shield had raised Mary Ann since she was an infant, they were good parents, and Mary Ann was happy? They would swear to that in court. They were all related to the Little Shields. Cousins, in-laws, cousins of in-laws: a whole web of relatives.

All the notes missed the main question: how had Eldon and Myra gotten custody of Mary Ann? Another relative, a social services employee, had gotten them some sort of paper that made them think they had custody. The relative had died, and the matter had been forgotten—a small child stuck in limbo. And the Little Shields hadn't called the police, because they didn't think they had to. The relative had taken care of the legalities. For five years, they stuck to the story they had created: Mary Ann had been placed in their custody as a foster child.

Was there no one who could swear to the truth, except for the woman who had left Mary Ann on a doorstep in the middle of a blizzard? Except for her, whoever she was?

She stared at the blank spaces around Lou Bearing's name. Three times Clint had talked to the man, yet he hadn't jotted down any comments.

Who was Lou Bearing?

She started through the Little Shields' list again, comparing it to the names on the calendar. Rosemary Little Shield was the last name on the list. Next to it, Clint had jotted the word *neighbor*. He had interviewed everyone in order. Nothing set him off course. Which meant Rosemary Little Shield had been the last person interviewed before Lou Bearing. And Lou Bearing could be her neighbor.

She stacked the sheets in order and placed them inside the file folder. She would have to follow Clint's trail, but she would start with Rosemary Little Shield.

16

SHANNON MARY O'MALLEY was her full name. Irish Catholic to the bone, like all of the family Father John had left behind in Boston. He thought of them often, and he kept them in his prayers, those people from another time, a lifetime ago. Seventeen-Mile Road unspooled ahead, the snow crisscrossed and rutted, soft and fluffy as cotton on the surface and sharp as knives below. He was aware of the girl's soft intakes of breath beside him. "Soli o siamo!" played softly between them.

It was after ten that morning when Shannon had arrived at the administration building, a blast of cold air trailing her down the corridor and into his office. She gripped a coffee mug in one hand. *Any coffee, by chance?* Sorry she had missed breakfast, but she hoped Elena wasn't offended. She'd overslept. All she really needed was coffee.

He remembered smiling. Looking up from the letter of recommendation he was writing for Justin Spearman's application to Creighton, and taking her in. Bundled up in a jacket twice her size, knit cap perched on the red hair that sprang over her shoulders, face flushed from the cold. She was like a breath of fresh air. He'd gotten to his feet and filled her mug with coffee at the little table next to the door. He made fresh coffee every morning for the bishop and himself when he got into the office, and usually by mid-morning, he made another pot. This was the second pot.

"Enjoy your evening out?" His voice had come back to him, tentative and insecure. He was on shaky ground in this parental role.

"Yeah, it was great." She had held up the envelope-thin laptop she grasped in her other hand. "I'm reworking my notes on our talk with Wilbur Horn. Strange how much more you remember, the more you think about something." She took a sip of coffee, then toasted him with the mug. "You don't know how much I needed that. Off to the office," she said, swinging into the corridor.

"Shannon, wait."

She looked back and for a moment he'd thought he glimpsed a flash of resistance in her expression, as if she had expected him to interrogate her about last night. He walked back to his desk and rummaged through the pile of papers he'd brought over from the residence. Dear Lord, being a parent was tough. Shannon was leaning against the door frame, drinking the coffee. He'd found the page he was looking for and carried it over to her.

"Oh, that! I found it on the internet some time ago." She had given a dismissive wave, coupled with a sly half smile, as if she appreciated his efforts, but she was the scholar here.

"I thought you might like to visit it."

That had stopped her. She tilted her head back and stared at him, as if a different uncle had appeared in front of her. "You mean . . ."

"It still stands west of Blue Sky Highway, near the foothills."

"Oh my God. Lizzie's house! Yes. Yes. How soon can we go?"

He'd told her to give him a minute to finish something, and she had clumped down the corridor in her heavy snow boots. He had heard her fiddling with the door to the little office he'd cleared for her. Then the door opened and closed. In ten minutes she was back, refilling the mug. Jacket still on, zippered up, scarf looped and re-looped around her neck, the knit cap pulled lower.

He had finished e-mailing the letter to the Creighton admissions office and closed the laptop. She was heading for the front door as he pulled on his jacket, grabbed his cowboy hat, and walked to the back office. He told the bishop that he and Shannon were going out, and the bishop said what he always said. He would hold down the fort.

Shannon was on the front stoop, stomping her boots with impatience. He followed her down the concrete steps glazed with ice, buttoning up his jacket as he went. Her boots left a trail of notches through the snow to the pickup. Inside, he jiggled the ignition and, under his breath, encouraged the old engine to turn over one more time. Finally it sputtered to life, a low growling noise, like that of a man waking after a long sleep.

Now, after that first outburst of excitement, Shannon settled into a dreamy silence in the passenger seat, gloved hands around the coffee mug she lifted to her lips now and then. Houses slipped past, silent in the cold air, lopsided piles of snow on the roofs, frost fringing the windows. Everything stopped in the winter, but Father John knew that wasn't true even as the thought crossed his mind. Pickups and cars bobbed down the frozen road toward him, some with headlights flashing through the grayness. From time to time, depending upon the direction in which the road bent, he glimpsed a trace of sunshine over the mountains.

"In case you're interested, James was a perfect gentleman." Shannon's voice erupted like that of an announcer on a radio program that had been off the air for a while.

"I wouldn't expect anything else."

"After we ate dinner, we went to his house."

His house.

"Used to be one of the ranch buildings behind the house where his mother lives. James insulated it, fixed it up. Put in a woodstove that keeps the place pretty cozy. He's very handy."

"Ah." He was learning more and more about James Two Horses.

"We talked for a couple hours." Four or five. "About everything. Have you ever met anyone you felt you could talk to for the rest of your life and never run out of things to say?" Father John felt her eyes playing over him. "I guess not. But let me tell you, it is a wonderful thing. I felt I could tell him anything. He didn't judge me or tell me how stupid I've been or how I should have made better choices. All that stuff. What do you think?"

He was thinking that James Two Horses had the makings of a good priest. He said, "I hope it was helpful."

She laughed at that. "What I ought to do and what I probably will do are different things for me. Always have been."

"You're talking about your . . ." He hesitated.

"Lover. You might as well call it for what it is. David is leaving. I've always known that. I wouldn't be surprised if he's moved out already."

Father John let the silence ride between them a moment. Then he said, "Are you all right?"

"Yes, of course. James let me talk it all out, all the dysfunctional aspects of David's and my relationship. When you step back and look at it, there was no other way it could end. Or should end." She took a long drink of coffee. When he looked over, he caught the sheen of moisture in her eyes before she turned toward the window.

He braked at the stop sign and waited for three trucks on Blue Sky Highway to pass, then took a right. There would be a cutoff ahead, not much more than an alley that could be obscured in the snow. He took his foot off the gas pedal to let the pickup coast, and he hunched forward, looking for the cutoff.

A truck turned out of the snowy field that ran between the highway and the foothills, brown and traced with snow. Father John tapped the brake and slowed to a crawl. As soon as the truck turned, he swung into the cutoff and maneuvered the pickup into the twin ruts sprinkled with dirt and black splotches of oil that zigzagged ahead. The white fields folded around them.

"Lizzie must have liked it out here," Shannon said, "in the middle of nowhere. Maybe people forgot about her and her white skin and freckles."

Father John smiled to himself. How easily the barriers between the past and the present slipped away when you took a step into the past, into those long-ago lives, and imagined yourself living them. It had happened many times when he was studying American history, researching the life of somebody no one else cared about. But he was caught up, as if he had stepped out of his own skin and into that of a man who had lived a hundred years ago, and he had known—*known*—how that man thought and felt and engaged the world.

And now Shannon was caught up in the life of a woman by the name of Elizabeth Fletcher Brokenhorn.

He came around a wide, lazy curve conscious of the rear tires slipping a little. He'd been thinking he should get new tires for some time now, as soon as the mission finances looked a little better. A perennial hope, he realized. The finances never changed. Random donations from people he'd never heard of. For a moment, he thought about the upcoming meeting in Milwaukee, the discussion on whether St. Francis Mission could continue to operate. He knew he had been putting off returning Father Jameson's call.

There it was, leaning sideways in the snow as he came out of the curve, the Brokenhorn cabin, a century of hand-hewn logs and resolve. Shannon let out a loud gasp beside him. He turned off the CD player; "Il balen del suo sorriso" faded into the quiet.

He was thinking he should have tried to reach Thomas Horn for permission to visit the cabin. He had called Wilbur, who told him to call his relation, Thomas, who looked after the old place, but Thomas didn't seem to be around. Father John tapped on the brake, searching the road ahead. No driveway, no cut into the waves of untouched snow. He stopped the pickup in a direct line from the cabin. "Hope you brought your snowshoes," he said.

Shannon was out of the cab, slamming the door behind her, before he had slid out. Still studying the expanse of snow, searching for any hint of an easy way across. Shannon was already striding into the field, snow banking around her boots and crawling up the legs of her jeans. Then she was running, yelling with delight, hands in the air, like a kid playing in the snow. He could feel the charge of excitement as he started after her.

The door hung slightly ajar, the windows gaped open, any glass that might have been in place at one time was gone. Shannon was yanking at the door, which squealed and creaked and held steady, frozen in place. Father John took hold of the edge, tugged upward until he felt the hinges settle into place, then pushed the door inward. He stood back, expecting Shannon to lunge inside, but she laid a hand on the frame and leaned forward, and he understood that she was stepping into the little house in her imagination, like Lizzie a hundred years ago.

He waited, not wanting to break the spell. Finally, she turned toward him and smiled. "Let's see what it's like."

It was freezing inside, as if the cold had burst through the open windows and expanded into something hard and permanent. Snow blanketed the floorboards. He clapped his hands together, conscious of the whoof his gloves made in the cold. Shannon was patrolling the rectangular perimeter, not more than fifteen feet by ten.

She stopped in front of a window that framed a view of the foothills and stared outside for a long moment. "Lizzie stood here," she said. "She saw this same view. Winter, spring, summer, fall—all the changing colors." She walked over to a wall with a round hole cut into the logs. "This is where she cooked. The stove stood here." She pointed at the hole and swiped at the snow with her boots, as if she might uncover evidence of a wood-burning stove. "She cooked everything. Whatever John could bring home. Whatever commodities they received from the government. She made bread from the flour they received. For a few weeks they would have bread, until the flour ran out."

She circled the area in front of the stove. "They slept here, the whole family. Lizzie and John over here." She gestured to the right. "The five kids here." A gesture to the left. "Huddling close for warmth, wrapped in buffalo robes." She glanced up with a start, as if she had just realized she wasn't working things out alone. "Don't you think so?"

"I hope so." Buffalo robes would have been scarce on the reservation. Sold off to traders long before for food, and impossible to replace. The great herds of buffalo were gone. It was likely that Lizzie and her family depended upon the thin woolen blankets they got from the government, along with the other rations promised in exchange for the Indian lands.

"Lizzie is so close. I can almost feel her presence here, in her home. Can't you?"

He smiled. He supposed she was right. If he let himself move into that realm of imagination—lose himself, as he did back in graduate school—then he supposed he could *feel* Lizzie Brokenhorn's presence. That was a long time ago.

The shot came like thunder that split the air and rumbled beneath the snow-covered floorboards. "Get down!" He took hold of Shannon's shoulder and pushed her to the floor; then, stooping low, he made his way to the nearest window. The field was open and quiet, their footsteps the only trace of activity. He moved to the side window, near the spot where the stove had been, and peered past the edge. He could see a pickup parked behind the Toyota, and a man standing next to it, rifle raised.

Another shot blasted across the field, and Father John dropped to his knees, his heart hammering. "Lie down flat," he said. *Dear Lord, don't let anything happen to her.* "I'm going out."

"You can't do that! Please, don't do that."

Hunching down, he worked his way across the floor and pulled open the door. "It's Father John from the mission!" he shouted into the white abyss. "I'm coming out." God, where was his handkerchief? He dug into the front pockets of his jeans, then the rear pocket, the other rear pocket, and finally pulled it free and, shaking it out into a small white frame, he reached around the door and waved the white handkerchief in the direction of the road.

"It's Father John!" he shouted again. His own name reverberated across the field and over the cabin. He got to his feet, sheltering next to the door frame, still waving the flag.

"No!" Shannon's voice sounded behind him, high-pitched in terror. "Don't leave me."

He stepped outside, holding the flag of truce. Waving. Waving. He could feel the man watching him. "I mean no

harm," he shouted. "I was visiting the Brokenhorn cabin."
He kept walking.

The man didn't move for a long moment. Then, he lowered the rifle and started stomping through the snow toward him. "Father John?" He came closer. "What in tarnation you doing here?"

Father John felt the tension leak out of his muscles. He recognized the man. Thomas Horn.

"Sorry about the warning shots," Thomas said. "Only way to keep trespassers from vandalizing the place."

"My apologies. We should have asked permission." Father John heard Shannon coming up behind him. Felt her rather than heard her. She approached silently in the snow. "This is my niece, Shannon O'Malley. She's researching the life of Lizzie Brokenhorn."

Thomas Horn gave a quick nod, as if Shannon were in a long line of folks interested in Lizzie. "I got your calls." The man turned and began stomping back toward the road. Father John took hold of Shannon's arm; she was shaking, and color had drained from her face.

"Sometimes grandmother's memory is sharp as ever." Thomas had stopped and looked sideways. Then he started off again, and they fell in beside him. "Other times, she can't remember me. I was waiting for the best time to get back to you. She's been real good the last couple days. I expect she'd like a couple visitors, you want to stop by now."

17

SHE WAS AVERAGE height, a little stocky, with rolls of flesh that bulged through a long-sleeved white tee shirt and rolled over the top of her blue jeans. *Full-figured* would be the correct term, Vicky thought. The figure of a middle-aged woman with a full resume of kids, ranch work, and part-time jobs to hold it all together.

"Come on in." Rosemary Little Shield flung the door wide open. She had a way of looking at you out of the corners of her eyes, which reminded Vicky of Rosemary's relative, Eldon. Rosemary was Eldon's mother's cousin, to be precise, which Myra Little Shield had explained when Vicky called to get the woman's address. Not that it mattered. All relatives were the same.

Rosemary lived on a ranch that ran into the foothills west of Fort Washakie, Myra had told her, then adding the rest of the story: Rosemary and her husband, Larry—also Little Shield, another distant cousin of Eldon's—had inherited the

ranch from her father. They had hoped one of their kids—
they had four—would stay on and help run the place, but
the kids had scattered. The way of kids these days—off
to college, a job in some city, forget they're Arapaho.
Larry ran the ranch. Took on a hired hand when he could
afford it.

"Clint said he was going to interview Rosemary," Myra
had gone on, "but we never heard what she had to say.
Knowing Rosemary, she told things exactly as they are. No
beating around the bush with her, and she saw Mary Ann
the week after we'd gotten her. She knows how much we
loved her from the get-go."

Vicky had asked if she or Eldon knew a man by the name
of Lou Bearing, and that had stopped the conversation.
Vicky could almost hear the condensed quiet that had gathered on the other end. "It's not ringing a bell," Myra said
finally. "Maybe Eldon knows him. Why do you ask?"

Vicky started to explain that Clint had interviewed him
after he'd talked to Rosemary, then stopped. There were no
notations, no indication Clint had actually spoken to the
man. Only the name written under three different days. It
was possible Clint had intended to interview Lou Bearing
and, for some reason, had changed his mind.

Myra had jumped into the silence. "I have to get back to
work. I'm leaving early this afternoon to take Mary Ann to
the dentist's."

Now, Rosemary Little Shield was directing her to a love
seat in the small living room and asking if she would like
a cup of coffee. "That would be nice," Vicky said, perching
on the edge of a cushion. Outside the temperatures hovered
below freezing, and despite the warm air blasting through
the Ford, she had been chilled on the drive across the reservation. She unbuttoned her coat and kept it on, huddling
inside the warmth, listening to the clinking, splashing
sounds coming from the kitchen.

Rosemary came through the archway into the living room, a mug in each hand. She set the mugs on the small table in front of the sofa and settled herself into a faded pink upholstered chair.

"Like I told you on the phone," Rosemary said, "I don't have a lot of time. I'm on the early dinner shift at the diner today."

Vicky said she understood. Ulrich's Diner in Riverton. She had eaten there many times. She supposed she must have seen Rosemary Little Shield there, another Arapaho woman working in town, a long drive every day. Women on the rez would go wherever they could find a job. It was the work that mattered, not the distance.

"So you've taken over Mary Ann's adoption case?" The woman had an open, matter-of-fact manner. There wasn't much time; the polite preliminaries had to be skipped. "That other lawyer spent a good hour here asking questions. He hung around so long that Larry came in from the pasture to see what was going on, so then he interviewed both of us."

And that was strange, Vicky was thinking. In his notations, Clint hadn't mentioned Larry Little Shield. It seems there was a lot that Clint Hopkins hadn't mentioned.

"Would you mind telling me what you told Clint?"

Rosemary lifted her shoulders in an exaggerated shrug. "What you'd expect, I guess. How Myra called and said they had a new baby to care for. Naturally, I was surprised, 'cause they'd just lost their baby. So I was thinking, where did this new baby come from? She told me they were foster parents, and they hoped they'd have the baby for a long time, like the rest of her life. That evening, Larry and I went over to see the baby. I remember we brought some stew I'd made. You always need food with a new baby. And Mary Ann was real new—you could tell. Tiny little thing. But alert, with big blue eyes that followed you around, watching you, like she was trying to figure everything out."

"Did it strike you as unusual that she was white?"

"You mean a white foster child with an Arapaho couple? I guess, but Myra said they thought the mother was Arapaho, and the baby happened to look more white than Indian, which would probably change as she grew. You know, the Indian side would come out. All I know is what I told Clint. Myra and Eldon were as happy as I'd ever seen them. There never was a couple more in love with a baby. I was so happy for them, after what they'd been through. Larry and I, neither one of us, wanted to throw any cold water, so we kept our mouths shut. But we were both thinking, soon as social services finds a white couple to take Mary Ann, the Little Shields will lose her."

"But it didn't happen. Didn't you wonder why?"

"You sound like that other lawyer." She gave a throaty laugh. "Like I told him, it didn't happen, and pretty soon the whole family just accepted Mary Ann as one of us. We figured Eldon and Myra would adopt her, and that's what they are trying to do."

"Did you hear any rumors or gossip around the rez?"

"Rumors? Like what?"

"Clint didn't ask about rumors?"

Rosemary shrugged. "There's always busybodies that's got an opinion and can't keep it to themselves. Sure, there were rumors, some of them real nasty, like maybe Mary Ann was stolen, or Myra and Eldon bought her from somebody. Nobody paid any attention. Mary Ann had a good home. It was all that mattered."

Vicky was quiet. Everyone on the list was related to the Little Shields, all of whom had probably ignored the rumors. Clint had no way of knowing what people might have said behind the family's back, but a judge would want to know. A judge would demand hard evidence to prove Mary Ann had been left on the Little Shields' doorstep. She felt a downdraft of weariness. Is that what Clint had experienced? A sense of the impossibility of proving Mary Anne had been left on the Little Shields' doorstep?

"Why did you suggest Clint talk to Lou Bearing?"

"Who?" Rosemary had sprung upright and was pulling on a jacket she had yanked off the hook "I just realized the time. I can't be late for my shift."

"The man Clint interviewed after he spoke to you." Vicky got to her feet and started buttoning her own coat.

"You mean Lou and Debbie Bearing? Don't really know them. Keep to themselves. Never seen them at the powwows or farmers' markets. Why would I send Clint to talk to them?"

"I thought they might be neighbors."

Rosemary threw a scarf around her neck as if she were throwing salt over her shoulder and could read the future based on the patterns in which the crystals fell. "Neighbors? What are you talking about? The nearest neighbor is a mile away."

Vicky looped her own scarf under her chin and followed Rosemary out into the frigid air. A sheen of frost lay over the Ford. She was trying to picture Clint's calendar. In the jottings below Rosemary's name, he had written the word *neighbor*. The following day he had written Lou Bearing's name for the first time.

Except there was no one who could qualify as a neighbor, and Rosemary had not suggested Lou Bearing.

"Hope you have good luck helping Mary Ann," Rosemary called over her shoulder as she turned toward the pickup on the far side of the stoop.

"Thanks for your time." Vicky's voice sounded sharper in the cold air than she intended. She veered in the opposite direction, toward the Ford, and was about to get inside when she stopped. She must have misinterpreted the sequence of Clint's notations. Neighbor could have referred to Lou Bearing's neighbor.

She swung about and started back across the yard, waving at the woman maneuvering the pickup into parallel tire ruts that ran out to the road. Finally the pickup rocked to a stop and the driver's window began a slow, jerky motion downward.

Vicky grabbed hold of the door handle. Her breath floated into the cab, a cloud of steam. "Who did you suggest Clint talk to?"

The woman blinked several times, as if she were trying to comprehend. "I didn't suggest anybody. I'm going to be late."

"Please. It's important. You must have mentioned someone."

She looked away a moment, then turned back. The tip of her nose was red with the cold. "It was just conversation. We were talking about the adjustment Eldon and Myra had made to take care of a baby, and the baby wasn't even their own. It's not like babies know the difference between night and day, so they're up all night, crying. You don't know what's wrong. I told him what Dina said . . ."

"Dina?"

"Dina Fowler. Worked the same shift at the diner. She'd come to work looking like she'd been up all night, and she didn't even have a baby. It was her neighbor's baby. Crying all night. I remember Dina saying she hadn't even realized the neighbor's were expecting. Then, one night, the crying started."

Neighbor. Clint had jotted the single word, and Vicky realized she had assumed that Lou Bearing was Rosemary's neighbor. He wasn't; he was Dina Fowler's neighbor. She said, "Does Dina still work with you?"

"Left a couple years ago after she and Matthew moved to Lander. She opened her own place on Main Street. Like I say, we were just chatting. I never expected Clint would go find Dina." The window began creaking upward. "I really have to go."

Vicky stepped back and gave the woman a little wave of appreciation. Hard pellets of ice and snow sprayed from the wheels as the pickup ground forward. Clint Hopkins had been a good adoption lawyer because he was thorough. Nothing was unimportant, no idle chitchat. Every comment might lead to something.

18

FIRE CRACKLED IN the wood-burning stove, a survivor from the nineteenth century, glowing red and orange and emitting heat waves into the small room. Traces of gray smoke escaped from the metal chimney that rose through an opening in the ceiling. Shannon was conscious of her uncle standing close behind her in the small room. A few feet away, slumped in a chair in front of the stove, was an old woman bundled in a Pendleton blanket, with a lined, leathery face and a pink scalp covered with strips of thin gray hair.

"Grandmother." Thomas Horn bent over the woman. The gentleness in his tone surprised Shannon, as if he were speaking to a child or someone quite ill. "Are you up for visitors?"

The old woman stirred and shifted about inside the blanket. "I love visitors."

"Father John from the mission is here. He brought his

niece." Shannon felt the man's eyes dance over her for a moment. "They would like to talk with you."

At that, Theresa Horn strained sideways and looked over her shoulder. Light flickered in her narrow black eyes.

Shannon watched her uncle move in a little closer, drawn to the warmth of the fire. The woman squared herself again in front of the stove. From somewhere in the folds of the blanket, she brought out a hand, speckled with spots and thin as paper, the fingers as crooked and fragile as dried sticks. Uncle John held her hand in both of his for a long moment. "How are you, Grandmother?"

Voice crackling like the fire, the old woman said she was as ornery as ever. Waiting for winter to blow away so her bones could warm up. "And who's this pretty thing?" She strained sideways again, and now Shannon felt the old woman's gaze traveling over her.

"My niece, Shannon."

"Oh, yes, so Thomas said. My grandson tells me what he wants me to know. He thinks I'm too senile to know what he's up to, so I always check." The old woman gave a little laugh that rumbled about the blanket.

Shannon stepped in closer to let the old woman take her in, make up her own mind as to what kind of heart beat inside this white woman. Good heart? Bad heart? A day on the reservation and its ways were taking hold of her. If Theresa Horn decided she had a bad heart, Shannon knew, they might as well leave, because the old woman would go as silent as an abandoned drum.

"I'm so pleased to meet you." Shannon leaned down—not too far, just enough to allow the old woman to bring her into focus. "Your grandson was kind enough to invite us over."

It took a moment, but gradually a smile worked its way through the old woman's expression. First the black eyes, then the mouth. She lifted a hand again, and Shannon took it, conscious of Uncle John watching her. Was her excitement contagious? She was holding a hand that had held Lizzie's hand. The small hand of a child then, when Lizzie was in her late fifties or early sixties. The hand of an old woman now, roughened and muscular.

"So you want to know about my grandmother." Theresa Horn retrieved her hand and hid it again in the blanket. "Thomas told me Father John called about bringing you by. You come from back east."

The old woman was sharp today; she hadn't missed anything. Shannon glanced up at Uncle John beside her. He was easy to read. Thomas hadn't returned his calls because his grandmother hadn't made up her mind whether she wanted to share her most precious possession—her stories—with a stranger. Even when Thomas brought them home, he probably wasn't sure how she would react.

"Chicago," Shannon said.

The old woman nodded. "Grandmother came from a place near Chicago. You have that in common, that and red hair. Oh, I remember reddish hair poking out of the calico cloth she wrapped around it. You'd better sit down." She motioned to the kitchen chairs Thomas had pulled over.

Shannon dropped onto one of the chairs and leaned forward, conscious of Uncle John taking the chair next to her and Thomas Horn hovering nearby in the shadows, close enough to hear everything. The old woman was saying something about her grandmother dying when she was seven years old.

Shannon felt a stab of disappointment. How much could the old woman remember? How much would be true?

"I remember how she hated her hair," Theresa said. "Hated her white skin. Used to try and hide them. My father got her light skin. His hair was light, not red like grandmother's. Never made any difference. He knew he was Arapaho, but I guess that was what bothered grandmother.

She knew she wasn't Arapaho, no matter what her heart said."

"It's wonderful that you have those memories." Shannon could feel her whole being reaching toward the old woman. This was as close as she would ever come to Lizzie Broken-horn, these people on the rez with Lizzie's blood in their veins.

"I may be old as the hills." Theresa gave another cracked laugh. "Some days I still got my marbles. What else you want to know?"

What else? Shannon threw another glance at the man beside her. Information is a gift. It was impolite to ask for a gift. Finally she said, "You actually knew her. I was hoping you could tell me if"—she drew in a long breath, then plunged on—"if you think she was happy."

The old woman sank farther down into the blanket until her chin disappeared. "Nobody asked questions like that back then. You were alive, so you were happy. Grandmother worked hard. She did her chores. She cooked our food every day. We ate stew. Rabbit, deer, elk, if Dad and Grandfather got lucky. Beef when we got our rations once a year. Beef on the hoof."

Another laugh erupted from the blankets. "I guess they thought, let those Indians play at being Indians and slaughter their food. One beef for a family. The men killed the cow and Grandmother went to work. She had a big knife, sharp enough to take off your finger, and she got down on the ground and skinned and butchered the carcass. Up to her elbows in blood when she finished. She cut off big slabs of beef that she pounded with the berries us kids found on the prairie. She stretched the beef out to dry on racks grandfather built. We had beef stew on real cold days in the winter, when we needed extra fat on our bones, she used to say."

"We saw her house." She'd been right, Shannon was

thinking. Lizzie had made the stew at the stove. "It looks like there was a stove inside."

The old woman shook her head. "Grandmother cooked over the big wood fire in the tipi. If we came inside to get warm, she put us to work. Go to the creek and get more water. Go clean the potatoes in the snow. She always had a bucket of wild potatoes and onions she dug in the fall. The dirt stuck to them like glue. By the time I got them clean, my fingers were frozen. Grandmother didn't take to excuses. If I complained, she told me to get back to work."

"She sounds very"—Shannon could sense the man beside her waiting, his breath suspended, while she searched for the word—"disciplined." She had almost said *tough*.

"She survived, didn't she? The old people kept us alive. Hunting, trying to grow crops on this no-water land, working all the time to keep our bellies filled. You want to know if she was happy? I'd say she would've been happier living free on the plains in the Old Time. But when she came to the people, the Old Time was gone, and the people were sick and hungry. Weren't any good times before or after the rez."

Shannon gave Uncle John a quick glance. *When she came to the people.* As if Lizzie Fletcher had come on her own.

The old woman had tilted her head back until her chin emerged from the blanket. Her gaze trailed the chimney to the ceiling. "I remember how she taught me to make fry bread. 'Pinch off a piece of dough,' she'd say. Those white hands of hers were quick and strong. 'Pat it out.' The old woman patted at the blanket until Shannon could almost see a ball of dough taking shape, round and fat and smooth like the photos she had seen of Indian women working in the food booths at powwows.

"'See?'" the old woman said, her hand still patting the blanket. "'Not like that. Like this!' Oh, she was a stickler for doing it right. Not worth doing unless you did a thing right. She'd toss the dough into hot oil and turn it with a stick until it was golden brown and sizzling. You could see the steam coming off it, and your mouth would start watering. She always kept pieces of fry bread in her necessary bag. When us kids got hungry and started crying, she'd pull out a piece of fry bread to shut us up."

Shannon sat back, reluctant to let the moment pass. Theresa Horn was deep in memories now, transported to another time. A child following her grandmother around, doing what she was told, hoping for another piece of fry bread. And where was her own mother? Tending to the crops, hunting for wild berries and vegetables, hauling water? Working. Working. She knew enough about tribal life to know it was the older women, the grandmothers, those whose work kept them closer to home, who raised the children.

"Lizzie sounds like a good grandmother," she said, wanting to keep the memories flowing, to hold the old woman in the past.

"We didn't think of good or bad. Grandmother looked after us. She taught us kids how to survive. How to tan hides and sew shirts and pants and dresses. She took us to the Sun Dance. Oh, I remember riding in the back of the wagon that bounced all over the place. Grandmother up on the buckboard handling the horses. They never gave her any trouble. She could turn and stop them whenever she wanted. She taught us to be respectful of the dancers 'cause they danced in the heat for three days without water or food. They made a sacrifice to the Creator so that He would take pity on the people. After the dancing ended, we helped Grandmother hand out the chokecherry juice so they could drink water and eat food without getting sick. She knew all these things, Grandmother did. She passed them on to us."

The old woman slumped downward until her chin disappeared again, and Thomas stepped forward, not saying anything. His look said it all: She's getting tired.

Uncle John stood up first, and Shannon rose beside him, reluctant to let go of the past. This old woman had known Lizzie Brokenhorn, held her hand, sat at her side, breathed in the essence of her. "Thank you," she said, but the old woman's eyelids had dropped down and she had receded into some other place. Perhaps she was still with Lizzie.

Shannon waited while her uncle shook hands with Thomas Horn and thanked him; then she did the same. The man crossed the room, opened the door, and Shannon stepped out first into the blast of cold air.

"SHE DIDN'T TELL me everything." Shannon watched the cabin, a dark smudge in the gray light, pass outside her window as they drove along Blue Sky Highway.

"What else would you have liked to know?"

"What else?" Shannon laughed. "E degio e posso," one of her favorite arias, was playing between them. "Everything else. Did Lizzie ever look at her white arms and legs and wonder who she was? Where she came from? Why she was different from her people? Why she resembled the white people in town? Did she wonder what they thought of her?"

"What do you think?"

"Of course she did. So did John Brokenhorn. He moved the family into the mountains at one point to hide her from white people who might take her. Recapture her." She slid sideways into the corner and stared at the man beside her, the clumps of reddish hair beneath the brim of his cowboy hat. They were alike; they were related; they came from the same tribe. What was it like for Lizzie to look at her Arapaho family—husband, aunts and uncles and cousins, all the people who gave her her place on the earth—and know she was different?

She straightened herself and stared out the windshield. It looked like snow again, the dark clouds hanging low, stationary and heavy, waiting to open up. She would spend the rest of the day writing out her notes, deciphering what she wrote, reading between the lines. Is that what history was about? The past that lodged between the lines?

And this evening? This evening she would see James Two Horses. Hamburger or pizza someplace. He would know a little restaurant with small tables that they could hover over, faces close, voices low, talking. She still felt the ripples of amazement that had run through her last night. She had never been able to talk to David like that, where she felt he was taking in every word, taking her seriously.

She turned into the passenger window and dabbed at her eyes. She didn't want Uncle John to see. God, she couldn't think of David without crying. It was as if his name turned on a faucet inside her. What a fool she'd been. She had always known it was coming. She had to give him that—he hadn't lied to her. But she had hung on, hoping for what? That he would change his mind, of course, fall in love with her, be unable to imagine life without her.

"Are you all right?"

She felt Uncle John's eyes on her. She couldn't hide from him.

She swallowed hard and tried to compose herself before she turned toward him with the most relaxed smile she could muster. "Sure. The research is going just as I hoped." She drew in a long breath, aware of the stuttering sound. "James and I are having dinner again tonight. I hope Elena and the bishop don't take offense."

Uncle John gave her a sideways glance. A glance, nothing else, but she knew that he knew everything.

She stopped the words crowding into her throat: *I might have been tempted to sleep with him last night if he hadn't said, "We'd better go. It's time I got you back to the mission."* It was the way it should be. The last thing she needed was to jump into another relationship after David. And

James was different, so much more solid and real. Any relationship, if it happened, would be like that.

Uncle John understood. She saw the truth in the throb of a tiny blood vessel in his temple, the way he glanced over and smiled at her. She felt raw and exposed, all her secret hopes thrown into the road for everyone to see.

"I'll let Elena know," he said.

19

THE FRONT DOOR sighed open into the warm, muggy atmosphere of the diner halfway down Main Street in Lander. Odors of hot grease, fried meat, and coffee hung over the counter that stretched along the rear. A few booths lined the plate glass windows on either side of the door. The place was empty. The lunch crowd, if there had been one, had moved on, leaving behind wet traces of boot prints on the yellow vinyl floor.

The bell above the door jangled into the silence for a moment before cutting off as Vicky let the door bang behind her and slid onto a stool. Through the opened door behind the counter she could see a woman bent into scrubbing the metal surface of a trestle table. The shiny circle widened under her hand.

Vicky took the menu out of the metal holder and flipped it open. The realization that she was hungry had come out of the blue. Toast and coffee this morning before she'd gone to the office, then nothing, and it was almost time for dinner. Living off adrenaline, chasing after Clint Hopkins, trying to escape the image of the dark figure suspended over the hood of the black truck. She squeezed her eyes shut a moment, forcing away the thought that she was two blocks— *two blocks*—from where Clint had died.

She glanced at the menu: hamburger, steak sandwich, turkey sandwich, grilled cheese. There was another thought that stayed with her, an icy hand gripping her: the truck had been waiting for Clint Hopkins. She *knew* it to be true. Clint had been murdered. Somehow it all converged on the last name on the calendar, Lou Bearing. Clint had met the man, spoken with him, and something Lou Bearing said must have sent Clint elsewhere. A man obsessed with uncovering the truth behind an infant's sudden appearance on a doorstep, doggedly interviewing one person after another, day after day, and then? Nothing. A calendar with three days x-ed out. Where had he gone? What had he done? Taken a break in the midst of an investigation? Put his feet up by a fire and smoked a pipe? She didn't think so.

She had been staring at the menu, lost in her own thoughts, and now the woman from the back was on the other side of the counter. She had set down a glass of water, and now she was tapping a pencil on the notepad cupped in her hand. An Arapaho with the prominent cheekbones, the little hook in her nose, the black eyes that seemed to take in everything and gave nothing.

"What can I get you? Sorry, we're out of apple pie."

Apple pie. Vicky hadn't yet turned to the dessert section. "Are you Dina?"

The woman stepped back, something new in her eyes, a flicker of interest. "Dina's Diner. This is my place. What's it going to be?"

"Grilled cheese." A hot grilled cheese sandwich struck her as the most delicious item on the menu. "Coffee."

Dina slipped the pad into the pocket of a white apron streaked with ketchup and mustard stains and the shiny residue of grease. The order was not worth writing down. She had already turned back when Vicky said, "I'm an attorney here in town. Vicky Holden. I'd like to talk to you for a few minutes."

The woman swung back. "I heard of you. The Indian lawyer. Were you working with the lawyer that got killed?"

"I've taken over one of his cases."

"About time, I say. He came in here last week, asking questions. Had me digging into the past, trying to remember what happened five years past, like that wasn't a lifetime ago. 'You must remember,' he told me, and sure enough, I remembered. He was working on an adoption case for an Arapaho couple. Well, he didn't have to say anything else. I figured he was helping the Little Shields adopt that white girl they'd been taking care of. I told him, you need to talk to Vicky Holden, the Indian lawyer. She'll know about tribal adoptions." She studied the surface of the counter and drew in a breath that puffed her cheeks. "Too bad what happened to him. Run down in the street like that. He seemed like a good guy."

She glanced around the diner, as if she wanted to make sure another customer hadn't materialized, before leaning in closer. "Let me get your grilled cheese. I'll join you for a cup of coffee."

Then she was off. Through the door, out of sight in the back, a refrigerator door swishing open and closed, metal clanking against metal, a faucet running. After a moment, new odors floated out to the counter—hot, fresh coffee and melting cheese. Vicky sipped at the water, conscious of the empty space in her stomach.

Dina reappeared, balancing two mugs of coffee with a plate piled with a grilled cheese sandwich, potato chips, and a dill pickle. She set them on the counter, then walked around and settled on the adjacent stool.

"You go ahead." She nodded at the sandwich. "It's late for lunch. You must be hungry."

Vicky bit into the sandwich, then took another bite. Is this what came from working in a diner—feeding people all day long—the ability to sense hunger? She took a sip of coffee, aware of the woman's eyes watching her, waiting until the time was right to talk. Until they were both ready. It was the Arapaho Way.

She finished half the sandwich, took a long drink of coffee, and rotated toward the woman. "I spoke with Rosemary . . ."

Dina put up a hand. "And she told you about the crying baby. Clint came around wanting me to tell him everything I knew. Like I say, it took a minute to figure out what he was asking about. But when the memories started coming, they were real clear. We were living outside Fort Washakie, Matthew and me. Nearest neighbors a little way across the field. Lou and Debbie Bearing. Arapahos. Real standoffish, didn't want anything to do with anybody. Never saw them go anywhere. Lou worked in the barn out back. Kept to themselves. Didn't have any kids. All of a sudden they had a baby. How'd we know? Never heard a baby crying like it was in pain, screaming bloody murder all night long. We didn't get any sleep for a week. I went over once and knocked on the door. They didn't even answer, just shouted from inside: 'What do you want?' 'Is there anything I can do to help?' I had to shout back. I remember it was freezing cold, and I was leaning into the door trying to get some warmth. They shouted back that they were fine, just a little colic. They were taking care of her. It wasn't gonna last long."

"Her? They said *her*?"

Dina pulled her lips into a tight line and nodded. "That was the last night we heard the crying. The next night was quiet as a grave. After that, I started watching their house when I was home, you know, their comings and goings. She drove a little car, and he had a pickup. They'd drive off for a while, then come back. I didn't see any sign of a baby. I wondered what had happened to the baby. I thought I should call social services."

"Did you?" This would be something, a social services inquiry from someone else about a baby who had appeared out of nowhere. Like the baby dropped at the Little Shields', except Mary Ann had not disappeared.

The woman was shaking her head. "We talked about it and decided we should give them a chance to explain, before we dragged in the"—she let a beat skip before she said— "authorities. We went over one evening after we'd seen them come home. This time Lou opened the door. Real friendly like, which surprised us. Says come on in, want some coffee? Matthew said we came over to see how their baby was doing. He said *their* baby even though we knew she wasn't theirs. Debbie never looked like she was pregnant, and we'd seen her outside a couple weeks before that crying started."

Vicky waited while the woman took a drink of coffee. Finally, she went on: "'Oh, wasn't our baby,' Lou said, like we was some kind of nincompoops didn't know the score. 'Some friends were visiting. Sorry their baby made so much racket. Yeah, we were real glad to see them move on.'"

"Did you believe them?"

"Clint asked the same question." Dina held the mug to her lips and peered over the rim, a faraway look in her eyes, as if, for a moment, she were back talking to Clint. "Now, I think, of course we didn't believe them. How could we? But at the time, what can I say? It seemed reasonable even though . . ."

"Even though?"

"We never saw any other cars at the house. No pickups

or campers, the kind of thing you see when folks come visiting."

Vicky took another bite of the sandwich. Lukewarm now, the cheese congealing against the toast. She washed it down with coffee. "Did Clint say anything?"

The woman laughed. The mug of coffee shook in her hand. "I got the impression Clint Hopkins wasn't much for saying what was on his mind. He kept his own counsel. I imagine he went to have a talk with Lou and Debbie. Wouldn't surprise me if they denied there was ever a baby at their house. Maybe we were having hallucinations, me and Matthew. Wouldn't surprise me if that's what they told him."

"When was the last time you saw him?"

"Clint? Never saw him again. Just that one time. You could tell how much he wanted that little girl to be safe with the folks that loved her, like he was going to do everything he could to make it happen."

Vicky pulled her bag around from the back of the stool where she had hung it and was groping inside for her wallet when Dina set a hand on her shoulder. "It's on the house. I'd like to see that little girl safe, too, so no one can take her away."

OUTSIDE, THE TEMPERATURE was dropping, the cold settling over the parking lot. Vicky pulled her scarf around her neck and sank inside her coat. Her fingers stiffened as she pulled on her gloves. *I'd like to see that little girl safe.* The words bounced around inside her head. Clint had wanted the same thing. It had gotten him killed. And now it was what she wanted.

She slid into the Ford and shut the door. It made a hollow thud in the cold air. The engine balked for a second before it finally turned over, cold air exploding from the vents. The sky, gray clouds edged in black, fell all around. Spring seemed so far away this afternoon, it might have been November. She realized that the tiny buzzing noise, like that of a mosquito, was her cell. She rummaged through her bag among the lipstick, combs, notepads, pens, tissues, keys—the detritus of her life—and pulled out the cell. "Vicky Holden" appeared in the readout. She pressed the answer button.

"Oh, I'm glad I reached you." A mixture of relief and anxiety ran through Annie's voice. "Betty White Hawk called back. A so-called friend of Vince's sent her on a wild goose chase. Betty went to the house the friend told her about, and nobody there had seen Vince in a week or more. You ask me, they're helping him. Betty said she's going to lose her job because she didn't go into work today. All she can think about is Vince."

"Did she mention Lou Bearing?"

"The guy from the bar last night? She went to his house this afternoon. He ordered her off his property. Said she was harassing him."

Vicky took a minute. She could see her breath curling into the cold air. "What is she going to do next?"

"She's hoping you'd tell her."

Lou Bearing. The name kept appearing like thistles in a patch of grass. The clock on the dashboard read 4:24. It would take forty minutes to drive across the rez to the Bearing house.

"Anything else?"

"You had a couple of walk-ins this afternoon that Roger took. Are you okay?"

"Yes, of course." The questions took her by surprise. "Why wouldn't I be?"

"You seem so, I don't know, distracted, ever since the accident."

Vicky started to say it wasn't an accident, then checked

herself. Was she the only one who believed it was murder?
She told Annie to lock up when she left. She would see her
tomorrow morning. Then she pressed the end button, put
the gear into reverse, and backed out of the parking slot. She
had to wait for a thin line of traffic to pass before she skidded onto the street. Exhaust from the truck ahead laid down
black lines over the snow, like paint. There was nothing in
Clint's notes except the name Lou Bearing. Nothing about
him. Who he was. What kind of work he did. What he had
told Clint.

Why did you leave it all in your head? The truck threw back
chunks of snow that slid down the windshield. Vicky fiddled
with the wipers until, finally, they swished the snow away. She
was heading out of town into the reservation. The snow-
streaked brown shoulders of the Wind River Range rose into
the gray clouds.

Lou Bearing, wife Debbie, no children—that was all she
knew. She drove to Fort Washakie and continued west, the
mountains looming closer. The Bearings lived on a road
outside town, with a big barn out back, Dina had said. "You
can't miss it."

20

VICKY TURNED OFF the engine and scanned the house. A rectangular house, wooden stoop at the front door, a faint light inside turning the windows iridescent. Whoever was inside would have heard the Ford, engine growling, crunching the snow. If the Bearings wanted company, they would open the door.

She gave it another couple minutes, then got out. The snow was banked around the stoop and piled over the steps, and she had to grip the rail to keep from slipping. She could feel the snow trickling down into her boots. The door bucked under her fist when she knocked. Draughts of icy air blew across the stoop. Silence except for the swoosh of the wind.

She had started back down the steps when she heard it: the loud, heavy clank of metal on metal. She stood still, holding on to the rail. The sound came again, like that of railroad cars coupling, or a trolley banging against a metal bumper. Industrial, city sounds incongruous on the open, snowy plains that stretched into the dark distance.

Vicky walked around the house and down the side, the cold working its way through her coat. Across an expanse of churned snow in back was the dark cliff face of a barn. Dim arrows of light escaped around the double doors that shuddered with the thumping noise. It was getting dark fast, shadows thickening across the snow.

She made her way to the doors, waited for a break in the noise, and knocked. The noise stopped, leaving an eerie quiet that lasted a half minute, as if whoever was inside had run out another door. She removed her glove and knocked again, pounding hard, the wooden doors shivering sideways. From inside came the sound of shuffling footsteps and a low muttering before the doors finally rattled apart on their metal rails.

The man standing in the opening was slim and hunched forward, backlit by the bright lights inside. He had black hair, cut short above his ears, and deep-set eyes that gave his face the look of a mask. A red scar, like the teeth marks of a saw, pulsated on one cheek.

"Lou Bearing?"

"Who wants to know?"

Vicky went through it all, keeping her eyes on the mask: She was Vicky Holden, an attorney. Could she talk to him for a few minutes?

"I'm busy."

"I represent a friend of yours, Vince White Hawk. And there's another matter . . ."

He sliced a thin arm between them, as if he were chopping wood. "That Rap is no friend of mine. Who told you that?"

"You were seen drinking with him at the Buffalo Bar and Lounge a couple of nights ago."

"So what? I drink with a lot of people."

"Could I come in?" The wind, sucked through the open

doors, was whipping around them. The man started backing up, and Vicky followed him inside. Floodlights attached to metal poles in the corners lit the barn like a stadium. Tools and crumpled rags littered the benches against the walls. In the center, a sedan listed sideways on blocks two feet high. Next to the sedan was a black truck, the front facing the rear wall, hood up. The air was thick with the smells of paint and metallic dust. She had stepped into a garage and body shop.

Lou Bearing reached past her and yanked the doors shut. "Make it quick." He spoke out of the corner of his mouth, his lips stiff, as if they were glued on. The jagged red scar, which ran from the corner of his mouth to his temple, pulled his left eye downward. He stared at her out of the right eye.

"Vince could be in serious trouble," she said.

Bearing swung around and walked over to one of the benches, then turned back. "Don't see how it's my business."

"There's a warrant for his arrest on a robbery charge." She could feel the cold gripping her. The barn was like an icebox despite the lights beaming down and a space heater that crackled and glowed red in the far corner. She pushed on: "He's gone into hiding. I'm trying to help him. I was hoping you might know where I can find him."

Bearing rubbed his hands together, impatience pouring off him. He didn't say anything.

"Who else did Vince drink with at the bar? Did he say anything about a drinking house?"

"Time for you to push off." Bearing's expression remained flat, unreadable, except for the scar, which glowed purplish in the light.

Vicky stood her ground. Everything about the man's demeanor said he was hiding something. If he knew where Vince might be, why wouldn't he say so? Especially if what he claimed were true, that he and Vince were not friends. What difference would it make to him? The man was as nervous as a cat.

A new thought hit her as she watched him: Lou Bearing did not want Vince found.

Then he was shouldering past her and pushing back the doors. Frozen air stirred around them. What had made her think Lou Bearing would tell her anything when he had stonewalled Vince's mother and John O'Malley?

She stepped farther into the center of the barn, ignoring the opened doors. "There is something else."

"There's nothing I have to say to you." The scar jiggled when he spoke. He was rubbing his hands, as if he could work warmth into them. Little beads of perspiration glistened on his forehead.

"I've taken over the Little Shield adoption case that Clint Hopkins spoke to you about."

"Don't know anything about it." Bearing dodged sideways toward the bench, picked up a hammer, and walked to the front of the black truck. "Get out of here." He spit the words over his shoulder.

"Whoa! What's going on?" A woman stepped into the doorway, then came into the barn. Something familiar about her, and yet Vicky couldn't remember ever meeting her. Another face on the reservation, at the grocery store, the gas station, lost among hundreds of faces. Arapaho with straight black hair showing beneath a cowboy hat pulled low over her forehead. She had a dark complexion, red-flushed with cold or anger, and little pillows of flesh below her deep-set dark eyes. She wore a bulky jacket that gave her a stuffed look, shoulders and chest bulging. So this was Debbie Bearing.

"Who are you?"

"Vicky Holden."

"Oh yeah. The Rap lawyer in a fancy office in Lander. We don't need any more lawyers around here."

"I'm representing the Little Shield family . . ."

"Nothing to do with us. You better leave."

"I know Clint Hopkins came to see you."

"I was gonna tell her . . ." Lou began.

The woman put up a hand and moved deeper inside, head bent forward; the doors jiggled behind her in the wind. She threw a warning glance at her husband. "I'll handle this." Then she squared her shoulders a few feet from Vicky. "If you know that lawyer came around here asking a lot of stupid questions, you know what we told him. Five years ago? Who remembers five years ago? So some neighbor says she heard a baby crying. So what? We got relations. They come and visit. Sometimes they hang around. I told that lawyer to stop bothering us."

Stop bothering us. Debbie Bearing swallowed hard, as if she could pull back the words. It was obvious this was not something she had meant to say.

"Clint came to see you two days in a row." Vicky went for the opening. She could see Clint's calendar, the black Xs on the following three days. "Then he came back a third time. Where had he gone? What new questions did he have for you?"

Lou Bearing looked frozen in place, a statue next to the truck. His wife was breathing hard, shuffling her feet on the hard-packed dirt floor. She took her time before she said, "How are we supposed to know what that crazy lawyer was after? Asking a lot of questions that had nothing to do with us. What do we know about the Little Shields? What do we care if they adopt a kid or not? You lawyers get your jollies pestering people. Made Hopkins feel like he was earning his big fee. Lou threatened to throw him out."

And that was it. Vicky knew by the nervous lift of Debbie Bearing's voice, the nerve jumping at the edge of her eye. She glanced over at the thin, stooped man braced against the side of the black truck, hammer dangling from one hand. She doubted Lou Bearing could have thrown out a big, fit man like Clint Hopkins. Clint had left because he had run into a wall, and whatever he had glimpsed behind that wall had led him to call her.

That night he was murdered.

"I also represent Vince White Hawk." Vicky went on, grasping at thin air. From the tiny flicker of light in the woman's eyes, Vicky knew that Debbie Bearing knew her client.

Debbie curled her lips against her teeth. She looked over at her husband a moment, then settled her shoulders inside the bulky jacket. "How we supposed to know every Rap on the rez?" Keeping her gaze on Vicky, she said to her husband, "You told her that, right?"

"Right." Lou's voice sounded shaky and uncertain. "Just because I had a drink with the guy doesn't mean I know him."

Debbie turned sideways and glared at the man, who looked as if he wanted to fade into the truck. "You drink with a lot of guys."

"I told her."

Debbie turned back. Her gaze was level and steady, as if everything had been cleared up. "Get out and leave us alone." She tossed her head in the direction of the doors and the wind whistling through the cracks.

The doors banged shut behind her as Vicky went out. She picked her way through the pencils of light around the corner of the house and out to the front, the light getting dimmer. The night was black with dark clouds that obscured the moon and the stars that usually lit up the sky. She lurched for the handle and slid inside the Ford, grateful for the familiar feel of the steering wheel in her hands, the cough of the engine turning over, and the flare of headlights that washed over her footprints in the snow.

She backed across the yard, turning halfway around to make out the tracks, not wanting to attempt a U-turn and get stuck. The Ford crawled down into the barrow ditch and up onto the road, engine growling and tires spinning. She drew in a sigh of relief and drove toward Lander.

She had accomplished nothing. Nothing to allay Betty's fears, nothing that might help the Little Shields. And yet she couldn't shake the feeling that behind the stonewalling and the indignation of Lou and Debbie Bearing, there was everything.

21

THE CELL WAS ringing. A muffled noise that emanated from the depths of her bag on the passenger seat and jolted Vicky out of the rhythm of the tires on the snowy pavement. Vicky slipped her earpiece behind her ear, not taking her eyes from the flare of headlights on the road. The ringing stopped. "Vicky Holden here."

A jumble of sounds: clanking glasses, a distant roar of guffaws, the shuffle of boots on a hard surface. "Hello." She heard herself shouting over the noise in what was probably a bar. A surge of anticipation ran through her. Vince could be on the other end. "Are you there?"

"Vicky? I got to talk to you." It was a woman's voice, aggressive and depressed at the same time, slurring the words, stumbling over them. The voice of Betty White Hawk.

"Where are you?"

"At the Buffalo. Waiting for Vince."

"You heard from him?"

"No. No." The aggression surged forward. "I'm going to find him."

"How does that help Vince? Your drinking."

Loud, raucous laughter erupted in the background. It was a moment before Betty said, "I'm waiting for Vince. Sooner or later, he's gotta come in. He likes this place. He drinks here. So I got to thinking, there's some stuff you don't know."

"You think it will help locate Vince?" Vicky kept her eyes on the road, the yellow headlights bouncing on the snow. It was surreal, the silence of the snow around her, the hum of the engine, and the stream of warm air flowing from the vents interspersed with the noise of the bar, the drunken meanderings of Betty White Hawk, who had convinced herself that her son would show up if she waited long enough and drank enough to keep believing. And now she was reminiscing, calling up stuff she wanted to talk about.

Vicky knew the way it would go. The nights that Ben Holden had come home drunk, the old memories flooding in and Ben wanting to talk and talk and talk. *Sit down, Vicky. I'm talking to you.*

"Vicky? You there? I gotta talk to you."

"It can wait until tomorrow." Vicky tried to blink back the image of Betty White Hawk making her way across the bar and stumbling outside when Vince didn't show up. Driving herself home.

"I keep thinking . . . I keep thinking, what if Vince is dead? I can't stop thinking . . ." She was crying, soft mewling noises like those of an infant.

"Stay there," Vicky heard herself saying. "I'm on the way." She could feel the tiredness clinging to her, pulling at her legs and arms. In fifteen minutes she could be home. Her own apartment, familiar and warm. She would scramble eggs, make fresh coffee. Be alone. Think about her conversation with Lou and Debbie Bearing, try to figure out their connection to Vince White Hawk and the Little Shields. That there was a connection, she was sure. But nothing made sense. And there was Betty, drinking, wanting to tell her *something*.

"Did you hear me?" Vicky said. "I'm on the way."

The neon sign with *Buffalo Bar and Lounge* in white letters and a large, yellow glass of foamy beer glowed on the sign ahead. Vicky pulled into the parking lot. It had taken almost forty minutes to get to Riverton. The sense of uselessness was like a physical presence beside her. Betty had probably left by now.

She slammed out of the Ford and made her way to the front door, the icy pavement pulling at her boots, as if she were walking underwater. The pounding noise of music cut through the frigid air. Before she could open the door, it swung out and two cowboys staggered past in the blast of a guitar riff.

"Well, now. What have we here?" One of the cowboys stepped sideways toward her, headfirst, as if he were heading off a straying calf.

Vicky dodged past and caught the door as it was about to close. "Hey, pretty lady," the other cowboy called as she stepped inside and pulled the door shut. The air was dim and smoky, vibrating in the music that poured out of speakers set along the ceiling. It took a minute for her eyes to adjust. Groups of cowboys and women in blue jeans and boots—laughing and shouting, hoisting bottles of beer and glasses of what was probably whiskey with ice cubes clanking—formed and dissolved around the table. A few couples were dancing on a small floor in the center, moving drunkenly together at half pace to the music. She couldn't spot Betty anywhere.

Then she saw her, small and vulnerable-looking, straddling a stool, propping her head on one hand, an elbow set on the bar for support. A half-filled glass of whiskey stood next to her elbow. Vicky started around the tables, slipping away from a cowboy who reached for her arm. She slid onto the stool next to Betty. The smell of whiskey invaded her nostrils and sank into her throat. She swallowed hard to counter the reflex to throw up. "You had better let me take you home."

Betty managed to lift her head a little, then let it sink back onto her hand. With her other hand, she gripped the glass and took a long drink. "I didn't think you were coming."

"How long have you been here?" Vicky wondered how many glasses of whiskey Betty had put down.

"Vince could show up anytime." Betty swiveled a little on the stool, then grabbed the edge of the bar to steady herself. "He's all I got, Vicky. I have to wait for him."

"He had three bottles of whiskey," Vicky said. "He's drinking somewhere else. When he sobers up, he'll call you." God, how many times had she said this to Betty? And who was she trying to convince? This drunken woman or herself? "He's not coming to the bar. I'd better take you home. You can wait there for him to call."

"He's going to die." The woman's face crumpled into the kind of grief Vicky had seen at funerals. Betty White Hawk was already mourning her son.

"You mustn't lose hope." Vicky tried for a calm, optimistic note, and yet she had the sense that she was missing something. Betty had wanted to talk to her, to tell her *something.* The music thumped from the speaker overhead and drowned out the sounds of ice clinking in the glass that Betty set down. The bartender had moved across from them, and Vicky realized he was waiting for her order.

"Coffee, black." She faced him. "Make that two coffees. We'll be at the table." She nodded toward a vacant table against the far wall, a good twenty feet from the nearest speaker. Then she took Betty's arm. "Let's go where it's not so noisy," she said.

It was as if the woman had climbed out onto a cliff and stood staring down at the abyss. "Vince won't see me over there. I have to stay here."

"I'll watch for him." Vicky took hold of the woman's arm and tried to nudge her upward, but Betty remained immobile, holding on to her place a moment before she started to lift herself off the stool. She fell against the bar and clawed at the edge, breathing hard. For a moment, Vicky feared she might pass out.

"I'll help you," she said, grabbing Betty's arm hard and propelling her upward. Then they were stumbling, both of them, around the tables, past the guffaws and loud, drunken conversations, past a table of cowboys.

"What we got here?" A cowboy jumped to his feet. "Let me give you a hand." He took hold of Betty's other arm and, as if he knew where they were headed, guided her, toward the vacant table. "Better get some coffee in her." He winked at Vicky. "Call on me anytime."

The bartender walked over, waited for the cowboy to head back to his own table, and set down two mugs of coffee. "She didn't finish her drink."

"Coffee is fine." Vicky nodded, then sat down next to Betty, who was blinking at the log wall, as if she were trying to figure out how the bar had disappeared. "Drink this," Vicky said, handing the woman a mug. "You'll feel better."

Betty took a long drink of coffee before setting the mug down. "I keep seeing Vince dead, and I can't take it, Vicky. It's going to kill me. I couldn't just sit there waiting for Father John or some cop to knock on my door with the horrible news."

"Vince has gone on benders before. He'll sober up, and I can still try to get the judge to send him to rehab."

"You don't know."

"What? What don't I know? What did you want to tell me?"

"I watched his Daddy die. Rickie. The love of my life." Moisture swelled in the woman's eyes. She made fists and punched at her head. "You know what that's like? To listen to the man you love gasping for breath? I can't ever get that hissing sound out of my head. I kept shouting, 'Don't die on me. Don't you dare die on me.' But I couldn't breathe for him. I couldn't get him air."

Vicky waited a moment before she said, "You told me Rickie died in an accident. You didn't tell me you were there."

"The pickup turned over and I crawled out, but Rickie . . . he was trapped beneath the steering wheel. It pinned him down like a big boulder. I couldn't . . ." Betty set her elbows on the table and leaned into her fists. "I couldn't get him out. I tried and tried. I pulled so hard, but he wouldn't move, and all the time he kept hissing. I screamed for them to come and help, but they went on. They drove away and left him to die."

Betty was crying hard now, and Vicky found a tissue in her bag and handed it to her. She waited while Betty swiped at her eyes and nose, then nudged the coffee mug toward her. "Try to sip a little more."

It was a moment before Betty lifted the mug and took another drink. When she set the mug down, Vicky said, "Who drove away? Who are you talking about?"

Betty looked at her with wide eyes blurred with tears. "Lou and Debbie. I hate them. I've stayed away from them since it happened. Vince was young when his Daddy died. I never told him about Lou and Debbie because I didn't want him to grow up with the hatred I lived with. When I heard Vince had been drinking with Lou right here in this bar, I thought I was going to go crazy. Lou's going to do to Vince what he did to his Daddy."

"What did he do?"

"I've been trying to forget."

"I know. But if Lou is going to do the same thing to Vince, you had better tell me what it was."

Betty drained the rest of the coffee, and Vicky motioned the bartender for a refill. After the bartender had moved away, she waited while Betty took a sip of the fresh coffee, giving her time to organize whatever she was about to say.

Finally Betty set the mug down and looked at her. "We didn't have any money. And Vince was getting bigger. He needed things. A lot of food, and he was always growing out of blue jeans and boots. Rickie wanted to be a good dad. He loved that boy. He got to talking to Lou Bearing—they'd gone to school together—and Lou said he had a job for him. Five hundred dollars. Well, that was a lot of money. All Rickie had to do was drive Lou and Debbie over to a car lot in Casper. They had picked out a car they wanted, and Lou knew how to start it. He was gonna drive the car off the lot and back to the rez with Debbie in the passenger seat, like they were just a young couple going to the movies."

Betty took another drink of the coffee, and Vicky could see she was starting to sober up. She was saying how she had gone along because she didn't want Rickie to go alone. And it would look better if it was a couple in the pickup. The cops wouldn't be so suspicious. Lou and Debbie were scrunched together in the backseat, giddy with excitement. It wasn't a new car they intended to steal. Nothing fancy. Lou needed an SUV for the parts. He could cannibalize it, fix up a couple of other SUVs that, she figured, he had also stolen. Lou knew what he was doing, Rickie told her. He'd always been good at fixing up old cars, making them like new.

"What happened?"

"We went to the lot. It was Sunday night, nobody around. Didn't take long, and Lou and Debbie drove out through a chain that was about a foot high. Snapped it in two. We started back to the rez. Lou wanted us to follow, stay close behind, in case of trouble and they had to abandon the car. They figured they'd jump back into our pickup and take off. It was crazy, the whole idea, but Rickie had five hundred bucks in his pocket. We were on Seventeen-Mile Road, and Lou was driving fast. Too fast, and Rickie tried to keep up. We came around that big curve, and the pickup skidded out into the other lane. There was a truck coming, and Rickie tried to get back into our lane. That's when it happened. We were all over the road, back and forth, out of control. I don't know how we missed hitting the truck. I still see it whizzing past. Next thing I knew we were rolling down the barrow ditch and out onto the prairie."

She started crying, big, racking sobs that shook her chair. Vicky placed an arm around the woman's shoulders. "I'm so sorry," she said.

"I tried to pull him out. I tried and tried, and Lou and Debbie kept going. They didn't even stop. I can't watch Vince die like that, Vicky. I can't."

"Do you think they're still stealing cars?"

"What do you think? They got Vince to help, just like they got his daddy. They paid him some money. Those sons of bitches. When I went out to beg them to tell me what they knew about Vince, they threw me out!"

Vicky sat back in her chair. The music sounded far away, as if it came from across the street. The bar had started to clear out, only a few cowboys and their girlfriends still hugging the tables. Nobody was on the dance floor. Vince had been drinking with Lou Bearing, a man who repaired cars and trucks in a barn, and Vince had come into some money. It made sense.

"I'll drive you home," Vicky said. "I'll have your car brought to your house in the morning." Annie would handle it, she was thinking. She would hire a couple of her relatives to retrieve the car.

"What would you have said to Lou if he had come in?" Vicky guided the woman out of the bar and across the parking lot. She placed her arm around her waist and turned her toward the Ford.

Betty stopped and looked at her. "Didn't you hear what I told you? If that sonofabitch came in, I was going to kill him."

22

FATHER JOHN SET the phone next to the laptop on his desk where he could answer it right away. He had spent most of the morning staring at it, willing it to ring, picking up at the first jangle of noise. Two calls, so far. Lucinda Oldman, wanting to schedule the baptism for her new son, and Grandfather Black Wolf, letting him know Grandmother was back in Riverton Memorial. Could he visit her? Yes, of course. Later this morning for sure.

Nothing from Shannon. No call, no sound of James's truck plowing around Circle Drive. It wasn't his business, he kept telling himself. Not his business at all if his adult niece chose to spend the night with a young man. And who knew? The truck could have gotten stuck in the snow. Maybe the engine wouldn't turn over. What else could Shannon have done but spend the night and wait until morning?

He set both elbows on the desk and blew into his fists. He had caught the glances between Shannon and James, the quick, warm smiles, like the remembrance of a private joke. Hadn't Shannon told him how wise and mature James was? He tried to tamp down the sense of alarm. Shannon, coming off a breakup, trying to hide the disappointment, confusion and pain enveloping her like a cloud. Back and forth he went between worrying and telling himself it wasn't his business. She was his brother's child, an adult, which meant she was part of him, too, an appendage he'd seldom thought about, until he'd begun to sense something was wrong.

He kept his eyes on the phone. Surely, it would ring. He had considered calling James's house, but that seemed intrusive. He had no right. He had every right, he decided, to confirm that Shannon was safe. He picked up the phone, scrolled to James's number, and tapped the call button. It took a moment before the ringing started, then three long rings before James's voice was on the other end. "Two Horses."

"I've been worried about Shannon." Father John picked his way through the words; he didn't want to sound like an overbearing busybody. "Is everything okay?"

"Everything's fine, Father." They both knew the real reason for the call. "We're on our way to the mission now. See you in fifteen minutes."

Father John pressed the end button. He got up and went down the hall, following the clack-clack of computer keys. Bishop Harry was bent over the small laptop. "Have a seat," he said, his eyes on the screen.

Father John dropped onto the hard wooden chair the bishop kept for counseling sessions—guaranteed not to make anyone want to linger. He waited a moment until the clacking stopped and the bishop shut the laptop and looked up. He had blue eyes as shiny as new marbles, lit with intelligence and humor. He nodded, an acknowledgement of the real reason Father John was there. "You're worried about her."

"She's having a tough time. It looks like she made a mistake with her last . . . relationship." Father John swallowed the word. What in heaven's name did it mean? A commitment with strings and end dates? Hardly a commitment at all. "I'm afraid she may be making another one."

"We all have to find our way, John. Often the price is a mistake. Can you save Shannon from pain?" He waited until Father John shook his head. "You can be her friend, her uncle, part of her family. Families must love unconditionally. I would also suggest"—he nodded four or five times—"that you trust her."

"What about James?"

"Ah, James. We've had two very interesting discussions. I believe he is making progress in discerning his vocation."

"Do you believe he has a vocation?"

"Without a doubt. The calling came to him like a bolt of lightning. St. Paul struck down on the road to Damascus. He knows he must serve the people of God, go where the Lord leads him."

The wind had come up, and the bare branch of a cottonwood tapped against the window, making an eerie, rhythmic sound. The old building sighed and creaked. "You're saying James has a vocation, but not for all of it."

"Precisely." The bishop gave him the benevolent smile he had probably bestowed on students in the school he'd run in Patna, India. "James also has a vocation for a family. He very much wants to marry and raise children. He must find his way."

"The diaconate."

"Or the Anglican priesthood. He must decide."

Father John looked over at the window, the cottonwood branch scraping back and forth. He watched the wind unfurl and lift the snow across the space between the building and Eagle Hall and wondered if he'd had a vocation for all of it twenty-five years ago.

"I've been checking the online news bulletins from the

province." The bishop sat very still. His voice had gone soft and inward. "The powers that be are gathering for what they call a planning meeting. Planning the future of the Jesuit missions."

Father John nodded. He supposed Father Jameson had called to let him in on what was going on. There hadn't been time to return the call. There would never be enough time, he thought, for the news that was most likely coming.

The front door opened and swooshed shut, sending a draft of cold air down the hall and into the small office. He got to his feet, conscious of the intensity of the old man's blue eyes on him. It was uncanny how the bishop could see through him, read his thoughts.

"You don't have regrets, do you?"

Father John turned around in the doorway. Regrets? How could he regret this? St. Francis Mission and the Arapaho people. He felt as if, all of his life, he had been on his way here. "No regrets," he said.

"JAMES HAS A wonderful idea." Shannon had already swooped her laptop off the desk in the closet-sized office and was in the corridor, laptop gripped to her chest, still bundled in her coat, gold-colored cap pulled down to her eyebrows. Red curls sprang from beneath the cap. Her eyes brimmed with enthusiasm. James stood behind her as if he had stepped back to give her center stage. "He's arranged for me to view an old movie Lizzie and her husband were in."

Of course, Father John thought. Dozens of Arapahos and Shoshones had gone to Hollywood in the early 1920s to be in the first cowboys-and-Indians movies. The Brokenhorns had been part of the troupe.

"Almost two years in Hollywood! Imagine. I'll be at the library in Lander, in case"—she stopped, as if she couldn't imagine why he might want to know where she was—"you know, anybody calls here, in case they can't reach me on my cell."

Father John smiled at this niece of his and walked her and James to the front door. He closed the door behind them, shoving it hard against the wind, then went back to his desk. A sense of relief flooded over him. A wise man, the bishop. They would find their own way, Shannon and James.

He had just begun to pay a few bills—not all of the bills stacked in front of him, since there wasn't enough money in the mission account, but those that had worked their way into the highest priority—when he heard the dual growl of engines. Shannon and James, driving off; someone else arriving. He wasn't expecting anyone, but parishioners were always stopping in. A chat, maybe a little counseling, a cup of coffee. He finished writing the first check. The engine cut off, leaving the whistling noise of the wind. Then the clack of boots on the steps, the pneumatic whoosh of the door opening. He recognized the footsteps in the corridor and was on his feet when Vicky rapped on the door frame and stepped into his office.

"I took a chance I'd find you." Snowflakes sparkled in her hair and on the shoulders of her black coat. She looked flushed with fatigue.

"Let me take your coat." He was surprised at the ease in which she shrugged the coat into his hands, something weighing on her mind.

"Coffee?" He was already at the small metal table behind the door, filling two mugs with the coffee he'd made that morning. He shook some powdered creamer into his mug. Vicky liked her coffee black.

He handed her a mug, then leaned back against the edge of his desk. She wouldn't sit down, he knew, preferring to sip at the coffee while she trolled about the office. Window, door, back again. She thought better when she was moving.

She had never actually told him this, but he knew it was true. He took a drink of his coffee and waited until she turned to face him.

"What do you know about Lou and Debbie Bearing?"

"I've met them a few times." This wasn't what he was expecting. He'd thought she might have some news about Vince White Hawk. Everything about her warned that the news she did have wasn't good. He had tried to call Betty last night, but she hadn't answered. He intended to stop by the school where she worked. "What's going on?"

"I think the Bearings are involved with Vince White Hawk's disappearance. He still hasn't shown up, and Betty is worried sick. She's . . ." Vicky hesitated, then plunged on: "She's falling apart, John. She's been drinking. I met her at the Buffalo Bar last night. She'd convinced herself that if she hung around there, Vince would come in."

"You think Lou and Debbie Bearing know where he is?"

Vicky had started circling again, sipping at the coffee. "Betty thinks Vince got his drinking money from them." She stopped again. "Ten years ago, the Bearings hired Vince's dad, Rickie, to help them steal a car in Casper and bring it back to the rez. Betty went along. She and Rickie were following the Bearings back to their place, speeding on Seventeen-Mile Road, when Rickie's pickup turned over. He was trapped behind the steering wheel. He died there. The Bearings drove on. They didn't stop to help."

Father John took a moment. The accident, as everyone called it, that had killed Vince's father, had happened a few months before he'd come to St. Francis. "Does Betty think the Bearings had Vince help them steal a car?"

"She says it's what they do. Steal cars for the parts Lou uses in the shop he's set up in his barn. When I went to see them—"

"You went to see them?"

"Yesterday. I didn't learn much. Lou was working on a sedan and a truck. A black truck. He and Debbie claimed they didn't know anything about Vince." Vicky was pacing again, working out something in her mind. "They're lying. But there's more, John. I think they also know something about the Little Shields and their daughter."

She stopped pacing, and this time she walked over and leaned against the desk beside him. "The Little Shields had hired Clint Hopkins to help them adopt their daughter. I've taken over the case."

He nodded and started to say how sorry he was about the lawyer, but Vicky was going on, something about how she had been following Clint's investigation. "I'm running into brick walls, but I'm convinced that"—she took in a gulp of air—"he found out something that got him killed."

He didn't say anything, waiting for her to pick up her thoughts again, arrange them in some kind of order that made sense. He had counseled Myra and Eldon Little Shield a few times. They weren't parishioners, but they had come anyway, worried sick that they could lose their little girl. He had encouraged them to seek a legal adoption. They must have hired Clint Hopkins. The *Gazette* had said Clint's death was an accident. It was clear Vicky didn't think so.

A moment passed before she drew in a long breath and said, "I've talked to Dina Fowler. She and her husband, Matthew, used to live near the Bearings. She told me they didn't have children, but she had heard a baby crying at their house for a week. It was in March, five years ago. The same time the Little Shields got Mary Ann. Eldon said they told you about it. He gave me permission to discuss it with you."

Father John waited while Vicky went over to the table, poured some more coffee, and resumed pacing. "A baby left on their doorstep," she said. "Myra's cousin worked for social services. She gave them papers that made them think they had temporary custody. I suspect the relative was trying to help them out, since they had just lost their own baby. The point is, they love that little girl. They want to adopt her. I believe Clint must have stumbled onto something that could complicate the adoption." She turned around and faced him again. "Clint Hopkins, the best-known adoption attorney in the county, asked me to be his cocounsel. An Arapaho lawyer. Whatever he learned, he believed the tribe would be involved."

"You're saying Clint could have learned where the child came from?" The Little Shields' biggest fear, Father John was thinking: that their child's natural parents existed somewhere, and cared.

"I'm saying that Lou and Debbie Bearing could know something about it." Vicky threw one hand in the air. "Five years ago, a neighbor heard a baby crying at their house. A relative's baby, the Bearings say, and who could disprove it? How could anyone connect Mary Ann to the Bearings?"

Vicky circled over to the window and looked out. "Lou is a nervous man. It's like he has something on his conscience that he would like to be free of. I got the sense he might have told me something if Debbie hadn't come in."

He'd had the same feeling the other night at the Buffalo Bar, Father John was thinking. Lou Bearing had shrunk away from him and Betty, holding on to the edge of the table, as if the table could protect him from their gaze, their accusations. A feeling was all it was, a second sense that came from years of watching people shift about in their chairs, avoid his eyes, clasp their hands together, and, finally, unburden themselves.

"I can go out to the house," Father John said.

Vicky gave him a quick smile. "I was hoping you would say that."

23

SHANNON STARED AT the image on the video. An ordinary-looking woman, leathered, wrinkled face with no makeup, no sign of concern about her appearance. *Take me as I am.* Staring out at the camera, unsurprised, as if this were normal, acting in a movie, pretending to be someone else. She wore a blouse embroidered with quills, a printed skirt that swished about her legs, and a headdress filled with eagle feathers she would have earned, Shannon knew, from the trials she had overcome. The headdress concealed her hair. Her eyes were light, her face pale.

Standing beside her was John Brokenhorn, wrinkled like Lizzie, but dark skinned with narrowed, defiant black eyes. His eagle-feathered headdress listed to one side. On the chest of his dark shirt were beaded and quilled pendants, gifts from Lizzie, most likely. And a silver peace medal with the hard-to-decipher image of some politician who had promised the Indians peace.

All of this, plunked down in Hollywood.

"She looks old and tired." James rolled his chair closer to Shannon's and hunched toward the photo.

"In 1922 she would have been fifty-nine."

"She had a hard life."

"Is that what you think?" Shannon turned toward him and smiled. She didn't know where James Two Horses had come from. Out of the blue, confident and assured, settled within himself. He had a vocation to the priesthood, he'd told her. But there were other vocations, other callings, he couldn't ignore. He'd been talking to the bishop, and the old man had helped him to see that he would have to find the way to honor all of his vocations.

Her heart had sunk when he'd first mentioned the priesthood. How silly, she told herself now. What had she expected? A man she had just met, even though it seemed as if they had always known each other. They had talked for hours last night, talked about everything. It was great, taking it slowly, getting to know each other. She had never met a man like James. He seemed to be part of her, connected by some invisible thread she hadn't realized existed. She remembered the faintest light shining in the window just before she'd fallen asleep on the sofa. When she'd awakened, she saw that James had draped a blanket over her. She could hear him moving about the kitchen. Smells of coffee and bacon drifted through the sadness that permeated her. This man, who seemed part of her, was considering the priesthood. Well, maybe she was kidding herself. Soul mates didn't exist, except in romance novels and fairy tales—the *forever afters*. She no longer believed in all of that.

She was glad for his presence now, the way he found her work—her project—exciting and interesting. Unlike David. *Who cares about what happened a hundred years ago?*

She cared, and part of coming to the reservation, she realized, was to be with her uncle, an historian who cared, and to do research where Lizzie had actually lived and be with the people she had loved. To find more than history. To find the *story*. And she had found James. He had suggested they watch a video of *The Covered Wagon,* one of the movies Lizzie and John Brokenhorn had been in. He arranged with the librarian at the Lander Library to set up the video. They were alone in the small, glass-enclosed room. Beyond the glass, the librarian—Nancy somebody, who James had gone to school with—stood behind a counter, in an earnest conversation with a young woman. People milled about, wandering among the stacks of books on the far side of the counter.

He turned toward her and smiled. "Ready to continue?" When she nodded, he pressed the forward button, and the images started moving again across the small screen. Indian warriors racing past on horseback, the long, winding wagon train coming over the prairie, all accompanied by the tinny plunking of a keyboard. The images looked grainy and unstable, as if sand were blowing through. Lizzie, huddled with the other Indian women in front of a tipi, stooping over a kettle, a little fire dancing beneath it.

At one point, James reached for her hand and squeezed it. "It must have been hard for her."

She was struck by the sympathy in his voice. She studied his profile for a moment: the dark eyes, almost black. The bump at the top of his nose, the high forehead, and the strong, wide chin, the generous mouth. Brokenhorn might have looked like this, so handsome that he had taken Lizzie's breath away.

"Living on the reservation?"

James shook his head. "Hollywood."

Yes, of course. She went back to watching the images flash past. "An Arapaho woman." She kept her voice low, parsing her thoughts over the ripple of piano keys. "Not really Arapaho. A white woman, born into a white family, plunked down among her own people for a while. White people everywhere she looked. On the streets and sidewalks, on the movie lot. She was surrounded by white faces."

She shifted toward James. "She must have wondered how her life might have gone had she not been captured. How could she have looked at the cars and houses and shops and restaurants and all the rest of Hollywood and not thought, What would this have been like? What would I have been like?"

"You think that in the two years Lizzie spent in Hollywood . . ."

"She might have regretted the way her life had gone."

James was shaking his head, giving her that thoughtful look she was getting used to, as if he had heard every word and was turning what she'd said over in his mind. "It wasn't her world. She had never known white towns and crowds of white people. The only white people she'd had contact with lived in Lander and Riverton, and I doubt she went to town very often. There were signs on the shopwindows then: No dogs or Indians allowed."

Shannon sat back. "She never wrote anything." The movie had ended, the screen shimmered gray, and James pressed another key.

"She would have been illiterate," James said. "Some Arapahos went to the school at St. Francis Mission, but most worked the ranches and farms. They had to work, or they didn't eat. Not many girls went to school." He gave a sharp laugh. "They had to do most of the work."

"It's impossible to know what Lizzie felt. All I have is conjecture and . . ."

"That's not history."

"Exactly. Besides, what was Lizzie supposed to do if she felt regrets or longings? Leave Brokenhorn? Leave the only life she knew? Whatever she may have felt, I think she would have kept silent and gone on."

THE SUN HELD all the way across the reservation. It had broken out that afternoon, a red disc that flared against the gray clouds moving across the mountains. Always welcome, the sun: warming the frozen air, licking at the ice at the edge of the roads. Father John squinted in the brightness as he drove toward Lou and Debbie Bearing's place outside of Fort Washakie.

He had stopped by Riverton Memorial first to visit Grandmother Black Wolf, who assured him she would be up and about and home, where she belonged, in no time. After that he had doubled back to Wind River school, where he had found Betty White Hawk in the break room, gulping coffee, jittery as a cat. No, she hadn't heard from Vince. Every day she worried that this would be the day her son could die.

Coming around a bend, he spotted the house and barn rising against the Wind River Mountains in the background, like the painting of a winter's scene in a Western museum. Except for something odd: a woman with long black hair was stomping through the snow in front of the house, arms waving, beseeching, clutching at the air. She flung herself about, shrieking like a trapped animal. He pulled a sharp turn across the road, bumped over the barrow ditch, and stopped a few yards from her. She paid no attention, lost in herself, shrieking and reaching for the sky, in some kind of primitive dance. A dance of grief.

Father John jumped out and ran to her. "What is it?" His own voice mixed with the woman's cries. "What's happened?"

She stopped moving and looked at him, eyes unfocused, skittering about. The shrieking died back into a gurgling noise. She wrapped her arms over her chest and started plucking at the sleeves of her jacket.

"Debbie?" he said, and the name seemed to grab her attention. She folded downward, sinking onto her knees in the snow, boots splayed behind her. She was sobbing.

Father John hunched down beside her. "Look at me, Debbie. I'm Father O'Malley from the mission. I want to help you. Tell me what's happened."

"He's dead." The woman spoke so softly, he had to lean forward, bracing himself with one hand in the snow. "Lou's dead."

24

FATHER JOHN PULLED his mobile out of his pocket and pressed 911. Crumpled beside him, Debbie Bearing seemed to be sinking deeper and deeper into the snow. There was one ring, then a voice asked what the emergency was. He gave his name and said he was at the home of Lou and Debbie Bearing, west of Fort Washakie. Lou Bearing was hurt. Possibly dead. Debbie was in shock. "We need an ambulance." Which could take a while, he was thinking. There were few patrol cars, few officers to cover the miles of empty space on the rez. "It's the house with the large barn in back."

"Where is the injured man?"

"I'm not sure." He wasn't even sure if the hysterical woman beside him knew what she was talking about. He leaned closer to Debbie, trying to get her attention. She had drifted off, gone somewhere else. "Where is Lou?"

She blinked at him, the effort to concentrate printed on her face. "The shop," she said finally.

"I heard," the voice on the phone said. "I'll hold on while you check."

"I'm going to give the phone to Debbie," he told the voice. "Talk to her while I'm gone."

For a moment, Debbie didn't seem to understand. She recoiled from the phone, an alien object from outer space. "Tell the operator what you've told me, Debbie."

She nodded, as if the sound of her own name had brought her back again, and reached for the phone. Her fingers were red and stiff with cold, and the phone started to slip. He closed her fingers around it, holding them there a moment, willing the warmth of his own glove into her hand. "Lou's dead," he heard her say as he got to his feet and started around the house toward the barn.

A light-colored pickup stood close to the house. The snow all around had been disturbed. A lot of footsteps; he wasn't the first person to have walked about today. He stayed with the footsteps down the side of the house to the barn, where the footsteps had churned out big, messy circles, as if a tractor had run through.

One of the barn doors had been pushed open, and the sun glinted on the metal railings. Inside looked as dark as night. Just across the threshold, he could see smudges of snow prints on a hard-packed dirt floor that bumped into the darkness. "Anyone here?" He was shouting into a vacuum, the sound of his own voice echoing around him.

He moved farther inside. The shadowy hulks of vehicles rose in front of him. He patted the wall on the left, then the one on the right. Finally his fingers found a smooth plastic plate with a switch in the center. Lights flashed on, streaming down from metal poles in the corners, flooding over a black truck and a dark sedan lined up in bays. Tools spilled over the worktables alongside the vehicles. More tools cluttered the benches against the walls and dangled from hooks on the walls.

He stepped toward the vehicles, scouring the areas in between, the spaces under the tables and benches, anyplace large enough for a body. Nothing out of the ordinary, nothing he wouldn't expect to see in a garage: little pools of oil here and there, glinting in the light; oil-smeared rags tossed onto the benches; coveralls hanging from nails.

"Anyone here?" He spotted what looked like a broken baseball bat lying next to the wall. He stooped over and picked it up, feeling his muscles tighten, bracing for the unexpected. Someone could be here, someone involved in Lou Bearing's death. Anything could have happened. A disgruntled customer, an argument that escalated into violence. Metal tools everywhere, easy to grab, slam into a scalp. My God.

He reached the wall and turned, moving down the side of the black truck toward the hood, his own heart pounding in his ears. Still nothing. Then, there, sticking out from below the bumper, was a boot, dirty and worn-looking, and, oddly, not out of place on the soiled dirt. Attached to the boot, a jeans-clad leg. Another leg angled under the truck. The body of a man sprawled facedown, light shining on the circle of scalp near the top of what was left of his head. Spreading around him was a dark, glassy pool of blood. Blood splattered the metal bumper like flecks of black paint and smeared the wall three feet away. The ashy smell of blood filled his nostrils, the smell of death.

It took a moment to absorb what he was looking at. The blue jeans and brown jacket, the outstretched arms, as if Lou Bearing had tried to save himself. There was a black revolver a few inches from his right hand. "God have mercy on your soul," he said.

He took a few steps backward, then swung around and started retracing his steps, walking slowly, searching the spaces and the shadows, gripping the bat, wanting to make sure no one else was there. He moved past the door and checked out the other side of the barn. Still nothing except the faint smell of blood and an odd change in the atmosphere the farther away he got from the body. He started along the side of the sedan and worked his way again toward the rear wall. A couple of brooms leaning against a table, metal pails stacked together, shelves lined with paint and aerosol cans, a container of brushes. He stooped down and looked underneath the vehicles, then glanced up at the rafters. Hiding places, but no sign of anyone, except for the body of Lou Bearing under the front of the truck.

Father John turned around and hurried out into the bright glare of snow and sun. He broke into a run around the house. Debbie Bearing was folded over in the snow. He could hear her moaning.

He knelt down beside her. She started rocking back and forth, moaning and mumbling, not making any sense. She gripped her knees to her chest, and he managed to pull the mobile out of her hand.

"Are you still there?"

"I'm here, Father." The voice came from far away, another reality.

"A man is dead in the barn. He was shot in the head."

"Lou Bearing?"

"His wife must have found him."

Debbie was still rocking back and forth. He leaned over and patted her shoulder.

"You're sure he's dead?"

Yes, he was sure, he told the voice. He knew death. So many deaths since he had come to St. Francis. Accidents, fights, gunshots. "He's dead," he said again.

"Try to keep the wife calm until the medics arrive." The voice was steady and certain. How many times had the operator given this advice? Wife, mother, cousin, friend—keep them calm. "Do you want me to stay on the line?"

"No. We'll manage."

He ended the call, slipped the phone into his jacket pocket. The woman was wobbling now, trying to get to her feet, to get a grip on the earth. "An ambulance is on the way," he told her. "Shall we wait inside, where it's warmer?" He started to take hold of her arm.

"No. No. No." Debbie swatted at his hand, then lifted her own hands overhead. The screeching began again, the besieging of heaven. After a long moment, she seemed to catch her breath. "Don't take me in there. I can't go back there."

"It's your home, Debbie," Father John said, trying for reason, logic. What was he thinking? "You can wait in my pickup," he said. It wasn't warm; he was never sure if the heater would turn on, and the engine had been cooling now for a while. Still, better than the snow.

She didn't protest. No screeching now, just low moaning and sobbing sounds. He held her arm and helped her onto her feet. She was surprisingly heavy for a small, compact woman. A solid build, thick arms he could feel through the weight of her jacket. She stumbled forward, boots skimming the snow, not connecting with the ground, and Father John placed his arm around her waist, holding her upright as they walked to the pickup. He lifted her into the seat, where she flopped back, breathing hard. Father John waited for the screeching to start again. It came at intervals, it seemed, the way grief came in waves. He reached behind the seat for the blanket he kept in back and pulled it around her shoulders, enfolding her in fleece. She was shivering.

"He left me." Debbie spit out the words, like something hard and bitter in her throat. "He promised he would never leave me. We were in it together . . ." She stopped, as if in that instant she realized what she was saying.

"In what together?" Father John kept his voice low.

"A team. The Bearing team—that's what we were," she said. "Lou and Debbie. Nothing was going to tear us apart. Oh God. Oh God."

"Take a deep breath," Father John said, and after a moment, that is what she did. Drew in a long breath, more docile now, following instructions, as if she had been lost out in the yard, circling and screaming, not knowing what to do, and now someone was telling her what to do. She let the breath out slowly, then drew in another.

"What will happen to me?" She looked up at him, then flicked her eyes away. "We had a pact. Why did he leave me? I was strong for both of us. God, he was drinking and going to bars, even though I told him I'd take care of everything. Don't worry. And everything was working out like I planned. Working out, working out." The words sounded like the click of a metronome.

"Debbie, what are you talking about?"

He wondered if she knew herself. She seemed rational and irrational at the same time, flailing at something that welled inside her.

When she didn't say anything, he asked if there was someone he could call. "Family or friends? They'll want to be with you."

She threw her head back and laughed. "I never thought he'd do it. I never thought he had the guts to do it. He told me lots of times he was done, fed up. This morning he started in. Shot his hand at the coffee mug, and spilled coffee, and said he was tired of it."

"Tired of what?" What was she trying to tell him, to get off her chest?

"Waiting. Tired of the waiting, and so end it. Shoot yourself, I don't care. He went out to the shop. He left so fast, I don't remember him going. He's sitting there with coffee dripping onto his jeans, and then he's gone, and I heard it. I heard the shot. I never thought . . . I never wanted . . . I killed him."

Father John patted the woman's shoulder again and told her to take another breath. This was as tough as it got. There were no words. *Don't blame yourself.* He expected her to start screeching again, reaching for heaven. This would take time. Years. "I'm very sorry," he told her. "There must be someone you want with you."

"Just us. Our team, Lou and me. We did fine, didn't we? Nobody else. Don't let anybody else in. We told each other we're enough."

Down the road, coming toward the house, coming fast, was the sound of sirens. A parade of vehicles: gray and white police cars, an ambulance, and a white van. They started to slow down. Father John stepped away from the pickup and waved them forward. One by one they turned, dipping into the ditch, then up onto the yard, snow spitting beneath the tires, sirens fading and finally shutting off, leaving only a faraway echo.

25

THE HOUSE LOOKED deserted. Holding its place in a row of other houses, cars at the curb, pine trees bundled in snow, and yet something different about it, as if the life had been sucked out. Vicky managed to fit the Ford between two sedans, then made her way up the unshoveled walk.

The door was flung open before she reached the porch. Lacy Hopkins leaned outside, face drawn, blanched with questions. "What is it?"

"Vicky Holden." A sheen of ice lay over the porch floor. Lacy stared around the edge of the door. No sign of recognition in her eyes, no memory of Vicky having been there the day after Clint's death. Another face in the crowd of people offering condolences. "I'm the lawyer who has taken over one of Clint's adoption cases."

Lacy nodded. A flicker in her eyes, like the effort to remember. Then she said, "I wasn't expecting company."

"I wanted to ask you about something." They were standing outside, like two women waiting for a bus, Vicky thought. Lacy looked disheveled, as if she hadn't slept in a long time. Sandy hair uncombed and ropy, hanging over the shoulders of her gray sweatshirt. Veins throbbed in the long neck rising out of the sweatshirt. Her face looked as dry as leather, her lips flaky.

She motioned Vicky inside, then reached around and pushed the door shut. The house was hot and closed-in, as if the air had coalesced into a tight ball. Vases of flowers stood about the floor and crowded the tops of two tables, permeating the air with the sweet, sickly odor of a funeral home. The French doors in the far wall were opened, and Vicky could see into Clint's study to the polished, empty surface of his desk.

Lacy was looking about, surveying the living room as if she were seeing the disarray for the first time—flowers, piles of laundry on the sofa, magazines jumbled with empty food cartons on the coffee table, boots and shoes kicked off on the carpet.

"It won't take long," Vicky said.

Lacy turned toward her. Surprise in her face now, as if she had just registered who Vicky was. "I guess you'd better sit down." She stepped over to the sofa, gathered up a pile of clothing and dumped it onto the floor. "I remember you now. You saw the accident."

Vicky nodded. "I'm very sorry."

"You don't believe it was an accident."

Vicky felt a little tremor of unease. "I told the police what I saw."

Lacy nodded. "It was you, then. A detective told me a witness thinks somebody murdered Clint. Asked me all kinds of questions. Who would want Clint dead? Any threats? Arguments or altercations? How was our relationship? Problems in our marriage? Oh my God." She was starting to cry, shoulders shaking. "It was an accident! Can't we leave it at that? Isn't that bad enough? Do I really have to deal with all the suspicions, the gossip?"

"I'm very sorry." There was nothing else to say. Vicky couldn't say she hadn't seen what she had seen.

"You're not the only one."

"What do you mean?"

"Some other witness, out of the blue, decided my husband was murdered. Why are you doing this to me?"

Vicky let the question invade the space between them. There were no answers, no platitdudes that might soften the blow. Finally, she said, "I'm trying to settle an adoption case Clint was working on. The Little Shields' case."

"You really believe I know about Clint's cases?" Lacy gave a hoarse laugh. "He kept them to himself. They were his life, all the little kids looking for homes. They were Julia and he was their"—she hesitated, staring at Vicky for a long moment before she plunged on—"warrior riding to rescue them."

"I've been following Clint's footsteps." Vicky picked at the words, moving through rocks and thistles. "I've talked to the people he talked to, and I've run into a dead end. There are several days unaccounted for on his calendar. I don't know where he went or who he talked to."

"My husband lived in his head."

A clock somewhere ticked in the silence.

"In his head. Always lost in a tangle of thoughts. Working things out. Planning. Plotting. Do you think he was easy to live with?" She gave another hoarse laugh. "It was like living with a robot."

Vicky flinched. Was that what she had become? A robot? Obsessed with her cases? With the people who found their way to her office? The drunks and addicts and petty criminals like Vince White Hawk, needing her help, taking over her life? Is that how the people close to her would describe her? Lucas in Denver, Susan in Los Angeles, her own children sending texts, leaving voice mails?

She realized the woman was talking about Julia being settled at school in Laramie, living her own life. "Clint didn't have to worry about her anymore, and I was . . . well, hereabouts somewhere. He barely noticed me."

Lacy looked away, her face rigid, like a mask with tiny cracks breaking beneath the surface. For the briefest moment, Vicky allowed herself to wonder if the barely noticed wife had grown tired of being a cipher in her husband's life. She must have heard the gossip about Clint and his young secretary. Every lawyer in town knew, Rick Masterson had told her. Surely Lacy knew.

Vicky could feel the words skittering away. A coldness came over her, and she realized she was shivering in the hot, flower-drenched house. The woman slouched on the chair across from her, gray sweatshirt bunched around her waist, a clump of hair hanging over one eye, wondering . . . what? If the lawyer working on one of Clint's cases thought she might have arranged her husband's death?

"I didn't kill my husband, you know." Lacy blurted out the statement. "There was a blizzard, and the truck driver didn't see him. It was an accident, a terrible, cruel accident. And here I am"—she lifted both hands—"with nothing to look forward to."

"Do you have family, friends to talk to?"

"Do you really suppose it might do any good?"

Vicky leaned forward. "Your husband cared deeply about a child named Mary Ann Little Shield. He wanted to see her legally adopted by the parents who have raised her. I'd like to finish the work he was doing. I need your help."

Lacy didn't take her eyes away, staring without blinking. After a long moment, she said, "I have no idea where he went, if that's what you want to know. Just packed a bag, placed his laptop in his briefcase. It was like, 'Oh, by the way, I have to go out of town on a case for a few days.'"

"Out of town? Did he say where?"

"Ask Evie. I suspect he told her." Lacy shrugged. "She's probably at the office. A young lawyer from Casper will close Clint's practice. I have no idea whether he'll keep Evie on or throw her out in the street where she belongs."

So Lacy had heard the gossip. Vicky got to her feet. "I'll keep you posted about the Little Shield case."

"You do that." Lacy nodded toward the door, and Vicky understood she could find her own way out.

VICKY SENSED THE presence on the other side of the door. A movement, an almost imperceptible shift in the atmosphere. She knocked again. A small tremor ran through the hard wooden door followed by a punctuation of silence.

"Evie?" She leaned into the door. "It's Vicky Holden." A moment passed before she heard the sound of footsteps approaching. She had called the office from her mobile on the way over. There was no answer, and she had decided to take a chance that Evie Moran was still there.

The door swung inward a few inches. The secretary stood in the opening, bracketed by the edge of the door and the frame. "I wasn't expecting visitors," she said. "I'm about to leave."

"This will only take a minute."

Evie dropped her eyes and let out a long sigh, as if the excuse were too familiar to bother responding. "The new lawyer will take over next week. You should talk to him."

"He won't be handling the Little Shields' case." Vicky waited a beat before she went on. "May I come in?"

The secretary yanked the door back. She looked older than her years, slumped with worry. Her eyes were red-rimmed, like the eyes of a clown, and her hair stood out in patches, as if she had been pulling at it. She wore a pink blouse that hung over the top of her jeans, and she was barefoot, long painted toes splayed over the carpet. Behind her the office looked swept clean, everything in place: the surface of the desk clear, the side chairs squared to the front of the desk, magazines arranged on a small table against the wall, books stacked on a bookcase. She swung around, walked behind the desk, and dropped onto the chair. "I've been through everything," she said. "I gave you what Clint left on the Little Shield case."

"There's a three-day gap in his calendar." Vicky perched on one of the side chairs. "I thought he might have taken time off to sort through the information he had, but Lacy said he went out of town on business. She didn't know where he'd gone."

"What makes you think I would know?"

Vicky shifted in the chair. This wasn't going to be easy. Something had happened between the two women since she'd last talked to them. They had been in shock then; Clint not yet dead twenty-four hours. But now? They'd had time to think, connect dots. She wondered if Lacy had seized upon the rumors and confronted the secretary. And how had Evie responded? By accusing Clint's wife of arranging his murder?

"Clint might have mentioned something." Stay with the subject at hand, Vicky told herself. Rumors, speculation—let the police sort them out. All she wanted were legal parents for a little girl.

"I told you, Clint didn't talk about his cases."

Vicky nodded. Clint Hopkins, a lawyer who lived in his head, allowed his cases to take him over, consume him, so that nothing else mattered. Like a robot, his wife had said. Programmed to focus on whatever case he was working on.

She tried a different tack. "I know Clint spoke to Lou

and Debbie Bearing on two occasions before he left town. The day after he returned, he went back to their place, and that night he was killed. I think he must have found something he thought they could explain. Something he asked them about. Why else would he have gone back?"

"Then you should ask them."

"I have. I'll have to find the answer somewhere else."

Vicky kept her eyes on the woman across the desk until, after a long moment, Evie Moran got to her feet. "This is my last day here," she said. There was a crack in her voice. "Everything's over. The new lawyer offered me a job, but I declined. Thank you very much."

Vicky stood up. "I think you know where Clint went."

The young woman was shaking her head. She squeezed her eyes shut against the moisture shining at the edges.

Vicky hurried on: "You don't want to tell me because you were with him." It was a guess, the kind of stab in the dark she'd taken when she could feel a client was holding back. "Tell me, Evie. Help me conclude the case Clint cared so much about."

Evie sank back into her chair, as if the air had gone out of her. She dropped her face into her hands and began sobbing, making little staccato noises. "Does everyone know? Lacy and you and everyone else in the world? Clint said it was our secret. He never told secrets. He never told anyone anything."

"Where did you go?"

"I was only there one night. He said he would be busy. There was someone he had to talk to." She dropped her hands and sat up straight, drawing on some new resolve. "He didn't say who it was. 'I'm still figuring things out,' he said. I knew if I showed up before Saturday, I'd never see him. He wouldn't even talk to me, he'd be so engrossed in whatever he was doing. So I waited and flew down Saturday night. We spent the night together and drove home on Sunday. It was beautiful. Snow everywhere. Just Clint and me alone in a white world. Then he was gone."

"Where, Evie? Drove home from where?"

"Denver."

26

VICKY COULD HEAR the beep inside her bag as she made her way down the icy sidewalk to the Ford. A new text message. The bright sun bore down onto the rooftops, but there was a chill in the wind that whipped at her coat. She dipped her head, tucked her chin into the collar, and tried to ignore the beeping noise, her thoughts on the three missing days. Two days driving back and forth to Denver; one day in Denver. But where in Denver? Who had Clint gone to see and why?

Clint had deleted everything on his laptop but the barest notes and names on his calendar. What had he found that he didn't want to come into anyone's hands, not even hers? Still, he had wanted to consult with her on the Little Shield case. He would have told her everything, Evie said. And what was that? What had he carried about in his head, unwilling to allow anyone to see?

Vicky gripped her coat close with one hand while she

opened the car door with the other. She slid inside and started the engine. She was shivering. He had gone to Denver, Evie said, and Vicky had pushed the girl. There must have been something that would give them an idea of what he did there.

Evie had gone into Clint's office and retrieved the laptop. Vicky had waited while Evie had called up the file on the Little Shield case. Nothing, the secretary said, except the notes. Then Evie had skimmed the list of files. No sign of Little Shield, Wind River Reservation, Arapaho.

Vicky had been pacing the small area between the desk and the door, conscious of Evie still hunched over the computer, the keys clicking. "I told you Clint kept everything in his head. He was paranoid his files would be hacked."

Vicky had stopped pacing, a new thought presenting itself. "What about the Web sites Clint visited before he went to Denver? They could tell us what he was looking for."

Evie had pulled back, tapped a couple keys, then hunched forward again, eyes boring into the screen. "Nothing." She exhaled the word. "Clint erased his entire history."

"What did he tell you?" She had pressed the secretary again.

"Nothing. He told me nothing."

Inside the Ford, Vicky retrieved her mobile, her hand shaking with cold. An image of the dark figure starting across the street in the snow played across her retinas. A dark figure, carrying a briefcase. Paranoid, controlling, thorough. And something else: elusive.

She ran her finger over the button and tried to concentrate on the text message. Her hand was shaking with cold. Annie: "Shooting at Bearing's place. Someone dead. Thought you'd want to know."

Vicky felt her heart catapult inside her chest. A shooting at the Bearings'. My God. And this morning she had gone to John O'Malley and told him she suspected Lou Bearing was hiding something. She knew John O'Malley. He would have driven out there to talk to Lou. He would have gone right away. For her. To allay her concern.

She could see Lou Bearing skulking about the barn, nervous, eyes twitching, yearning to tell something. To unburden himself. Confess. The man's discomfort had been as palpable as another presence. She had defended clients like that, shifting in their chairs, wanting to tell everything, get it off their chests. Finally blurting out the sad, terrible truth.

Lou Bearing had been like that, until Debbie walked in, determination and resolve propelling the woman, enough for both her and for her husband. And everything had changed. Lou's demeanor, the yearning that had shone in his eyes, the longing to set down a heavy load.

Is that what happened? Debbie Bearing had walked in on a confession? And a man was dead? The man who had heard Lou Bearing's secret?

Vicky realized that, somehow, she had pulled away from the curb and was driving down Main. A blur of snow piled over the street and wrapped about the buildings. She swiped at the tears bristling on her cheek. She could feel her heart thumping. God. God. What if she had sent John O'Malley to his death?

She had to get ahold of herself. She was talking to herself out loud, her own voice echoing in the void of the car. Admonishing herself. *Get a hold on. Get a hold on.* Anything could have happened. Lou himself could have been shot. Someone else could have come to the barn. She fumbled in her bag for her cell and pressed John O'Malley's number. Three rings, then the familiar voice saying to leave a message. She tossed the cell on top of the bag.

John O'Malley could still be at the mission, in a meeting, a counseling session, nowhere near the Bearing place. She turned onto Seventeen-Mile Road and drove toward the blue billboard rising into the sunshine and blue sky. The words

looked watery: *St. Francis Mission.* She swung left and sped
down the tunnel of cottonwoods, rear wheels sliding in the
snow, and turned toward the administration building, her
heart pounding. Her mouth had gone dry. The red Toyota
pickup was gone.

She jerked to a stop where the Toyota had stood, flung
open the door, and ran up the steps. She slammed herself
against the heavy oak door. "John!" She shouted into the
corridor, into the emptiness of his office. "John. Are you
here?"

"What is it?" The bishop listed down the corridor from
the back office. "What's happened?"

"Is John here?" John O'Malley was not here; she could
sense his absence. The Toyota pickup was gone.

"I'm afraid he's gone out." The old man couldn't quite
hide his own worry. "Left a couple hours ago. Is everything
all right?"

"I don't know. I don't know." Vicky had swung back
toward the front door when the door across the corridor flew
open. The tall, red-haired woman—a girl, really, the serious
look on her face almost comical—blocked the corridor.

"What's happened to my uncle?"

"He went to talk to someone. There's been a shooting.
I'm going over there."

"I'm coming with you," the girl said, and Vicky could
hear the click of footsteps behind her as she yanked the door
open and ran down the steps. She had started to back the
Ford onto Circle Drive when Shannon O'Malley pulled open
the passenger door and jumped onto the seat. A black jacket
half on, half off. She wiggled about, jammed both arms into
the jacket, and pulled the fronts closed.

"You think Uncle John's been shot?"

Vicky hunched over the steering wheel and peered past
the windshield, barely registering the question, the girl's
voice nothing but background noise.

"I don't know," Vicky managed. She was at the end of the cottonwood tunnel, sliding into the turn back onto Seventeen-Mile Road. A horn sounded, brakes squealed. She jammed her foot down hard on the accelerator and sped away from an oncoming pickup.

For a long, blessed moment, Shannon was quiet. Vicky was aware of the girl staring straight ahead, watching the road. It could take thirty minutes to get to the Bearing place. She had lost two minutes checking the mission. Two precious minutes. She wondered if an ambulance had been called. There was a chance the victim was still alive. Oh God. Let him be alive.

"It's dangerous here."

Vicky flinched. The girl's voice had startled her out of her own thoughts. She had forgotten the girl was there.

"Life is dangerous," she said.

"Uncle John is great." And then she went off about the research she was doing and how John O'Malley had been helping her, how he really cared about a captive white girl who had become Arapaho more than a hundred years ago. Background noise to the name pulsing inside Vicky's head. *John O'Malley. John O'Malley.*

"Why would anyone want to shoot a priest?" the girl said.

The road unfolded ahead, mottled gray asphalt plunging through the whiteness. The reservation looked deserted, empty, except for a trail of smoke rising out of chimneys here and there.

It took a moment before Vicky realized the girl was waiting for an answer. What an absurd question. No one would want to harm Father John O'Malley. He was a man of the people; he belonged here. "No one. No one," she said, trying to blink away the image of Debbie Bearing, the hot hatred in the woman's eyes.

"You think someone did."

"I want to make sure he's all right."

Shannon went quiet again. This time Vicky felt the girl's eyes boring into her. "You love him, don't you?"

"Everyone loves him." Vicky waited a moment, scanning the road ahead for the junction with Blue Sky Highway. Easy to miss with snow everywhere; more minutes would be lost. She slowed for the turn, then picked up speed again, heading southwest. She turned onto Highway 287. The rooftops of Fort Washakie appeared like dark smudges on the horizon ahead. She glanced over at Shannon O'Malley. "It's not what you think."

The girl took her time. Then she said, "Well, that's too bad."

Vicky felt her muscles stiffen. This girl came from another time, another world, where people did what they wanted to do and nothing else mattered. Nothing else was allowed to get in the way, not vows and conventions and expectations . . .

The noise of a siren grew louder. She saw the flicker of red and yellow lights, slowed down, and jittered to the side as the ambulance tore past. Shannon was up partway on her knees, stretching backward, eyes following the ambulance. "It could be Uncle John."

They were a short distance from the Bearing place, and Vicky made a decision: They would go on, find out who was in the ambulance. Then she would follow it. Follow it to hell.

She pulled out into the lane and kept going. Shannon was still twisted about. "We should turn around."

Vicky didn't say anything. Looming through the glare of sun and snow was the Bearing house and the barn behind it, a pair of dark buildings set back from the road with vehicles parked in the yard. She could make out a police car and a blur of people walking about. She slowed again, came around a short curve and swung left, bumping over the barrow ditch and up into the yard past a couple of sedans and other vehicles toward the red pickup. She jammed on the brake, slammed out of the Ford, and started running, barely aware of the surprise in the faces turned toward her. Past the little groups of people, around the cars. She stopped. The rear door of the police car hung open. There was a muffled squawk and a hiss of radio noise. And then she saw him: getting out of the backseat, his cowboy hat brushing the top edge. Coming toward her now. "Vicky," he said.

"Oh my God. You're alive." She was trembling; her legs felt numb, as if she were standing on air. She felt the warmth and strength in his arms as they wrapped around her and pulled her to him.

After a moment, she stepped back, and it was Shannon's turn, hugging him, sobbing. "We were so worried."

So many eyes on them, Vicky realized. At least a dozen people gathering around, boots shuffling in the snow. A plainclothes officer had gotten out of the other side of the car and was watching over the roof. A spectacle. Two women sobbing over a priest.

"Come over here." Vicky felt him lift her hand. Then he took Shannon's hand and led them toward the front of the house, away from the others. "Lou Bearing is dead. Debbie found him in the shop this morning. It looks like he shot himself."

"I knew you would come here . . ." Vicky began, wanting to explain, yet knowing it wasn't necessary. She could see in his eyes that he understood; the moccasin telegraph had the news already. She had tried his cell, but he hadn't answered. Then she had gone to the mission to find him. He wasn't there, and Shannon had insisted on coming with her.

"I was finishing the statement to the police." He gave a nod in the direction of the police cars. "Debbie's on the way to the hospital. She's in shock. I'm going over there." He looked at both of them a long moment, then he reached out, and Vicky felt herself pulled into his arms again. Then Shannon, crowding in. "You're all right?"

"We're fine." It was Shannon's voice, muffled against his jacket.

Vicky didn't say anything.

27

THEY WERE STANDING inside the door as if they had seen her turn into the driveway. Annie and Roger, expressions edged with anxiety. "You okay?" Annie said.

Vicky pushed the door closed. She could feel the dry heat blowing through the vents. Of course she was okay. Why wouldn't she be? She started to slip out of her coat, and in an instant, Roger was behind her, taking the coat, hanging it on the rack next to the door.

"We heard about Lou Bearing," he said. "Debbie's in the hospital with shock. The news is all over the telegraph."

How efficient the moccasin telegraph was. The news had reached the office before she had. She wondered what else Annie and Roger had heard. It wasn't just a matter of text messages and phone calls. Now it was videos. She closed her eyes for a second, trying to erase the video of herself throwing herself into John O'Malley's arms. That should stir up a lot of gossip.

"I went to the mission this morning," she began. A feeble effort to explain. What did it matter? People would believe what they wanted to believe. "John said he would have a talk with Lou. I was afraid I had sent him to his death." She drew in a long breath, feeling calmer now, more like herself. "He went to the hospital to check on Debbie."

Because Debbie had no one, she was thinking. No one she seemed to care about. No one who cared about her, except Lou, who was gone. But this was Vicky's family, Annie and Roger. And the kids, Lucas and Susan. Living far away, but part of her nevertheless. She had *someone.*

"Are you hungry?" Annie might have been addressing a small child. "Roger brought in sandwiches. Egg salad?"

Perhaps that was the emptiness inside her—hunger. Breakfast had been hours ago. She couldn't even remember what she had eaten before she'd left for the office.

"Egg salad sounds delicious." She gave them another smile, these two solicitous people—this family—and went into her own office. She had *someone,* she told herself again. John O'Malley was a priest. He cared for those who had no one.

Annie was behind her. She stationed herself at the corner of the desk and waited while Vicky sat down and turned on the computer. "What's the rest?"

"Lianna Blue Hawk canceled her appointment this afternoon. I guess she's not ready to divorce Joseph. They're trying to reconcile."

"And when will she be ready?" Vicky stared at the icons peopling the computer screen. "When he's knocked her senseless?"

Annie nodded, a blurred motion at the edge of Vicky's vision. "I told her you'd see her when she changed her mind. Lester Duwalt dropped in without an appointment. Claims highway department wrongly terminated him because he took time off for his grandfather's wake. Roger saw him.

You have an appointment with Doris Rides Fast at five. She didn't say what about."

Roger materialized beside Annie and set down a paper plate with a sandwich and chips and a mug of coffee. The musty odor of hard-boiled eggs mixed with the aroma of fresh coffee. Vicky glanced up and nodded her thanks.

"Let us know if you need anything else," Annie said. They were backing out of the office, around the opened beveled glass doors, these two friends of hers.

Vicky swiveled about, giving them her full attention. "Thank you," she said. "For everything."

Roger pulled the doors shut, and Vicky went back to the computer. She was running up against mountains. Everywhere she turned, she encountered an outcropping of rocks. Vince White Hawk, still missing. He could be a thousand miles away. He could be in a drunken coma or dead. And Mary Ann Little Shield, lost in a place as gray and amorphous as a snow cloud, with parents not legally her parents. People who loved her and who might lose her.

She forced herself to concentrate on the new information Evie Moran had given her. Three missing days on Clint's calendar that weren't missing after all. He had been in Denver. A night there with his secretary, a day driving back to Riverton, and he'd told her nothing. And yet, he must have had a reason to go to Denver.

She held herself still, barely breathing. Clint had visited the Bearings before he left and had gone back to see them as soon as he returned. Something he had learned from the Bearings had sent him to Denver. Clint must have stumbled onto something. And he had been killed because of it.

It all came back to Denver. She typed in "Denver Wind River Reservation 2011" and strained toward the screen, willing a connection to come up. A chamber of commerce site appeared, followed by things to do and see in Denver, festivals, and races. A similar site popped up for the reservation.

Powwows, rodeos, parades, drumming groups, dancers. Nothing that might explain a connection between Denver and an infant left on a doorstep on the reservation.

Vicky sat back and tried to focus on something else: a shadowy thought circling in her head, something Shannon O'Malley had mentioned. She had pushed it away, her own thoughts focused on the fact that someone was dead at the Bearing house, and John O'Malley had gone there. Now she felt herself slowly coming to attention. Shannon's voice sounded in her head as clearly as if the girl were sitting beside her now: *Uncle John's been a big help to me. He gets it, you know? Not everybody does. My own father wonders why I care about a captive white girl who became Arapaho.*

Captive white girl! My God, the reality was as obvious as the Wind River Mountains looming over the reservation, and Clint Hopkins had seen it. Lou Bearing must have divulged something that made Clint scour the internet and go to Denver. Divulged too much! Whatever Clint had found, he had tried to erase it, except for his calendar and notes. Had he expected her to follow in his tracks, should something happen to him? Hoped she would latch onto the truth and help Mary Ann? If she didn't, Mary Ann Little Shield would remain in that gray, indefinite place.

She typed in "Missing Infant Denver 2011." A new set of Web sites, several pages long, materialized. Culled from stories in newspapers, radio, and TV, two or three internet news sites, several blogs. She tapped on an account from the *Denver Post* and read down the page.

MOTHER KILLED,
INFANT ABDUCTED IN CARJACKING

A tense carjacking Monday ended in the death of a twenty-nine-year-old Denver woman, Louise Adler Becket, and the abduction of her five-week-old daughter,

*Elizabeth Louise. Jason Becket, husband of the de-
ceased woman and father of the infant, has offered a
$25,000 reward for information leading to the safe re-
turn of his child. "I will never stop looking for her,"
Becket said.*

*Witnesses said the incident occurred in Cherry Creek
North, the popular upscale shopping area. At about five
p.m. Louise Becket parked her late-model Honda SUV
in front of a series of shops. A pickup immediately pulled
in alongside the SUV, and a man and a woman jumped
out. They accosted Mrs. Becket as she was attempting
to remove the infant from the rear seat. The man alleg-
edly subdued the victim while the woman took her purse
and got behind the steering wheel of the SUV. She
backed out and drove down the street with Mrs. Becket
hanging on to the rear door in a futile attempt to rescue
her infant. Witnesses said the woman slipped under
the wheels of the SUV. According to Denver Police Detective Tim Martinez, she was pronounced dead at the scene.
The man fled in the pickup, following the SUV, and both
vehicles headed east toward Colorado Boulevard.*

*Witnesses describe the carjackers as medium height
with dark hair and dark complexions.*

*Police have issued an alert to law enforcement
throughout Colorado and neighboring states. Anyone
with information on the missing infant, the dark-colored
SUV, or a light-colored Chevrolet pickup is urged to
contact their local police immediately. Police are con-
cerned that the longer the infant remains with the carjackers, the greater the danger she is in.*

Vicky read the article again. She felt as if the breath had
been sucked out of her, as if the beveled glass doors and the
snow-covered ground framed in the window were closing in.
Elizabeth Louise Becket, a white infant—a captive—stolen

from her family. Whose father had offered a twenty-five-thousand-dollar reward for her return. Was that the story of Mary Ann Little Shield?

She glanced through the other sites. Repetitions of the newspaper article with something new added: police mock-ups of the two carjackers, according to the descriptions of witnesses. Dark hair and dark eyes, indistinct features. Indian, Hispanic, Asian. They could be Debbie and Lou Bearing or a thousand others.

There were pages of Web sites. Week after week, and still no news of the missing infant or the dark-complexioned carjackers. But no news in the months after the carjacking did not mean that Elizabeth Louise Becket—or her body—hadn't been found sometime in the past five years.

She closed the sites and typed in the same search string for Denver in 2012. An anniversary article popped up: "One year ago today, five-week-old Elizabeth Louise Becket was abducted in a carjacking in Cherry Creek North that left her mother, Louise Becket, crushed under the wheels of her SUV. Despite a five-state alert and ongoing search for the carjacked SUV and the Chevrolet pickup one of the carjackers drove, neither the vehicles nor the infant have been located. 'I know my baby is out there somewhere,' said Jason Becket, husband of the dead woman and father of the missing infant. 'She is all I have left. If anyone knows of her whereabouts, I beg you to contact the police.' He said the $25,000 reward he had offered following the incident will stand until his child is found."

Vicky repeated the search for the following years: 2013, 2014, 2015, 2016. Fewer articles appeared each year, a gradual tapering into a vacuum of inevitability and even acceptance, like the gradual tapering of grief.

She started a new search, this time for Jason Becket. He would still be in Denver, she was certain, and Clint Hopkins had gone there to talk to him. The search took only a few minutes, and she had located the man. The photograph showed a handsome man with a broad chin and curly hair and something undefined in his eyes, like a visible mote. Jason Becket owned several restaurants, including the Thirty-Second Street Bistro, judged the best bistro in Denver two years running. Vicky jotted down the telephone number, picked up the phone, and called.

She glanced at her watch while a phone rang somewhere in Highland, the northwest section of Denver, not far from where she had lived when she practiced law in a downtown skyscraper, before she'd come home to the reservation.

"Thirty-Second Street Bistro." The voice on the other end sounded cheery and enthusiastic. There was a faint background noise of clinking glasses and buzzing voices

Vicky asked to speak to Jason Becket. There was a muffled sound, as if a hand had been placed over the receiver: "Is Jason here?" A second passed, then the woman said: "Who's calling?"

"Vicky Holden. I'm an attorney in Wyoming."

She should hold, the woman said. Several minutes passed, the line inert, and Vicky had started to wonder if they had been cut off when a man's voice said, "This is Jason." There was an edge of impatience to his voice. "What is this about?"

"My name is . . ."

"Yeah, I got it. You're an attorney in Wyoming. Is this about Elizabeth?"

"Yes."

"You'd better have something definite. No more theories and possibilities, no more gossip. There was another Wyoming attorney here last week, asking a lot of questions. If you know something about my daughter, let's hear it."

"Mr. Becket, the lawyer you spoke to, Clint Hopkins, has been killed. I've taken over an adoption case he was working on. It's imperative that I meet with you." She should have checked the flight schedules, she was thinking. Flights out of

Riverton in the winter could be erratic. She plunged on: "I can be in Denver tomorrow." She would drive, if she had to.

"Killed!"

"He was struck down by a truck. The police believe it was an accident. I saw it happen. I believe it was deliberate. Could we meet tomorrow?"

"God! Why would anyone kill him? He seemed like a nice man. A little tense and, frankly, a little confused. I wasn't sure what he was trying to sort out and put together."

"Can we meet tomorrow?"

"Yeah, sure. Come to the restaurant. You know where it is?"

Yes, she told him. She knew where it was.

She had just replaced the receiver when the phone rang. Annie, saying Rick Masterson was on the other line. Vicky waited for the clicking noise, then she said, "Rick?"

"How about dinner?"

Dinner! Another conversation between two people who had witnessed the same incident and seen different things. "Sorry," she said, starting to explain that she was leaving town tomorrow and had a lot to do.

He cut her off. "Look, Vicky. I've been thinking about Clint's death. I believe you're right. It wasn't an accident."

Vicky let a couple of seconds go by before she said, "What changed your mind?"

"Clint, himself. Something he said at the meeting started to bother me. He told me he intended to bring you in on an adoption case to make certain the little girl would be settled with people who loved her, in case . . ." Vicky could hear the in and out of his breathing. "In case something happened to him."

"Something happened?"

"An hour later, he was dead. I realized I'd seen what appeared logical. An accident in a blizzard. I've told the police what Clint said. Look, Vicky, I'm sorry that you and I got off to a bad start, and I'm sorry we can't get together this evening. I have to go back to Cheyenne tomorrow, but I'll be here in a couple of weeks on another consultation job. May I call you?"

Vicky tried to picture the man who had sat across the table from her two nights ago. Sand-colored hair, earnest-looking face. A man who could reconsider, acknowledge other possibilities. "Of course," she said.

28

FATHER JOHN PEERED past the windshield wipers at Seventeen-Mile Road, blurred in the falling snow. He could barely see a car length ahead. It had started snowing sometime in the middle of the night and showed no sign of letting up. All around, the prairie and sky merged together, indistinguishable. Beside him, Shannon hunkered down inside her jacket with a scarf around her neck that billowed upward and connected with the knit hat, leaving a slit for her eyes. He jogged the heater knob, turning it on and off in an attempt to wake it up. Finally, the heater choked out a burst of warm air. "Giorni poveri vivea" played softly between them.

"Should warm up in a bit." He hoped that would be the case. All winter the heater had operated with a mind of its own. Inside all the layers of wool, Shannon was shivering.

"How far do we have to go?"

He glanced over and gave her a quick smile. "A Boston

girl, complaining about the cold? Not far, fifteen minutes."
Probably longer, he was thinking. He kept the pickup at a
slow, steady pace, watching for oncoming vehicles to burst
out of the white haze. He had just gotten to the office that
morning and was making coffee, measuring out the grounds,
when the phone had rung. He had darted over to his desk
and managed to grab the receiver before the caller was
shunted to voice mail.

"This is Daisy Blue Water . . ."

"Hello, Grandmother."

"Ah, Father. How's the weather at the mission?"

Always the polite preliminaries first, even in a phone
call. Father John smiled. "It's still snowing," he said. Only
a handful of people at Mass earlier, and he didn't blame
them for staying home. In fact, looking out at the wrinkled
faces of the elders, snuggling inside their jackets against the
chill in the church, he'd wished they had stayed home.

Daisy was going on about how she had gotten home yesterday from visiting her granddaughter's new daughter in
Billings and how her grandson's boy had come over to shovel
the walks before he went to school and how he would pick
up groceries for her that afternoon. When Father John said
she had a good family, she gave a sigh of contentment. And
then she came to the point: "My relation Wilbur says you
want to talk to me about my grandmother."

He explained that his niece, Shannon, was doing research
for her dissertation on the captive Fletcher girls. She was
here to research Lizzie Brokenhorn.

"Lizzie," Daisy said. "Grandmother loved that name soon
as she found out it was hers. When you want to come over?"

He had suggested later that morning, and the old woman
had agreed. Shannon hadn't come to the office yet. He suspected James had brought her back late last night. They had
been spending a lot of time together. Getting to know each
other, Shannon had told him. He knew Shannon: the minute

she came in and heard Daisy had called, she would want to see her.

And now Shannon sat with her hands encased in big furry gloves, resting in her lap. She stared straight ahead. He could feel the thoughts building inside her, searching for an outlet. He waited.

"I hope you don't disapprove of me," she said.

He shifted his eyes toward her and gave her another smile. "I'm proud of you and the work you're doing. I'm proud you think history is worth devoting yourself to."

"Oh, come on, Uncle John." He could feel her eyes lasering him. "James and I are together as much as we can be. We're taking our time. I want you to know we haven't started an . . ." She hesitated. "What you would call an affair. Our relationship's not about sex. I mean, it's bigger than sex. It's not that we don't want to sleep together. It's not the time, yet."

He glanced over and gave her another smile. "I know you'll make the best decision for yourself."

"You like James."

"Yes, I do."

He glanced sideways again. She was shaking her head, dipping her face deeper into the scarf. When she spoke, her voice sounded muffled and blurred: "I got a text from David yesterday. He's already moved out. Packed up his stuff, which pretty much was everything in the apartment, and poof! He's gone. The rent is paid for the month. In other words, I have a month to get my stuff out of there. That ought to take about an hour." She lifted her chin, and he saw that she was crying.

"I'm sorry."

"Breakup by text. Isn't that the best? No big arguments, just, So long, it's been nice to know you. I think there's an old song about that."

She was running a furry glove over her cheek, mopping at the moisture. "I'm not that sad, really. I mean, we had already broken up. We had an understanding. We would only stay together while it was"—she paused—"convenient. It's just that I didn't expect it to be so . . . bloodless."

Turning onto the highway, gripping the steering wheel against the back tires that were slipping about, Father John took a moment. The outskirts of Riverton—warehouses, garages, trailer homes—punched through the whiteness. "What about James?"

She was quiet for so long, he feared he had overstepped the sense of intimacy she had established. He was not her father.

"I think I'm falling in love with him."

He looked over at her, and she caught his eye and smiled. "He is so not called to be a priest."

"Falling in love . . ." He let the words settle between them.

"He's a good man," Shannon said. "One of the best I have ever met. He's . . . well, he's mature. He's not looking for a convenient relationship. He wants us to be together, to love each other for the long term. He's a forever-after guy. You'd approve, wouldn't you? Forever after?"

Father John was about to say he was glad she and James were taking their time, when she said, "I can write my dissertation anywhere, isn't that what you told me? I have all my research on the computer, the records and documents on Amanda Mary and Lizzie, the interviews with descendants. As soon as I finish the research on Lizzie, I can start writing. Two white girls captured by the Indians with completely different lives. Is it okay if I do it here?"

For how long? Father John was thinking. How long would there be a guesthouse and a mission? "The guesthouse is yours—"

She interrupted. "I told James you'd say that. I'll have a friend pack my stuff and send it. It won't be a big box, I promise. James and I, well, we can continue to get to know each other, see where we're going."

He was driving down the side streets of Riverton now, through a residential area: bungalows set back from the street, snuggled in snow, snow lining the curbs, banked against the parked cars. A forever-after guy, she had called James. That was what she wanted. Not the Davids who broke up by text. Not the commitments with strings attached, but the real thing. Maybe it wasn't really so different from the way it had been when he was Shannon's age. He had loved her mother then. He had wanted to marry her. Forever-after. He kept his eyes on the snowy asphalt ahead, aware of Shannon's presence filling up the cab: the daughter he might have had.

"You know she loves you, don't you?"

He felt as if Shannon had tossed a hard, icy snowball that caught him in the solar plexus. He didn't say anything, and she went on: "I saw the way she reacted yesterday when she thought you might have been killed."

He started to say they were friends, he and Vicky. They worked together. But Shannon shot out a furry glove. "Oh, please. I heard it yesterday from her. You're just friends and all that BS. There must be some way . . ."

"There is no way," he said. He found the brown-frame bungalow he was looking for, turned in alongside the curb, and gave his niece a reassuring smile. The commitment he had made was forever. "No way," he said.

"I WAS TOUCHED when Wilbur called me." Daisy Blue Water sat upright in a chair with flower-print upholstery and worn armrests, a small, ancient woman, fragile-looking, with a wrinkled face. She held her head high, a duo of paleness—light-brown hair fading to gray, cropped close to her head, and ghostly blue eyes. He would have taken her for a white woman if he hadn't known she was an Arapaho grandmother. She kept her hands clasped in the lap of her red skirt and crossed her feet, a prim and reserved posture left over from the mission school, he thought. So many of the elders who had gone to St. Francis School retained what the nuns would have called "good deportment."

"I'm sure Grandmother would be surprised to think anyone cared about her life. Apart from her family, naturally."

Shannon scooted herself to the front of the sofa cushion beside him. He could feel her excitement. "I understand you knew her."

"Oh, yes. I have very clear memories, even though I was very little, you know. She died in 1928. I was five years old."

Father John could see Shannon doing the calculations in her head. Daisy was ninety-three years old. Living in the home she'd occupied for fifty years, cooking meals as she had always done, visiting her new great-grandchild. She had family close by, descendants of Lizzie Brokenhorn, looking out for her.

Shannon leaned toward the old woman, concentrating on her story: how her grandmother used to pull her onto her lap and sing to her. "She liked to bake cakes. Her cakes were terrible, tasted like plaster and hard as stones. Naturally, all us kids ate them anyway. They were sweet, and we had powerful cravings for sugar."

Shannon slipped a photo of Lizzie and John Brokenhorn from her bag, a photo she'd found on the internet, she'd told him earlier. She popped to her feet, handed Daisy the photo, and sat back down. "Is this how you remember her?"

"Oh my." The old woman held the photo with her fingertips, as if it were a sacred object. "It's been years since I've seen this. It looks just like I remember her, and Grandfather, too. Only the photo makes her look darker. Her hair was very light and fine, like silk. I used to love to brush it. She had eyes like clouds, the faintest blue, and skin as white as winter. One time I asked her why her skin was so white, and she told me something was wrong with my eyes. She was brown, she said, like the rest of the people. But I had the same color of skin and light hair. I remember showing her my arms and asking why I had white arms. She would say, 'Don't think about it. You'll be brown soon enough.' She was right. In the summers I turned brown, but the brown would go away, and in the winter I looked white again."

Shannon glanced over at Father John, questions lighting her eyes. It wasn't polite to ask for the gift of information. He felt a surge of pride, the way she leaned back now and waited.

After a moment, Daisy said, "Oh, Grandmother knew she was white. She learned her story when Amanda Mary found her in 1902. She'd been looking for her for thirty-seven years. She never gave up hope. She wrote letters to the army, even wrote to Custer. It would get back to her that a trader had spotted a white child in an Indian camp, but when soldiers went out to look, the camp would be gone. Vanished into the plains. Amanda Mary kept at it. The woman had grit, I say."

Shannon waited a moment before she said, "I believe Lizzie also had grit."

"Oh, yes." Daisy was staring across the room, a distant look in her eyes as if she had gone somewhere else. "Especially when she finally met her sister. Amanda Mary rode the train to Casper and took a stagecoach to the reservation. A hundred miles, bouncing over the plains. Must have taken her back to her own time in captivity. It was brave of her to come. You want some coffee? I put a coffee cake in the oven."

The old woman pushed to her feet and steadied herself against the back of the chair a moment. Then she pushed off toward the kitchen. Father John stood up. "May we help?"

Shannon was close behind the old woman, and Father John followed. A few minutes later, they were seated at the dining room table, mugs of coffee and slices of coffee cake all around. Odors of warm cinnamon and sugar melted into the fresh coffee smells. "Thank you," Shannon said, sending a smile toward Daisy at the head of the table.

Father John could sense the urgency in Shannon's silence as they ate pieces of cake and sipped at the coffee. Finally, Daisy set her fork down and clasped her hands around her mug. She had long fingers with short, pale nails. There was a small gold band on her left hand.

"Grandmother never told me about meeting Amanda Mary, but my mother was there. She sat beside the interpreter that came from the agency. Grandmother never learned English, but my mother had gone to the mission school, so she knew English. She told me Grandmother was very upset. She didn't want to know she was white. Inside, she was Arapaho. Amanda Mary told her she was her sister. Grandmother's name was Elizabeth Fletcher, but their mother called her Lizzie. She was two years old when the Cheyennes attacked. Amanda Mary said they rose up out of the bushes along the creek, out of the ground. They were everywhere. She was holding her baby sister, Lizzie, in one arm. And she was holding their mother's hand when their mother slumped to the ground, and she saw the arrow in her chest. Next thing she knew, a warrior grabbed Lizzie. Mother said Amanda Mary cried when she told the story. "She had feared her baby sister was dead, but there she was, sitting beside her on a wooden chair Grandfather had made."

Daisy took another bite of cake, another sip of coffee. Letting the story live for a while, make its own way into their minds. After a moment, she went on: "Amanda Mary had come to take Lizzie home, back to her own people. She said Lizzie would live in a big house and wear pretty dresses and eat meat and potatoes every day. She would learn English and read books. They would be together again, two sisters, the way it was supposed to be.

"Grandmother started crying, Mother said. She talked so soft the interpreter had to keep asking what she said. She told Amanda Mary that she was home. She was with her people. She had her husband and children. She said something else . . ."

Daisy paused, sipping at her coffee, the pale eyes cloudy with memories. "She told Amanda Mary she was content. Well, it must've broken that woman's heart. Mother said Amanda Mary was real quiet. Just got into the stagecoach and went bouncing off."

Daisy set her mug down and smiled around the table. Back in the present now. "From then on, Grandmother called herself Lizzie."

29

VICKY HADN'T EXPECTED Lucas to meet her. She had called him last night to let him know she would be in Denver for a short time, to tell him she regretted not being able to spend more time.

"I get it, Mom," he'd said. "You're working on a case." She could hear the rest of it in his voice: she was always working on a case. He hadn't said he'd be waiting when she got off the airport train and followed the crowd up the escalators into the bright lights of the terminal. People everywhere, and there he was, standing just outside the railing. So handsome, like his father, that it took her breath away. She ran over and hugged him, then hugged him again. "What are you doing here?"

"I took the day off." He had already grabbed her bag and walked her across the terminal. "At least we can spend time together while I drive you around. Where to?"

By the time they were out of the airport and on the highway, warm air was filling the black BMW. She had told him the name of the restaurant she was going to in North Denver, and he had nodded. It made perfect sense that a case she was working on should take her back to the neighborhood where she had once lived.

"You okay, Mom? You look a little tired."

"I'm fine," she said. "And you look wonderful. Everything okay with you?"

"Better than okay." Lucas kept glancing between her and the highway. She could sense the turmoil inside him, the way he'd been when he was little, fidgeting to tell her something. And then he told her: Adrienne, the most wonderful girl in the world, had agreed to marry him. "You're going to love her, Mom. She's everything I ever hoped for, and what do you know? The crazy girl's in love with me."

Vicky stared at the highway, the open, snow-swept fields on either side, the flat-roofed commercial buildings spread ahead. The memories came crashing in. The vast, open plains; the hot summers on the rez; the rodeos and the bucking broncos; the hamburgers sizzling in the food booths; the smells of dust and coffee. And the cowboys—Indians from reservations all over the West—and none could ride a bronco or a bull longer than Ben Holden. And she, crazy girl, had loved him.

Now, beside her, was his son, an IT expert at a software company in Denver who sat at a desk in front of a computer all day. His sister, a graphic designer in Los Angeles, engaged to a white man. Ben would be proud of their accomplishments. He was always proud of his kids.

She shifted sideways so she could take him in, the whole reality of him. "You're so like your father."

"Mom! Come on." He looked over at her, wide-eyed. "I'm like you. I'm not like him."

He remembered too much, she thought. The drunken

Ben, the shouting and the flying fists, and everything falling apart—their family, the way things should have been. "Wedding plans?" she said.

"We're thinking June, a year from now. You'll love her, I promise."

"I promise I'll love her."

He would bring Adrienne to the reservation in the summer, as soon as it was sunny and warm, so she could see it the way he remembered it, Lucas was saying. They would go to a powwow, ride horses across the plains. There should be a carry-in dinner at Blue Sky Hall—didn't she think?—with the elders and grandmothers and friends he'd gone to school with. Yes, Vicky said to all of it. It would be a trip into the past.

They had left the highway behind and were in North Denver. Stop-and-go traffic down Federal Boulevard, Victorians and bungalows set back behind pines dusted with snow, women pushing strollers down the sidewalks, all as she remembered.

Now they were on Thirty-Second Street, heading west, the mountains rising like ice floes into the sky ahead.

"Looks like the restaurant." Lucas had slowed down, searching both sides of the street for an empty space at the curb. A long line of cars snaked past the restaurants and shops that occupied the string of Victorian houses. The BMW rocked to a stop. "Call me when you're finished," Lucas said as she got out.

The restaurant was packed. Every table taken. Groups of people, impatient looks on their faces, jammed the desk inside the front door. Laughter punctuated the low hum of conversations as plates clattered together and waiters hurried about. Vicky managed to make her way to the desk and told the young woman with black hair wrapped about her head like a ribbon and crayon red lipstick and bored eyes that she had an appointment with Jason Becket. The woman flinched backward. She started to say something about Jason being very busy when Vicky interrupted. "Tell him Vicky Holden is here." She waited while the woman picked up a receiver and repeated her words.

A couple of minutes passed, then a good five minutes. Vicky had stepped back from the crowd waiting for tables. Across the restaurant were two doors. One to the kitchen that expelled waiters hoisting loaded trays, and one that never opened. She kept her eyes on that door and, finally, it swung inward.

She could have picked Jason Becket out of a crowd. Blond hair, light complexion, a long nose and prominent chin, and a familiar look about him. It hit her with a thud: the man was the large, masculine version of Mary Ann Little Shield. He worked his way around the tables, and she went to meet him, holding out her hand. "I'm Vicky Holden."

His grip was hard, his expression businesslike. He ushered her through the door into a hallway paved with gray vinyl. Beyond the window at the far end, she could see a red delivery truck parked next to a Dumpster. Another door on the right opened into a small office, files and papers stacked everywhere, a pair of side chairs, shelves, a desk.

In a quick, efficient motion, Jason swept a chair clear and pulled it closer to the desk. He gestured for her to sit down, edged past the desk, and dropped into the seat he had probably just vacated. A pair of silver-framed photos stood at the corner of the desk. One, an infant wrapped in a pink blanket. The other, a pretty, dark-haired woman and Jason with a small boy on his lap.

"What do you know about Elizabeth?" His tone was flat, blunt, as if he didn't believe she knew anything. So many starts and stops, so many hopes dashed over the years. *I will never stop looking for her.*

Vicky unbuttoned her coat and loosened her scarf. The ceiling vent made little rattling noises as it emitted waves of warm air. He had not offered to take her coat. Clearly, Jason Becket did not expect the meeting to last long.

She took a moment before she said: "I believe Clint Hopkins told you about a white child who came to the reservation around the time your daughter was abducted."

"How shall I explain?" he began. "I told Clint I can't allow myself to get excited. There have been too many false reports, too many false sightings." He picked up a pen and began jabbing it against the mouse pad next to the computer. "What happened to Hopkins?"

"He was run down in the street the night after he returned from Denver."

"Accident?"

She took a moment before she said, "I don't think so. I saw it happen."

"You think it has something to do with the child?" A faint note of hope sounded in his voice, difficult to conceal.

"I'm trying to piece together the information Clint had gathered. It would help if you could tell me what you told him."

"He knew the facts; he'd read the newspaper accounts. He asked me to go over them." Jason shrugged. "My wife was running errands in Cherry Creek. She'd taken Elizabeth with her. I've always suspected it was her last stop because she kept Elizabeth on a regular schedule, and in thirty minutes or so, she would have wanted to be home to nurse her. You must have read the newspapers."

"Newspapers don't print the whole story."

He shifted forward, looking out of the corners of his eyes, watching something unfold beside him. "The carjackers, a man and a woman, came up when she was leaning into the backseat to get Elizabeth. They struck her on the head, knocked her down. The woman got behind the wheel and started driving. My wife managed to get up. She ran alongside the car and held on to the door. She was trying to save

Elizabeth when she slipped beneath the wheels and was killed. The man drove off in a pickup. They kept going. They didn't even stop."

They didn't even stop! Vicky could hear Betty White Hawk's voice looping through her head. A rollover crash, her husband trapped beneath the steering wheel. Lou and Debbie Bearing had driven on.

"There were witnesses," Jason was saying. "They gave the police descriptions. Nothing helped."

"Did they say anything that wasn't reported?"

"The carjackers were Indians. Oh, they looked Indian in the police illustrations, but the police wanted to keep their options open. Hispanic. Middle Eastern. But one witness got a close look at them. Laura Clement. She came out of a store as they started driving away. She heard my wife screaming and saw her fall under the wheels. She ran over to her, but there was nothing anyone could do. She said she would never forget the carjackers' faces. She could identify them."

"Did you tell Clint this? That a witness could identify the"—she drew in a breath—"killers?"

Jason nodded, his gaze still turned sideways. Then he faced her. "I told Clint I need a connection. I need to know how the child got to the reservation. I need proof she is Elizabeth. I've been through hell. The FBI is still on the case. Nothing," He stopped, allowing the weight of the word to settle between them. "I have a new family now. Sarah and I were married three years ago. We have a little boy, Josh. I've found some peace. I can't put myself through the agony and uncertainty again, not without proof."

Vicky sensed the conversation winding to an end, that Jason Becket was about to jump to his feet. He said, "Do you have that proof?"

"No." Vicky had been about to say, "Not yet," but she had swallowed back the impulse. She may never be able to find the proof. She may never be able to connect Elizabeth Becket to Mary Ann Little Shield.

She hurried on, not wanting the conversation to end. "What did Clint say?"

"Clint Hopkins was a man of few words. I didn't get the impression he liked to give anything away. He said he would talk to people on the reservation and get back to me."

"With the connection?"

"I presume that's what he meant."

"There's one more thing," Vicky said. Jason Becket was on his feet, and she got to hers. "Did he say how he had found you?"

"It was the first question I asked him. I got a half answer, something about how he had heard some things on the reservation."

Heard some things. Had Clint put it together? A baby crying at the Bearings'? A woman leaving a baby on a doorstep, a man repairing cars in his barn? A man who needed parts? All it had taken was an internet search. Starting close to home, branching across Wyoming, then to neighboring states. He'd spent a lot of time on the internet, his secretary had said. It's where he did most of his research.

Another possibility slid into her mind: Lou Bearing, a man struggling with a secret, longing to unburden himself. What had he told Clint?

Jason Becket walked around the desk and set his hand on the doorknob. He turned to her. "If you find a connection . . ." He paused, searching for the words. "I will want tests, you understand? I will want definite proof. I want my child back. *My* child. I will do everything to get her back."

Vicky left the restaurant feeling weak and slippery-footed. She had called Lucas from inside and waited until the BMW pulled up before she let herself out into the cold air. She held on to the door for support as she slid onto the seat. Elizabeth's mother had held on to the door. This was what Clint Hopkins had run into, the possibility—the likelihood—that Mary Anne Little Shield was Jason Becket's daughter. She did not belong with the people who had loved her for five years. Clint had wanted the adoption to be final. For Mary Anne's sake, so she could never be taken. Abducted again.

And yet there was a white man who could be her father. She understood why Clint had come to her. How would the tribe react? A child who had been part of them turned over to a white man, a stranger she didn't know? Tribal adoption laws were clear-cut. No Arapaho child could be adopted outside the tribe without tribal permission. What about a white child who had been living as an Arapaho? Would the tribe enter the case on the side of the Little Shields?

"I take it your meeting didn't go the way you hoped."

Vicky could feel her son's eyes on her, and she tried to pull herself back. "It's complicated," she said.

30

TRACES OF SNOW clung to the kitchen window and shrouded the residence in silence, interrupted occasionally by the sounds of the bishop puttering about upstairs and Walks-On snoring in the corner. Father John poured coffee into a mug, stirred in a quarter cup of milk, and headed back to the study. The lights around Circle Drive glowed in the window behind his desk.

He dropped into the old leather chair that, over the years, had taken on the contours of his body and stared at the interview with Amanda Mary Fletcher on the laptop. Published in a review of American history more than a hundred years ago, a few months after she had met Lizzie. "Well, I can't say for sure the white woman I talked to was my sister. There is no proof. She calls herself Kellsto Time, which means Killing Horn, and says she is the wife of Brokenhorn. She says she is Arapaho, and denies any memory of our family. She doesn't speak English, so I was required to take the word of a half-breed interpreter. I wouldn't be surprised if that Indian, Brokenhorn, hadn't bribed the interpreter to put words into Lizzie's mouth."

"What do you plan to do next?" the interviewer asked.

"I will wait, and I will pray, as I have done for thirty-seven years. I will pray that, if she is Lizzie, she will get word to me. I trust my sister knows I am waiting for her. If she is my sister."

FATHER JOHN GLANCED through the interview again. A sense of longing, disappointment, and even denial rang through Amanda Mary's words. And yet, she seemed certain that if the wife of John Brokenhorn was her sister, she would find a way to come to her. She would wait.

Her sister never came. And yet, Daisy Blue Water had said her grandmother took to calling herself Lizzie after the meeting. For the first time, she had acknowledged she was white. Still, she had stayed on the reservation, a white Arapaho woman.

"There's a lot about Amanda on the internet," Shannon had told him on the drive back to the reservation. She had found whatever was there, all of it now on her laptop, all the research and interviews. She had been filling in the gaps on the reservation, pulling in the human story left out of the records. The fact that Lizzie had cried when she met her sister—no record had mentioned that.

He shut down the laptop and swiveled toward the window. The wind drove the snow against the glass like shotgun pellets. His thoughts circled back to Shannon. Perhaps she would be another white woman married to an Arapaho. He smiled at the idea. It was an old story.

He couldn't shake the image of James in the sacristy getting ready to serve Mass, before Shannon had arrived. Earnest and conflicted, pulled toward the priesthood and pulling away. The priesthood wasn't what he had expected. Oh, Father John understood. It wasn't what he had expected, either.

Aware of another presence in the small room, he swiveled back and watched the bishop drop onto a chair that listed sideways under the old man's weight. He gripped a mug of coffee in both hands, lifted it to his lips for a moment, then set it on a small table. "Thought I might find you here," he said. "Trouble sleeping?"

Father John supposed that was the case, although he hadn't yet gone upstairs. An unsettled feeling had taken hold of him, as if the day were still moving toward something. So much unfinished, hanging in the air. Vince White Hawk still missing. Lou Bearing dead, and Debbie in shock. An Arapaho couple trying to adopt a white child. All unconnected, and yet he couldn't shake the notion that, somehow, they were mixed up together.

"How is the widow?"

Father John snapped back to attention. The old man seated across from him had a way of reading his mind. He told the bishop that, by the time he had reached the hospital, Debbie Bearing had already been released. He had driven back to the house and parked outside. She didn't come out, even though he'd had the feeling she was there, which meant she did not want company. He tried to blink back the image unreeling in his head: the woman flailing about the yard, howling at the sky.

"Vicky thought you were the one who had been shot." The bishop had narrowed his eyes on him. "She was quite upset."

"Yes, I know." Father John started to explain that Vicky had asked him to stop by the Bearings' place, then swallowed back the explanation. The circumstances didn't really matter. It was the fact that Vicky feared he had been killed. There had been times when he had felt the same terrible dread about her.

"You're very close."

"We're friends." Dear Lord, the bishop and Shannon both knew the truth. Was it that obvious? He thought of the way Vicky had thrown herself into his arms when she saw he was alive, and all the people standing about, watching. The moccasin telegraph had probably been jammed.

"You are a good priest," the bishop said.

"I pray every day."

"Not that the love you feel for each other will be taken away, I hope. The love of another always blesses our lives."

"For the courage to honor my vows."

"The day will come when you will have to leave the mission." The bishop shook his head. "When we'll both have to leave. There are rumors . . ."

"I've heard them." He had logged on to the province newsletter himself earlier this evening. The meeting had been held, a gathering of Jesuits and benefactors, to discuss the direction to take in the future, to test the air. It was clear where the discussions would likely lead. "The Jesuit province may have to close the mission," he said. "Not enough priests. Not enough money. What else is new?" He tried to make light of it. "It's always been a possibility."

"It will be hard for you to leave."

"For you, too."

"Oh, yes, but I've packed up and left before." The bishop got to his feet and hooked the handle of his mug in one finger. "I feel sleep coming on," he said, shuffling toward the door. Halfway across the study, he turned back. "We must always be ready to go."

He was bent-shouldered, moving across the corridor, taking the stairs one heavy, purposeful step at a time. The bishop had fallen in love with St. Francis Mission, with its people and its history and its silent emptiness. They were alike, Father John thought.

He could hear Walks-On snoring in the kitchen, deep into whatever dreams the night would bring. It was as though the day had finally collapsed. Father John was about to snap off the desk lamp and head upstairs when the phone rang. He glanced at the name on the small screen: Betty White Hawk. His muscles tensed as he lifted the receiver. "Father John."

"Thank God you're there." The voice lifted in hysteria. "You have to come right away." She started sobbing, garbling the words. "They're going to kill him. You have to stop them."

"Betty, listen to me. Take a deep breath and tell me what's happened."

She was crying hard, gasping for breath. A couple of seconds passed before she gulped out her son's name and told him the police found the house where Vince was hiding. "Somebody snitched him out. They're going to kill him."

"The police are not going to kill him, Betty. They're going to arrest him."

"Don't you get it?" The hysteria reached a higher pitch. "Nobody's going to arrest Vince. I know my boy. He'll shoot his way out, and they'll kill him. You have to stop them."

"Where is he?"

She gave a tangled set of directions. Seventeen-Mile Road, Yellow Calf Road, the first cutoff. A shack by the river. "I'm almost there. I can see the police lights, all red and blue. Oh, God. God. Don't let anything happen to my boy."

"I'm on my way," Father John told her.

THE PLANE JUMPED and rocked in the snow falling outside. It had been late leaving Denver. At one point, it had looked as if the flight would be canceled because of the weather in Wyoming. Vicky had thought she might have to call Lucas and ask him to come back for her. Finally, the flight had been posted. Late, but still taking off.

Vicky clutched the armrests, as if the armrests might steady the bouncing plane. The man seated next to her was snoring. God bless him! A lucky man to sleep through this. She closed her eyes against the snow smearing the window and tried to ignore the creaking noises. The images came to her out of the darkness: A white girl growing up Arapaho. A dark figure with a briefcase flying over the hood of a truck. Lou Bearing longing to lay down a heavy burden. And now, a man grieving for his lost child.

Coincidences. Betty White Hawk said that Lou and Debbie Bearing stole cars for parts, but that didn't prove that they had carjacked a car in Denver. A witness claimed she could identify the carjackers. After five years? Any defense attorney could establish enough doubt to discount the identification.

She knew what she had to do. She had to inform the adoption court of the possibility that Mary Ann Little Shield could be Elizabeth Becket. Tests would be made. She felt an emptiness opening inside her. Either the Little Shields or Jason Becket could lose a child.

Vicky's eyes snapped open. The plane had begun lurching back and forth. The man beside her shifted in his seat. Vicky tried to ignore the rocking plane and focus on Clint Hopkins's actions after he came back from Denver. He'd called her, arranged a meeting, and gone back to see Lou and Debbie Bearing.

And that was what had been bothering her. What had he hoped for? That Lou and Debbie would admit to carjacking a car in Denver, killing a woman, and driving off with an infant?

They would never have admitted anything. Except that Lou . . . She could still see the image of the slim man with narrow shoulders leaning against the truck as if he had been caught in a tornado. How long would Lou have resisted the pressure to tell the truth? Is that why Clint had gone back? Hoping Lou would break down, unburden himself?

Now Lou was dead.

But Clint had died first. Clint, who had put the pieces together, the coincidences, all except for the last connection between a crying baby and a baby left on the Little Shields' doorstep. He must have confronted Lou and Debbie about the carjacking, the abducted baby, the witness who could identify the carjackers. What he knew could have sent Lou and Debbie Bearing to prison for the rest of their lives.

Vicky sat up straight. Another piece of the puzzle clicked into place. She could imagine Lou Bearing and Vince White Hawk, hunched over beer at the Buffalo Bar and Lounge, Vince listening to a proposition, just as his Dad had done ten years ago. *Easy money. You need money, don't you? Take care of a little job.*

The pilot's voice boomed over the intercom. They would be on the ground shortly. Temperature twenty degrees, snow falling. A cold night out there, folks. The lights of Riverton flickered through the snow clouds, foggy and remote from the new image gripping her: Vince White Hawk with a stash of money, hiding out on the reservation, on the run from murder.

Vince would never surrender.

31

VICKY FOLLOWED THE man who had sat next to her down the metal steps and across a swath of snow-blown concrete. A blast of frigid wind went straight to her bones. Inside, the terminal resembled an aquarium in the bright lights. She was still shivering as she made her way through the small crowd beyond the baggage trough.

She didn't see them at first, but there they were: Annie and Roger, hurrying forward, worry etched on their faces. The roads must be terrible, Vicky thought. She had left her own car in the parking lot, but here they were, good friends, come to fetch her.

Then she understood it was something else by the way Roger swung her bag out of her hand and started for the door, and Annie fell in beside her. "It's Vince." Annie kept her voice low, throwing a glance toward the people milling about. Vicky could feel a knot tightening in her stomach. The sounds of greetings and conversations surged around them, and Annie didn't say anything else until they were through the door.

"They found him." Annie stayed close beside her, the two of them picking their way along the snowy trail that Roger stomped out toward the short-term parking. "He's been holed up in a drinking house. A so-called friend snitched him out. Police have surrounded the house, and Vince is refusing to come out. He has a gun, and he's threatening to kill himself."

Roger held the doors of his SUV open while Annie got into the passenger seat and Vicky lifted herself onto the rear seat. She pulled her scarf around her chin and snuggled into a little warmth.

"We figured you'd want to get out there right away," Roger said, turning on the ignition, looking over one shoulder as he backed the SUV out of the parking space. She could see the worry lines below the cap pulled halfway down his forehead.

"Betty's beside herself." Annie joined in, straining around to catch her eye. "She's scared to death Vince will either kill himself or come out shooting and let the police do it. He's terrified of going to prison."

"Where is she?"

"She's at the house by now, I'm sure. She must have called a half dozen times to see if you'd gotten back yet."

They were driving through Riverton, past the restaurants, shops, gas stations shimmering in the falling snow. Vince. Vince. She had worked out a deal with the prosecuting attorney. All he'd had to do was come with her and surrender. He would have been in rehab now. Safe in rehab.

But Vince had wanted to drink, and the force of it—the sheer need for alcohol—was stronger than anything else. Where had he run into Lou? At the bar where Betty had gone looking for him? And Lou had recognized the force of want in his eyes. He had *smelled* it. He'd offered Vince money for a simple job: follow a man with a briefcase, wait for the best opportunity, run him down.

Roger made a right onto the reservation. The windshield wipers made a lazy, droning noise against the snow at the edges of the cleared crescents. Ahead, the sign for St. Francis Mission looked blurred and wavy. Betty would have called John O'Malley, and he would have gone immediately. Vicky could feel herself relax a little. John would do everything possible to keep Vince alive.

THE BLUE AND red lights on a cluster of police cars swirled in the snow. Several yards behind the cars stood the house itself—a shack, really—a collection of logs and sticks left over from the days when the government believed shacks were good enough for Arapahos. Thick snow lay over a roof that might collapse at any moment, except the roof had held on through decades of winters. It would hold on tonight, unless a volley of gunshots blew it to pieces. Vicky shivered at the thought.

Roger maneuvered the SUV through the barrow ditch and into the yard. He stopped behind one of the police cars. An ambulance stood nearby, an ominous sign, preparation for the worst. Vicky got out and slammed the door, searching the little groups of people milling about, BIA police in bulky uniform jackets, ear flaps dangling from their caps, plainclothes officers bundled in sheepskin jackets.

She spotted John O'Malley over by a floodlight mounted on a metal tripod. As if he had felt her eyes on him, he broke away from a group of officers and started toward her. Voices all around were subdued and tight, and it struck her that the voices of the enemy in the Old Time must have sounded like that before the warriors swooped down on a village.

She had started toward John O'Malley, snow blowing in her face, aware of Annie on one side, Roger on the other, when Betty White Hawk—hatless, hair streaked white, face twisted in hysteria—jumped in front of her. "You've got to stop them!" She was shouting, throwing her arms about, gloves dangling off her hands.

Vicky took hold of the woman's shoulders. "What's happened?"

"He's going to kill himself if they"—the words sounded like a long wail; she waved a flapping glove around—"don't go away. He wants them to leave him alone."

She was aware of John O'Malley beside her. Annie and Roger had stepped away to give him room and, behind them, she could see Michael Lefthand, the BIA police chief, and another officer start over.

"We've been trying to talk him into coming out," John O'Malley said. "He wants to talk to you."

"Then we have to go in."

"Not going to happen." The police chief shouldered in beside her.

"Vince is desperate, Michael. I'm his lawyer. I have the right to talk to him. Father John is his pastor. We have to convince him to surrender peacefully. He's facing a charge of attempted robbery. It's not worth a life."

"I get it, but Vince is not listening to anybody's pleas." The chief threw a glance sideways. "No offense, Father. We have a SWAT team ready to take that shack and bring him out."

"They'll bring out a dead body," John O'Malley said. "Is that what you want?"

"Nobody needs to die tonight." Vicky stared at the chief until she was sure she had his full attention. "Let us try."

The chief lowered his head, considering something about his boots. A clump of snow slid off the brim of his hat. A couple of seconds passed before he looked up. "You get one chance. If Vince White Hawk refuses to talk to you, we go in. Got it?"

Vicky nodded, and she and John O'Malley followed the chief over to the floodlight. He took a megaphone from another officer and handed it to Vicky. "One chance," he said.

The megaphone was heavy, unbalanced. Vicky held it to her mouth and pushed it up with her other hand. "Vince, it's Vicky." Her voice boomed around the yard as if they were in an echo chamber. "Father John and I are coming in."

Silence. The shack might have been empty, left with nothing but ghosts.

"No going in unless he's on board," the chief said. "You could be walking into a bullet."

"Vince, can you hear me?" Vicky heard her own voice, swollen and shaky. "I have to know if you hear me. Open the door a little." She waited. The door remained fixed, shadowy and flimsy-looking. God, the SWAT team would overpower it in a second. "Vince! We can help you. Let us help you."

Still nothing. "Better let it go." It was Roger's voice behind her, joining in. "It's too dangerous."

She glanced up at John O'Malley. In his eyes was the same resolution that had gathered inside her. She tilted the heavy megaphone upward again. "It's just Father John and me, Vince. You know we're not armed. We're coming inside to talk to you."

"No, you are not," Chief Lefthand said.

Vicky pushed the megaphone into his chest and started across the yard after John O'Malley, who was already halfway to the shack. A flurry of movement and the sound of angry voices erupted behind them.

"Vince! We're coming." John O'Malley's voice came back to her in a freezing blast of wind. "Open the door. Nobody's coming in but us."

He had reached the door now, Vicky so close behind she could feel the warmth of his jacket. The door trembled under his fist. Nothing but the hushed silence that had settled over the shack and the yard, as if she and John O'Malley were alone. Two or three seconds passed—a lifetime—before she heard the clicking noise, and John turned the knob. The door creaked open. "Vince!" he called.

John O'Malley stepped inside, and she was right behind him, moving into a tiny space of shadows and gray light framed in the front windows. Over in the corner, a space heater emitted a red glow. A blanket, the only other sign of human habitation, had been tossed near the heater. Seated cross-legged on the bare wooden floor a few feet away, the red glow playing over his face, was Vince White Hawk, hands shaking, dangling off his knees.

Vicky got down on one knee beside him, conscious of John O'Malley sinking beside her. "Let us help you, Vince," she said. He wore the same dark sweatshirt he had worn the last time she'd seen him. Torn jeans, exposing bony, bruised-looking knees. Tucked inside the waistband of his jeans was the black metal handle of a pistol.

"You can't help me." The words came like a hoarse cough.

"I'm going to see that you are taken to the hospital." God, the man needed help, whatever he had done. Day after day of steady drinking. He could have been dead. "I'm going to try to work out the same deal with the prosecuting attorney. You'll plead guilty to harassment and he'll drop the attempted robbery charge. You'll be sentenced to jail, but you'll spend the time in rehab."

"It's your chance for another start," John O'Malley said.

Vince didn't move. He might have been a sculpture in a park. *Indian Sitting Alone.* Without looking up, he said, "You don't get it."

"Oh, I get it," John O'Malley said. "I've been where you are. I know all about second chances. And one thing I know for sure: you don't turn them down."

The floodlight burned through the window behind her,

and white light striped Vince's face and sweatshirt. He might have been behind bars, she thought.

Vince lifted his face, blinked into the light, and tried to scoot backward. The effort tipped him sideways, and John O'Malley set a hand on his shoulder to brace him. Vince was shaking. The space heater was no match for the cold air that invaded the old shack. Vicky got to her feet, scooped up the blanket, and wrapped it around Vince's shoulders. He shuddered into it.

"Nobody's gonna make me a deal."

"There are no guarantees," Vicky said. "I'll do my best."

"They think I killed somebody."

"You tried to rob somebody," John O'Malley said.

Vicky took a moment before she said, "Did you?"

Vince rocked backward, as if she had struck him with an anvil, eyes wide with fear, jaw moving with the impact of words trying to escape. One hand reached for the gun. "You'd better get out of here. Get out, both of you."

"I'm your lawyer," Vicky said. "Whatever you've done . . ."

"Nobody's gonna believe me. Even you think I killed that man." He gripped the gun and yanked it out. "I'm warning you. Get out!"

"Take it easy, buddy." John O'Malley's voice was calm, normal. "Put the gun away."

Vince was waving the gun like a flag. He kept his eyes on Vicky. "The cops'll never believe me." Tiny bits of spittle peppered her face. "I'm not going to prison for a murder I never did."

"I know what happened to Clint Hopkins." And she did, Vicky realized, as if the figures in the scenarios she had imagined had reassembled themselves. It wasn't Vince behind the wheel of the black truck. Either Lou or Debbie Bearing had been driving, because Vince had taken the money and disappeared.

"You didn't kill him." Vicky sat down on the floor, not

taking her eyes from the gun. Steadier in Vince's hands now. "Lou offered you money to do a job, isn't that right? You were desperate for a drink, so you took the money. But you didn't have it in you, did you, Vince? You couldn't kill a man."

John O'Malley had turned toward her, and she could see in his expression that he understood part of it. She hadn't had time to tell him what she had learned in Denver. The same truth that Clint Hopkins had uncovered, the truth that had gotten him killed.

"Clint Hopkins knew enough to send the Bearings to prison," she said. "They wanted him dead."

Vince was blinking into the light again, all the muscles of his face creased in concentration. "Lou never told me what the guy did. Just said he'd be at a meeting in downtown Lander later that night. He always carried a briefcase. I was supposed to wait for him to come out . . ." He gulped, as if something hard had lodged in his throat. "Lou gave me a thousand dollars. Said there'd be another thousand after I did the job. I took the money and . . ."

"Disappeared," Vicky said.

"I'm not a killer."

"Give me the gun." John O'Malley held out his hand. "It's your second chance, buddy." A long moment passed— Vicky could hear her heart hammering in her ears—as the dance went on: holding out the gun, pulling it back, holding it again, and, finally, setting it into John O'Malley's hand.

"We're going out together," he said. "Vicky and I will go first. You'll be right behind us."

Vince moved his head in what passed for a nod, then made an effort to get to his feet, scooting forward, trying to push himself upward. A great effort that came to nothing until John O'Malley took hold of his arm and lifted him up.

At the door, John O'Malley shouted that they were coming out, that Vince was unarmed. There was a change of plans then, since Vince was stumbling and weaving about. Vicky stepped out alone into the flood of white light, the falling snow like black flies in the light. Walking behind her, John held on to Vince.

"Your mother's waiting for you," she heard him tell the young man.

32

THE WOMAN CAME out of the house and ran toward the car parked in front. Coat open, sides flapping in the breeze that stirred the snow and sent little white clouds spiraling upward, head bare, scarf blowing around her neck. Betty White Hawk, a dark figure against the bright sunshine that had emerged this morning and scrubbed through the last of the snow clouds.

Vicky pulled the Ford in behind the car. A mixture of surprise and expectation flashed across Betty's face. She stood in the opened driver's door, stopped in motion. Vicky slammed out and walked over, boots crunching the snow.

"I been waiting all morning." Betty sounded tense, accusatory.

"I've been at the prosecutor's office." Vicky closed in on the woman. "I came as soon as I could."

"How is he?"

"Vince is in the hospital. He's under arrest."

"The deal?" Betty looked as if she might jump out of her skin. She slapped away the scarf that blew across her face and blinked into the brightness. The sun had set the snow ablaze.

"Peters withdrew the deal. He's upset over last night's standoff. Vince didn't help himself by hiding out and threatening to kill himself."

"I know. I know." Betty lifted both hands in supplication. "He's my son, and I love him. All he could think about was getting a drink. You said you'd help him."

Vicky let a long moment tick by. Betty didn't know the rest of it: Her son had accepted money to kill a man, had declined to do the job, and had taken off with the money. Neither did Peters, which, if the truth ever came out, would mean charges of conspiracy to commit murder and probably a host of other charges Peters would be happy to come up with.

"I'll meet with him after he's had time to think. A guilty plea means Peters wouldn't have the expense of a trial. In exchange, Vince would serve his sentence in a treatment facility."

"Guaranteed?"

"It's what I'm asking for." And hoping to conclude, she was thinking, before Peters became aware of Vince's role in a homicide.

Betty swung around and looked away, through the glare of the sun at the blowing puffs of snow. "We both trusted you."

"I'm doing my best."

"I have to get to work. If I don't show up today, I'm toast." Betty started sinking onto the seat, her attention directed to the steering wheel, the ice-crusted windshield.

Vicky leaned into the opened door. "There is something I need you to do."

This got the woman's attention, and her head jerked around. "Visit Vince? They won't let visitors near him."

"I want you to tell the fed what you told me about the Bearings and the death of your husband."

Betty's mouth went slack. She squinted into the sun. "I never told anyone, except you."

"It's important. A child's future is at stake."

"It happened a long time ago. What does it matter? I gotta go."

"It matters, Betty. There's something else I have to put together, then we'll go to see the FBI agent together."

The woman gave a quick, dismissive laugh. "I lost my husband that night. I lost Rickie. All I have left is Vince and my husband's reputation. He was a hero to folks around here, a great husband and a great dad. And he lost his life in a senseless accident. You want me to take his good name from him? Tell the fed he was a thief?" She started crying, her voice shaking. "My son's going to prison. Treatment facility, whatever. He's going *away*. And you want me to destroy all I have left? Everybody thinking how lucky I was to have had such a good husband?"

"Please think about it." Vicky felt the door yanked out of her hand. The subject closed now, the conversation over. The engine sputtered into life and the car jolted forward, then swung into a U-turn, and gunned across the yard, snow spitting from the tires.

ST. FRANCIS MISSION was quiet, drenched in the sun, the buildings sharp against the blue sky. The Toyota pickup stood nosed against the front stoop of the administration building. Vicky pulled in alongside and hurried up the steps. John O'Malley was coming across the office toward her as she came through the door.

He reached out and took her hand. "I've been expecting you."

Last night, so much had been left unsaid after Vince had finally agreed to surrender. What choice did he really have? And they had walked out together, the three of them, into the crowd that pulsed about the floodlight. The rest of it had happened fast: Chief Lefthand pulling Vince's hands behind his back, clamping on handcuffs, and pushing him down into the police car. She remembered shaking with cold and uncertainty as the car drove off. Vince on his way to the Fremont County Detention Center, where it would be up to a doctor to decide if he needed hospitalization. But he was alive.

She had been aware of Annie and Roger moving in close. They would drive her home and, as they started toward Roger's SUV, she had nodded at John O'Malley and mouthed the words: "Thank you." Then they had driven off, and Vicky remembered shaking with cold all the way to her apartment in Lander. It had taken hours to warm up, hours before she fell into an exhausted, black sleep. By morning the Ford had materialized in the parking lot. She wasn't sure when Annie and Roger had picked it up at the airport.

Now she dropped onto a side chair and let her coat slip from her shoulders while John pulled up a twin chair and sat across from her. "How is Vince?"

That was all it took for the words to rush forward. She told him everything she had told Betty: Vince in the hospital, the prosecuting attorney reluctant to cut another deal, her own hope—faint, unrealistic—that he would come around and she could get Vince committed to a treatment facility.

John O'Malley hadn't interrupted, had just nodded, understanding it all. Finally she jumped up, brushed past him, and walked over to the window. The mission grounds looked quiet and peaceful. Beyond, the reservation stretched into the blue sky, the sun beginning to sink, and the shadows turning the snow blue-gray. She looked back. John had abandoned his chair and was half sitting on the edge of his desk, waiting.

"Is it about the Bearings?"

She nodded and told him what she had learned in Denver. A man trying to pick up his life after his wife was murdered, his child stolen. She could still see the photo in the silver frame: Jason Becket, a dark-haired woman, and a small boy, and the other photo of an infant snuggled in a pink blanket. She told him about the carjacking in Denver five years ago, the young mother trying to get her baby out of the backseat and slipping under the wheels. The carjackers were a man and a woman, possibly Indian. They had driven on: the woman in the stolen car, the man in the truck.

"There was a witness who claims she can identify the couple," she said.

"It was five years ago."

"A traumatic event like that is probably etched in her mind." Vicky started circling the space in front of the desk.

"You think it was Lou and Debbie Bearing."

She didn't stop, just told him what Betty had said about her husband's death. "They were car thieves. That's how Lou got parts for the cars he fixed. Only in Denver, they got something more. An infant strapped into the backseat. They had killed a woman and driven on. Driven on! With an infant in the backseat!" She stopped. A chill began at the base of her spine and shot into her neck. "What if they had panicked and abandoned the baby? Left her in a trash barrel, thrown her into the weeds. Anything."

"But they didn't. They took care of her." She heard the touch of compassion in John O'Malley's voice, as if he had seized on a small, decent thing.

"And when their neighbor asked about the baby crying every night, Debbie told her not to worry. It wouldn't last much longer. My God, John. The baby had become a problem. She could link them to the death of her mother. They had to get rid of her. Drop her on a doorstep and drive off. But the Little Shields might have called the police. The Bearings took a huge risk, John. A huge risk."

Vicky started pacing again, wearing a circle around the center of the office, trying to corral her thoughts, all the coincidences, the connections. There was still a crucial gap, the piece she couldn't put into place.

"Why the Little Shields?" She stopped pacing and faced him. "Why take the infant to them? Myra told me they knew of the Bearings, but they didn't *know* them. They had never spoken to them. Yes, they had lost their own baby, and news would have spread on the moccasin telegraph, but other couples had lost children. They weren't the only bereft couple on the rez."

"Unless . . ." Vicky dropped onto the chair, feeling lightheaded, the air knocked out of her with a new thought working its way into her mind. "Unless the Bearings hadn't gone car stealing at all. They had gone baby snatching. Baby snatching for a bereft couple. In Denver, a big city, far from the rez. No one would connect an abduction in Denver to the reservation."

John perched on the chair in front of her and leaned forward, everything about him tight with concentration. She could feel him trying to arrange this new theory into a plausible, cohesive order, some kind of logic. "There isn't any proof, Vicky." *A terrible thing to contemplate, to accuse someone of.* She could read the message in his eyes. "They didn't know one another. Why would the Little Shields believe the Bearings would do something like that?"

Vicky was quiet a moment, aware of John O'Malley watching her, seeing *into* her. "In any case," she began, arranging her thoughts, listening to them tumble out, word by word, "I have to tell the Little Shields what I learned in Denver. Tests will determine if any of this makes sense. Jason Becket may not be Mary Ann's father after all, and then . . ." She threw out both hands. "None of this speculation will matter."

33

I AM COMING with you.

John O'Malley did not have to say it out loud. Vicky
knew he would go to the Little Shields' with her. They had
confided in him, and he had counseled them. They had given
her permission to bring him in on the case. And now he
would go with her. What was it? Moral support, physical
support, or just to let the couple know that she was not the
only one who may have stumbled onto what could be a terrible truth.

She shrugged into her coat while he set his cowboy hat
on his head and yanked his jacket off the coat tree behind
the door, pulling it on as they headed down the corridor and
into the afternoon, the pale sun stippling the grounds. "Let's
take my car," she said. The Ford had a heater that worked.

They crossed the empty, white spaces of the reservation
in long periods of silence, thinking the same thoughts: the
ramifications of this latest theory, a possible deadly connec-

tion between the Bearings and the Little Shields. But where was the proof? She had to keep in mind there was no proof.

Two figures were in the yard, a man and a small child. Rolling balls of snow that grew in circumference and left narrow tracks of dirt that crisscrossed the yard. Yellow hair hung beneath the child's pink cap and fanned across her shoulders. The man's face looked flushed, reddish brown with the effort of pushing an enormous ball toward some kind of enclosure in front of the gray-sided house. A snow fort, Vicky thought. And in a corral on the side of the house, a small pony.

Eldon Little Shield looked up and waved as Vicky steered the Ford off the road and into the yard. The child did the same, a wide grin spreading over her face, as if they were friends, coming to help. A sinking feeling hit Vicky as she pulled in behind a gray pickup.

"Your secretary called to let us know you'd be stopping by." Eldon stood outside the door as Vicky swung it open. "I left the shop early. Didn't want to miss you."

Mary Ann huddled beside him—all pale skin and wide blue eyes—and Vicky wondered how much she knew. Children knew everything; they were spies, spying on adults, spying on their own lives. And yet the hesitancy, the worry frowns in Eldon's face were absent in hers. "Good to see you, Father." Eldon waved them both toward the house. "Myra's waiting."

The house had a tidy, lived-in feel, a newspaper tossed on a coffee table, a bronze framed photo of Mary Ann on a table, jackets hung on a rack behind the door, odors of hot chocolate radiating through the warmth. Myra emerged from the kitchen as Eldon took their coats, adding them to the pile on the rack, a large squishy outcropping that bumped against the door. "You bring us good news, I hope," he said.

The child had sprinted to her mother, who was removing her hat and scarf, the mittens crusted with ice, the pink jacket soggy with snow. Whispering something about hot chocolate and cookies, she steered the child into the kitchen. Mary Ann was giggling.

Eldon nodded toward the sofa and a pair of chairs with oak armrests, an Indian blanket folded over the back of one. "Coffee? Hot chocolate?" The affable host, the smallest sense of uncertainty in his voice.

"No, thank you," Vicky said. She exchanged a glance with John O'Malley, who also waved away the offer. She dropped into one of the chairs while he perched on the other. This was not a social call; the information she had gathered in Denver, the theories and conjectures, none of it good. Out in the kitchen the child gave a carefree burst of laughter; metal clanged against a hard surface.

"I have new information about your case," Vicky began. "I know you've spoken to Father John . . ."

"Yeah. Yeah." Eldon waved away the rest of it. "Any news you got, I want Father John to hear."

Myra was back, and the couple settled together on the sofa, Myra leaning toward the kitchen, half turning toward the child. She gave Vicky a conspiratorial glance, mother to mother. "Put her in front of the iPad and she'll sit for hours." She shot a glance at her husband. "She can't hear us. She's lost in a game."

Eldon leaned forward and clasped his hands between his knees. "What did you find in Denver?"

How did he know? Vicky tried to scramble through the last couple of days. There was only one way Eldon could have known about the Denver trip. Annie had said that Debbie Bearing called yesterday, and she had told her Vicky was out of the office. Out of the office. Following Clint Hopkins' trail. Debbie must have concluded she had followed the trail to Denver, and she had told Eldon.

"I'm afraid it's not good news," Vicky began, reaching

for the words. "I've learned that an infant was abducted in a carjacking in Denver five years ago."

"That can't have anything to do with us." Myra worked her hands in her lap, kneading them together.

Eldon remained silent.

"It's possible that infant was your child, Myra," John O'Malley said.

"Crazy talk." Eldon jerked upright, a warrior on alert to an approaching enemy. "Denver's a long way from here."

"The family's name is Becket." Vicky pushed on. The whole story had to come out; light had to be thrown on the truth. "The father has never stopped looking for his child. He wants her back."

"You mean, he thinks Mary Ann is his child? He wants to take her from us? From her home? From her people?" Myra's voice cracked, and for a moment Vicky thought she would burst into tears. Instead she drew in a long breath, drawing on some inner reservoir of strength. "Mary Ann doesn't have anything to do with his baby. Her mother lived on the rez. She brought her to us because she wanted us to raise her. That man in Denver can't have her. He can't take her away."

A wild, high-pitched shriek broke across the room. Mary Ann stood in the kitchen doorway, arms flailing against the doorjambs. She shrieked again, mouth opened. "No! No! No! I won't go! Don't let anybody take me away!"

Myra jumped to her feet. "Oh my God," she said, gathering up the child, lifting her into her arms, cradling her, the child screaming now, face twisted in pain, wet with tears. Myra carried her into the kitchen, kicking the door shut as she went. The door gave a loud thwack that sent invisible waves through the atmosphere.

Eldon was on his feet. "Do you know what you've done? Do you have any idea?" He stepped forward, fists clenched, and John O'Malley got to his feet. Vicky stood up beside him.

"Take it easy," John said. The muffled sounds of a sobbing child came from the kitchen. "We're trying to find the truth."

"It's not her! Maybe some kid got abducted, but it's not her. There's no proof, no evidence."

"There was a witness," Vicky said. "The witness can identify the carjackers. They were Indian, a man and a woman." She hesitated, then plunged ahead. "I think they were Lou and Debbie Bearing."

Eldon didn't move, a statue frozen to the rug spread over the vinyl floor.

"You knew that, didn't you?" John O'Malley said, keeping his voice low and confidential, the confessor urging the penitent forward.

Then something happened: a crack in the man's composure and assurance.

Eldon drew in his lower lip and turned away. He stared across the room, past the window, out to the icy, white expanse that ran to the sky, the truth crashing around them.

"You don't know." His voice was shaky. "You don't know how it was. Coming home from the hospital alone. Our baby girl dead in some steel freezer, never to be with us, grow up in her home, let us love her, be our family, be everything." He started to cry, his words thick with tears. "Myra couldn't take it. She just couldn't take it. 'Why us?' she kept asking. 'What did we do that was so bad our little girl was taken away?' She got worse and worse, crying all day, staying in bed and crying. Then I found her in the kitchen, a big glass of yellowish liquid in her hand. I knocked it to the floor because I knew. I knew what it was. The bottle of bleach was on the counter."

The man shifted himself around until he was facing them. "I could never leave her alone. I called the relatives.

They came over and stayed with her, so I could go back to work. Somebody here day and night. Never alone."

"You contacted the Bearings." John O'Malley pushed on, low, rational tone. "Was it Lou? A man who ran a body shop in his barn, repaired cars, the same kind of work you do. You must have known him. Did he come to your shop looking for extra work?"

The two men locked eyes for a long moment, then Eldon broke away. "Scavenger, that's what he was. Coming around begging for old parts we didn't want. The boss sent him out to the yard to get rid of him. Let him take the junk so we didn't have to haul it away. That's what he used on the cars he worked on. Mostly junk. The rest, he stole, I figured. How else did he get any new parts?"

"He stole cars, so you thought he could carjack an infant for you," Vicky heard herself say.

Eldon took a step sideways, into another persona. He gave a large, raucous laugh. "You can't prove anything. It doesn't matter what Lou might've told you. He was a drunk and a liar. Nothing but a scavenger. You pay him a few dollars, he'd tell you anything."

"Or do anything," Vicky said.

"You got nothing. Debbie says I had anything to do with what they did in Denver, I'll deny it. Her word against mine."

"Mary Ann's mother died trying to save her," Father John said.

Eldon dropped his head and leaned forward, as if a hard gust of wind had caught him in the back. "I don't know anything about it," he said. "You don't have proof. All I know is our baby was on our doorstep; somebody left her. That's all I know."

"The adoption court will want proof that Mary Ann was abandoned. I will have to inform the court about Denver. The court will order tests . . ."

"No!" Eldon stood straight, shoulders back, chest thrust

out. "I will not allow tests on my child. Nobody's taking her from us, you hear me? No court. Nobody."

"There's a chance the court could order a joint custody," Vicky said. "The tribe could get involved since Mary Ann's being raised Arapaho and believes . . ."

Eldon lifted a fist, and Vicky flinched backward, half aware of John O'Malley moving between her and Eldon.

"You hear yourself?" Eldon was shouting now, barking out words. "Court. Joint custody. Like hell!" He checked himself, drawing in a long breath. The child was still sobbing in the kitchen, a muffled noise that wafted past the closed door. "This is my family we're talking about. They're all I've got, Myra and Mary Ann, my two girls." He moved sideways and fixed his gaze on Vicky. "We wanted Mary Ann safe, so nobody could take her away, and you come here with joint custody? We don't need you. You're not our lawyer anymore, understand? Get out of my house, both of you."

IT HAPPENED IN an instant, like a flash forward, Vicky aware of the weight of John O'Malley's arm around her, sheltering her from the angry, fist-clenched man, guiding her to the door, grabbing their coats and shrugging into them as they crossed the yard, the door slamming hard behind them. She was shaking, and John took the keys from her hand and said he would drive. Then they swung around and were out on the road that stretched ahead into the blue-denim dusk coming on.

Neither one spoke. Thoughts on the same track, Vicky knew. Revisiting the same pieces of information, plugging in the vacant spaces. "Lou and Debbie took care of the baby until the time was right," she said finally, blurting out another supposition. "They waited for instructions from Eldon. It had to be snowing, a blizzard, with no chance Myra would recognize the vehicle or Debbie Bearing running away."

"What about Clint Hopkins?" John kept his eyes straight ahead, steering the Ford down the narrow road.

"He must have figured out what took place in Denver and confronted Lou and Debbie. He was thinking about Mary Ann. I think he hoped I could convince the tribe to step forward on her behalf, so that she would remain Arapaho. At the very least, we might have worked out an arrangement where Mary Ann's biological father and the Little Shields shared custody. Of course, that assumes Clint never realized Eldon's part in the abduction."

"There's no proof, Vicky." She felt John's eyes on her. "Even if Debbie accused Eldon of hiring them, Eldon would deny it. It would be her word against his."

Vicky didn't say anything, her own eyes trained on the road unfolding ahead, nothing but empty space and sky. "She would deny that Lou hired Vince to run Clint down in the street like a dog. When Vince took the money and ran, someone else had to do it. And . . ." She took a moment, allowing the logical conclusion to present itself. "Lou was already weighed down with guilt. Debbie was the strong one."

Letting a few more seconds tick by, she watched the road, but she saw something else now: Lou Bearing leaning against the black truck. The hood lifted, the tool table nearby. He had been repairing the truck from whatever damage Clint Hopkins' body had inflicted. She said, "The truck is in the barn."

John had been quiet for some time, and she glanced over. He kept shifting his gaze to the rearview mirror. She turned sideways and looked out the back window. "How long has that black truck been there?"

34

FATHER JOHN DIDN'T reply. When *had* the black truck appeared out of nowhere? He'd noticed it a good five minutes ago, but when had it appeared? After he had pulled out of the Little Shields' yard and started toward Seventeen-Mile Road? Had it been parked down the road, waiting for them to leave?

"Did Debbie Bearing know you went to Denver?"

"I haven't talked to her," Vicky said, her voice tight with uncertainty. She sat twisted about, her gaze on the rear window. Then, a rush of certainty: "She called yesterday, and Annie told her I was out of the office. She must have figured I went to Denver and she told Eldon."

The truck was speeding up, gaining on them, the front bumper gray and solid-looking. The headlights had flashed on, yellow spotlights in the darkening dusk. He could barely make out the figure behind the steering wheel: jacket collar up, dark scarf bundling the lower half of the face, cowboy hat pulled low. It could be a man or a woman. He pressed down on the accelerator.

The truck shot forward, and Father John pressed harder, trying to maintain space between the two vehicles. He wasn't used to the Ford, the way it responded. It felt steady in his hand, but the road was patched in snow, ice glistening like puddles of rain. The truck didn't want space: it loomed in the rearview mirror.

"Hold on." He leaned onto the pedal, aware of the white needle shaking upward: seventy, seventy-five, eighty. The truck stayed close. Enormous, a black monster risen out of the empty white spaces. The Ford, small in comparison, a bumper car. Eighty-five. Ninety. Too fast for the road conditions. It was getting darker, harder to see beyond the headlights. The truck kept coming closer.

"She's trying to run us off the road." Vicky's voice was high, close to panic. He could feel the wheels slipping, hydroplaning, almost airborne, and he knew she felt the same sensation. "We can't outrun it."

The loud thud jerked the Ford sideways. The car started to spin out, and it took all his strength to turn the wheel into the spin until they were headed straight again, but down the wrong side of the road. The speedometer jumping at ninety-two now.

"Turn off ahead," Vicky shouted. "We have to go cross-country."

He couldn't speak, all his attention focused on the road and the truck coming in for another hit. He tried to spurt ahead, but the Ford was going all out, and this time the hit was square, encompassing the entire rear end.

The Ford jerked forward, shaking, wobbling. He gripped the wheel hard and let up on the gas a little. The truck stayed close behind. Then the Ford righted itself, and they flew ahead, steady and straight.

The truck had dropped a car length behind, but it was

still there, relentless. Vicky was right. He was going to have to drive off the road onto the wide expanse of empty land. But a sharp move at this speed would turn them over. The truck was roaring in close again, and this time, the hit came on the right, a noise that shattered the air. He heard Vicky scream as they spun out, snow spattering the windshield. No time to turn into the spin. The Ford was on its own trajectory, like a bucking bronco, and they were soaring over the barrow ditch and plowing through the snow. Twenty, thirty yards before he managed to rein in the vehicle and bring it to a stop. His heart thumped in his ears. They were still upright.

He looked over at Vicky. She was blanched, driven back into her seat. "Are you okay?"

"I'm okay." She had been holding her breath, he knew, and now she let out an explosion of air.

Later, when he tried to work it out, he wasn't sure when he had heard the crash, the squealing brakes, the thumping tires, the grating scrape of metal against metal. When had he gotten out, expecting the black truck to be coming for them over the snow? But it was then that he saw the two vehicles: the sedan clinging to the road, the black truck overturned in the snow. Black plumes of smoke rose over the truck.

Vicky pushed herself out and started running toward the road, high-stepping through the snow, arms outstretched for balance. He took off after her, then passed her, the whole scenario passing again in his mind: spinning out into the oncoming lane, headlights bouncing ahead. Dear Lord, he never saw the other vehicle. The driver had seen them, though, and swerved into the other lane.

The black truck, going ninety, ninety-five miles an hour, had been coming in the other lane.

He was breathing hard, sliding down the side of the ditch, forcing his way up the other side and out onto the road.

Vicky stayed close behind; he could hear her shouting into her cell: Accident. Seventeen-Mile Road. Send ambulances.

He ran to the sedan first, the right front accordioned into a jumble of metal shards hissing and sweating in the heat that radiated off the vehicle. The left side, the driver's side, was mangled. He could see the man slumped over the steering wheel; no one else inside. The man was moving, head lolling. Somehow he had managed to turn the sedan just enough—inches—so that the back took the brunt of the crash.

"Hold on!" Father John yanked at the door. Stuck, jammed into the frame. He yanked again, one boot propped against the lower frame, and felt it give a little with a sharp squeaking noise. He tried again, throwing all his weight into the effort until the door came loose. He managed to open it a foot, enough to wedge his shoulder behind it and push. He could feel the man's eyes on him and sense the panic.

He leaned inside. "Where are you hurt?" The man was Arapaho, a familiar-looking face, most likely from one of the get-togethers, not one of his parishioners. Blood was running down his forehead.

"I don't know." His voice sounded stronger than Father John had expected. "Everywhere."

Father John pulled his handkerchief out of his jeans pocket and pressed it against the man's forehead. It started to fill up with blood. He refolded it and pressed again, adding pressure until the bleeding slowed. "Can you hold this?"

The man nodded. He gripped the handkerchief and clapped it to his forehead.

"I'm not going to try to get you out," Father John said. There could be spinal injuries, head injuries. "An ambulance is on the way. The medics will tend to you."

The man gave a little nod and seemed to settle back, bleeding and in shock but alive. Alive, thank God.

Father John slid down the ditch on the other side of the

road, then clawed his way upslope to the truck. The wheels were spinning against the sky. Cab smashed, windows blown out, shards twinkling in the half-light, and inside—Debbie Bearing, upside down, dangling from her seat belt, slumped sideways. Vicky was hunched close to the broken window.

"Help me," Debbie kept saying over and over, a kind of litany.

"The ambulance is coming," Vicky told her. She glanced up at him. "I've been telling her, but she doesn't understand. She's delirious."

"Help me."

The door had been jammed into the roof, the window space smashed to half its size. It would take a crowbar to open the door, and even then, it might not budge. For half a second he thought about reaching inside and releasing her seat belt, but she would fall onto the crushed roof. The window was too small to pull her through.

"Try to hold on," he said, but he could see she was letting go. Letting go of life. He thrust his arm inside, found the woman's hand—cold and limp—and squeezed it. "Breathe with me, Debbie. In. Out." He exaggerated his own breathing, gulping in air, blowing it out. "In. Out."

Her breathing sounded labored and faint. She was looking up at him out of the corner of her eye, past the scarf tangled around her head and caught somehow on the steering wheel, tethering her to the truck. He could see the spasms in her neck muscles.

"Breathe, Debbie. In. Out." He glanced over at Vicky, and in her eyes, wide with shock and fright, he could see the truth: It was useless. The woman was dying.

"I'll pray with you." He turned his attention back to the woman dangling upside down. The wind made a low moaning noise around them. "Dear Lord, merciful God, forgive me my sins." He wasn't sure if her lips were moving silently or if it was part of the spasms in her neck. "I place my soul in your hands. I trust in you."

She went still. Lips not moving, eyes straight ahead, focused on something else, another reality. Father John could feel the life going out of her, and yet her hand remained the same, limp and cool. "God have mercy on your soul," he whispered.

He let go of her hand; she would have to go on alone. He retrieved his arm, aware of the glass shards catching and tearing at his jacket, and stood up. The sound of sirens came from the distance, but the wind could imitate that eerie, distant wail. They were in the middle of the reservation, miles from the nearest ambulance, the nearest patrol car. It would take a while before help arrived. He had to go back up to the road, see about the injured man and keep him company. He was a priest. Wasn't that what he did? Dig inside himself to find encouragement and hope for someone else?

He turned to Vicky, waiting beside him, eyes fixed on the lifeless body of the woman inside the truck, the woman who had wanted them dead. The woman who had killed and killed.

He put his arms around Vicky and drew her close, allowing the warmth of her to warm the coldness inside him. Thank God, they were both alive.

35

VINCE WHITE HAWK stood beside her, sleepy-eyed, drugged, bent forward, as if he were leaning into the wind, but he wore a suit, a snappy blue tie, and a white shirt with the collar jutting out from around his skinny neck, all of it the work of his mother. She had wanted her son presentable for the court hearing.

"Mr. White Hawk, you are charged with attempted robbery." A routine matter for the district court judge who shuffled through a pile of papers in front of him before looking up. "Mr. Peters?"

Jim Peters got to his feet. He took a moment to marshal his thoughts, then he said, "Your honor, prosecution and defense have reached a disposition of this case. We have agreed to ask the court to release Mr. White Hawk on a personal recognizance bond to be cosigned by him and by his mother, Betty White Hawk. As a condition, Mr. White Hawk will enter a sixty-day program of addiction recovery and rehabilitation. He will be taken to the rehab facility immediately.

"After he has successfully completed rehab, we have agreed to reduce the attempted robbery charge to a misdemeanor charge of disturbing the peace with a stipulated sentence of one-year probation, on the condition that he remain sober during that time. We have reached this disposition in view of the fact that Mr. White Hawk voluntarily came forward and provided the Lander Police Department with essential information that enabled them to clear up the murder last week of Clint Hopkins. In addition, Mr. White Hawk's mother has also provided information that enabled the FBI to solve a five-year-old abduction and murder case in Denver."

The judge worked his lips around silent words for a moment. "Ms. Holden?"

Vicky got to her feet. She could hear her heart pounding. In the meeting this morning, she hadn't been sure whether Peters would accept her request to ask the court for bond and rehab. After every argument she had made, he had reminded her that Vince could not be trusted. Finally Peters had agreed.

"Your honor, we agree with the prosecuting attorney."

The judge took his time before he said, "I'm also inclined to agree." He looked up and fastened his gaze on Vince for a moment. "The attempted robbery charge will stand until Mr. White Hawk successfully completes rehab and remains sober for thirty days. I am going to set a return court date for that time. If your client has met the conditions, I will grant the prosecution's motion to reduce the charge to a misdemeanor. He will enter a guilty plea, and I will accept the probation sentence. However, if he violates probation by substance use, he will be sentenced for such violation. Is that clear?"

"Yes, your honor," Vicky said.

"Mr. White Hawk, you will now be transported to the treatment facility in Rock Springs. Good luck, and don't let me hear of you in trouble again. This court is adjourned." The judge banged his gavel and swept through the doorway behind the bench, black robe swaying.

Vicky turned to her client. The sheriff's deputies were already approaching to whisk him to a van waiting outside the courthouse. "You have a second chance," she said.

Betty pushed past the deputies, grabbed her son, and started hugging him. "Thank you," Vince said, mouthing the words over his mother's shoulder, and Betty jerked around. "Yes. Yes. Oh, Vicky, thank you for giving me my son back." She let him go then, and kept her eyes on the deputies escorting him down the aisle and out the door.

Jim Peters stepped over. "Let's hope your client can stay sober and out of trouble." He shook his head at the improbability.

"He's going to be just fine." Betty threw her shoulders back and lifted her head, on sure ground now. "All my son needs is a chance."

Peters gave a mock salute and stepped back to the table. He gathered up the papers, slipped them inside a briefcase, and left the courtroom.

Vicky walked out with Betty, who seemed calm, wrapped in a new reality she could accept. Vince off to treatment, sure to recover, come home, live a good life, be her son.

VICKY DROVE NORTH on Highway 287, through the bright noon sunshine, a feeling of spring in the air. Snow glistening in the fields. She lowered the window a few inches and breathed in the faintest smells of spring: wet soil, sagebrush stirring into life, the freshness of the wind.

The sedan was turning in to the yard when she crossed the barrow ditch. A light blue, sporty-looking car with green and white Colorado license plates. Jason Becket had called two days ago. The FBI had concluded the investigation into the murder of his wife and the abduction of his child. The witness—a mother herself, out shopping for a few things for her own children—had gotten a good look at the carjackers. She would never forget their faces, she said. They still appeared in her nightmares. She had positively identified photos of Lou and Debbie Bearing. Without a paternity test, there was no proof that Mary Ann Little Shields was Elizabeth Becket, but there was a preponderance of evidence.

Vicky had not been involved. Everything was confidential that Eldon had told her and Father John—a lawyer and a priest. The whole story—the human story that Eldon had blurted out—would probably never be told: his wife, suicidal; his desperation to replace a lost child; a scavenger and carjacker coming around the shop. Not anyone he *knew*, not a relative or connection that could be traced to him.

It had taken several phone calls and meetings to persuade Betty White Hawk that it could help her son if she told what she knew about the Bearings. Vicky had arranged a meeting with Ted Gianelli, the local fed. She had gone along, reassuring Betty every step of the way.

Vince had been eager to tell the truth, hoping for a deal that would keep him out of prison. He had talked to both Gianelli and the police in Lander, filling in the gaps. Vicky had held her breath when he admitted to taking money to kill Clint Hopkins, then going into hiding, but the prosecuting attorney had declined to file any further charges. Vince had come forth willingly; he had helped to solve Clint Hopkins's murder as well as a five-year-old crime, and he was already facing charges for his own clumsy attempt at robbery.

Vicky slammed the door behind her and started across the yard through the piles of snow and rivulets of water. Jason Becket got out of the car and came toward her, a dark

shadow silhouetted against the grayish house. He held on
to her hand a moment as if she were a connection to his
child, then tossed his head back at the house. "So this is
where Elizabeth lived," he said.

"I'm sorry." She left the rest unsaid: *They're gone*. She
had told him when he called that the Little Shields had fled
the reservation. The FBI had already notified him.

"When?"

"A week ago," she said. "I told them what I had found. I
told them there would have to be tests. I believe they left
that night."

"Before I could get to her." Jason looked about, taking
in the wide, snow-stippled yard, the great empty spaces.
Then he stepped over to the blocks of snow melting in the
sun. "What's this?"

"A snow fort. The day I came, Eldon and"—she
hesitated—"the child were building a snow fort."

He drew in his lower lip, eyes sunken in thought. "She
could have everything. A big house with a swimming pool.
All kinds of lessons—music, tennis, horseback riding. Does
she like horses?"

Vicky said she didn't know, but there had been a pony in
the corral out back, and she didn't know an Arapaho child
who didn't love horses.

"She would be a beautiful debutante, like her mother."
He tossed his head toward the house. "Can I see inside?"

Vicky walked over to the front stoop, which was wet from
melting snow. The house belonged to Myra's aunt, according
to the moccasin telegraph, a piece of information wedged
among the speculations about why the family had abruptly
fled the reservation. Myra's aunt threw them out? They
moved to Denver? Oklahoma? L.A.?

Vicky tried the knob. Of course Jason would want to see
the inside, and it had crossed her mind to call the aunt, but
what would she have said? Mary Ann's natural father wanted

to see the house his child had lived in? That would have sent a rush down the telegraph. Besides, no one locked their doors on the rez. Anyone should be able to find shelter in a storm.

The knob turned in her hand and she stepped into the living room, Jason Becket behind her, so still that she turned around to check if he had come in.

The furniture was still there: sofa against the wall, a couple of chairs and small tables, a deep-backed TV that jutted into the middle of the room, but no signs anyone had lived here. A vacant place on the table where the photo of Mary Ann had stood.

"She watched TV in here." Jason sounded distant, lost in thought. He crossed the room and leaned into the kitchen. For the first time, Vicky saw the vinyl flooring, popped at the edges; the worn tablecloth hanging around the thin legs of the table; the countertop, scarred and stained.

She heard herself saying that the child had an iPad and she liked to play games at the kitchen table.

Jason turned and started down the hallway. A glance into the first bedroom: double bed, washed-out chenille bedcover. He walked to the second bedroom at the end of the hall and stepped inside. Pink everywhere: pink bedspread and pink canopy with blue and yellow flowers that looked hand embroidered, white dresser and small vanity, lamps with frilly pink shades. Everything else was gone. No stuffed animals or dolls or toys. The sliding door on the closet was open, the closet empty.

Jason was quiet for a long moment, taking it in. "They love her," he said as if he were talking to himself.

"They love her very much." The rest of the story, Vicky was thinking, would never be told: the man who loved her had arranged for her abduction.

"Then she's lucky. She has two families who love her." Jason backed out of the room, and Vicky followed: down the hall, across the living room, and into the warmth of the sunshine.

"I'll never stop looking for her." He swung about, as if he could preempt any questions she might ask. "The FBI is on their trail. They are looking in every state, watching flight and train reservations. I've hired my own investigators. I've found her now—God, it's been so long. I've come so close, so many times, but I've finally found her. I know who she is and I know who *they* are. Eventually . . . eventually I will bring her home to her real home with her own family. I will never stop."

"She's Arapaho," Vicky heard herself say.

"I know. She'll have to spend time with them. They love her and . . . she loves them. We'll work something out. Summers on the reservation." He threw out a hand and waved to the great, vacant spaces; the immense blue sky. Then he gave a little wave, walked over to the sedan, and got in.

The engine gunned and stuttered in the patches of snow, then the sedan bounced across the barrow ditch. Vicky watched it speed down the road, spitting out rocks and ice until it was a tiny dot in the distance, a black fleck in the sun.

36

THE FRONT DOOR flew open, followed by the thump of footsteps. Father John glimpsed the brown van outside the window as he got up from his desk. He turned into the corridor as Shannon swept past.

"My things!" In an instant, she took hold of the clipboard the deliveryman held out and scribbled on the page. "They're here," she said, swinging around as the man in the brown trousers and jacket let himself out. "I told you, Uncle John: I travel light. Two boxes. Hardly enough stuff to notice."

He offered to take the cartons to the guesthouse, but she gave a little wave and shook her head. "James is coming by in a little while. Another counseling session, not that it's doing much good." She shrugged her shoulders in the direction of the bishop's office down the corridor. "All that talking about what James really wants. I can tell you what he wants. He wants us to be together!"

"Then I'd say James and the bishop are making progress." Father John smiled. Who wouldn't love her? So open and unaffected, yet more settled than when she had arrived, deep into writing her dissertation, consumed with the stories of two sisters—one white, one Arapaho—and in love with James Two Horses.

Yes, James would take her cartons to the guesthouse. He would help her. He would look after her.

"I'm beginning to understand Lizzie." Shannon walked beside him along the corridor; they might have been strolling through the cottonwoods to the river on a sunny day. "It just came to me. You know how it is. You spend days and weeks and months living with someone in history, and you begin to understand what must have happened, how the person must have felt. You *know* the truth, even though it isn't spelled out in any historical record. But you know it."

They had passed the door to his office and were standing outside the storage closet he had set up for her. He could see the small desk wedged against the wall, layered with papers and folders, a scattering of pencils, pens, and paper clips, a coffee mug, the detritus of a dissertation. "Tell me about Lizzie," he said.

"Here's the thing, Uncle John. She wanted to go with her sister. She wanted to visit her own beginnings, see the home where she had lived, sit at the fireside where her parents had sat, walk the same grounds, gaze at the same stars. She wanted to touch that part of herself, but she was frightened."

"Frightened? Of Brokenhorn?"

"Oh, no." Shannon shook her head, as if the idea were absurd. "Brokenhorn loved her. He was devoted to her, and from what the descendants have said, he never mistreated her. He was proud of her, and yes, he worried the whites would take her away. He vowed never to let that happen. He even moved his family into the mountains at one time, where no one would find them. Yet Lizzie met with Amanda Mary, and I believe Brokenhorn approved, because he knew Lizzie was frightened. He knew she wouldn't leave him and the children, not even for a short visit."

Father John could feel the excitement rolling off the young red-haired woman beside him. It took him back to his own days as a graduate student, such excitement at finding something new, something no one else had ever realized, at comprehending. "You're saying Lizzie feared that if she went with her sister, she wouldn't be able to return."

"She wouldn't know how to return. Think of it: an Arapaho woman, living on the plains, riding a stagecoach to Casper and taking the train all the way to the Midwest. She wouldn't know how to get back. There wouldn't be any horse tracks on the plains for her to follow."

"Nevertheless, you believe she wanted to go?"

Shannon shrugged and pushed on, full of the wonder of it, the contradictions and pain in a woman dead more than a hundred years. "She was changed after meeting Amanda. The descendants say so. She insisted everyone call her by her white name, Lizzie, not Kellsto Time. She bragged to the other women that she had a home somewhere else, other people who loved her. When she went to Hollywood, she went with Brokenhorn and a trainload of Arapahos and Shoshones. She got to see the white world, but Hollywood wasn't where she had come from. She wouldn't have been frightened. She knew Brokenhorn would bring her home."

"Interesting theory." He felt like a teacher again, discussing a student's paper. "You'll need evidence."

"You know how it is. Truth has a way of coming out. You discover it first because you *know* it, and eventually the evidence catches up, proves you were right all along." She looked up a moment, studying the ceiling. "Daisy Blue Water has agreed to meet with me again. I think she likes remembering her grandmother. Who knows? Maybe she'll remember how her grandmother had wanted to go with

Amanda, but had been too scared." She gave him a wide smile. "Let's hope she remembers before I finish writing," she said.

Father John retraced his steps into his own office. The click-click of Shannon's computer started before he sat down at his desk. Another white girl, his own niece, falling in love with an Arapaho, living on the reservation, becoming Arapaho. He smiled at the idea. And James, who had thought he wanted to be a priest, wanted a life with her. James would conclude his counseling sessions, which would leave the bishop without a project. Yesterday, when he'd stopped in the office, he'd found the bishop reading a recipe book. The old man had glanced up, excitement in the watery blue eyes, and asked what Father John would think of pork ribs with plum chutney and roasted potatoes.

He had gotten a call later from a young couple thinking about getting married, circling around the pluses and minuses. He suggested they talk to the bishop, an expert at helping young people choose the path forward.

From outside came the thrum of tires on gravel and the steady roar of an engine. He swung around, went over to the window, and watched the tan SUV pull in beside his pickup—the car Vicky had rented while the Ford was being repaired. She was out in a flash, shoulders forward, making her way to the front steps. He met her in the corridor.

"I heard the good news a little while ago." He was ushering her into his study, taking her coat. He hung it on the back of the coat tree and told her that Betty had called. He could still hear the voice at the other end of the line, thick with relief and joy.

"Vince is in a treatment center in Rock Springs. He has a chance."

Father John nodded her to the chair, but he knew she wouldn't relax. She would travel around his office, pacing out her thoughts. They were traveling people, she had once told him, the Arapahos.

"Coffee?" The coffee he'd made that morning had gone stale; it would take only a few minutes to brew a fresh pot.

"Thank you." She gave him a smile. It surprised him, her acquiescence. It meant she would stay awhile; something else was on her mind.

He retrieved the glass pot from the table behind the door and carried it into the miniature kitchen off the corridor. On automatic, the same routine every morning and again during the day, depending upon his visitors. By the time he perched on the edge of the desk, watching Vicky stroll about, the smell of fresh coffee filled the office.

"Let me," Vicky said. And she was behind the door, pouring two mugs, stirring powdered milk into one, which she brought over to him. "I just met with Jason Becket."

He sipped at the hot liquid and waited. She had told him earlier about the FBI investigation and the preponderance of evidence that a man in Denver named Jason Becket was the father of Mary Ann Little Shield. He remembered the cascade of emotions that had washed over him: a father about to find his child; a couple about to lose theirs. It hadn't surprised him that the Little Shields had disappeared; wasn't that what Brokenhorn had done when he thought the whites might take Lizzie? Disappeared into the mountains? The moccasin telegraph had the news before Vicky had called to tell him it was true.

"How is he?"

"Devastated." Vicky stopped at the window, looked out, and sipped her coffee. "To come so close! It must be like losing her all over again."

So close. In his mind was the image of Daisy Blue Water recounting an old sorrow. Amanda had come so close to finding her sister only to lose her.

"He'll never stop looking." Vicky turned toward him. "The world is a small place today. So much media. It's difficult to hide. Still, it could take time. Mary Ann may be grown up before he finds her."

"She may find him."

Vicky smiled at him again, and he knew she'd had the same thought. "One day she'll look into the mirror and see blond hair and light eyes and say, *Who am I? Where did I come from?* And Jason Becket will be waiting."

She started pacing again—the door, the chairs, the window, and back again—something else on her mind, working out the best way to bring it up. He waited, and after another tour about the office, she stopped. "Is it true, John?"

He knew exactly what she meant. "It's a rumor." He tried to shrug it off, a nuisance. "There are always rumors." He dipped his head toward the corridor lined with framed photos of the earliest Jesuits at St. Francis Mission, his predecessors, strong and courageous and faithful men he had tried to emulate. "I suspect they heard the same rumors in their time. The Jesuits are always worried about having enough priests, enough money for their missions."

"Is it true?"

Vicky would not be put off; he could not cajole her, pretend it was nothing to worry about, the way he had been pretending to himself. He pushed off the desk and went to the window. The afternoon sun flared over the mission grounds, a spring sun, pale yellow, not yet in full control of its powers. Walks-On was asleep in front of the residence.

He turned around, facing her. "I believe, this time, it's true."

"Which means you will leave." The words hung like a heavy weight between them. "The people need you here. I need you. How can you leave?"

Father John looked back out the window. It was the question he had been wrestling with in the middle of the night. How could he leave? Oh, the actual leaving, the physical part, would be easy. Packing up—a couple of cartons, smaller than those that contained Shannon's belongings; The O'Malley's traveled light. Mostly books and CDs, his old CD player, a change of clothes, an extra pair of boots, Walks-On's bed. He could pack in thirty minutes, drive around Circle Drive and through the cottonwood tunnel the last time, Walks-On seated beside him, staring out the window, never dreaming they wouldn't be home by dark. The easy part he could do. He wasn't sure how he could do the hard part, and he knew, when he looked around at Vicky, that she understood.

He perched again on the desk. "You know," he said, trying to make sense of it in his own mind, the story he had told himself in the middle of the night, "whatever time we get with the people we love is precious, no matter how long it is. Fifty years, twenty-five, ten." He had been at St. Francis a little more than ten years now. "A slice of precious time that belongs to us for a while, and then is gone. We are always going. All of us."

Vicky took her time finishing her coffee, then she set the mug on the table behind her and turned toward him. Pinpricks of light danced in her eyes. "I'm not one of your parishioners you can cajole with your logic and your philosophy. I don't care about slices of time. I don't care how precious it is. When it's over, it's over. What is important is now. It's all we have."

"Then we have what matters, Vicky. We have the present. Nothing will happen overnight. Closing a mission takes time, and this is a bureaucracy we're talking about. Bureaucracies move at glacial speed. I've learned not to worry—I've told myself: wait until you know whether you have something to worry about. We're here now, in the present."

"Waiting," she said.

"Yes, in the present."

AUTHOR'S NOTE

The story of Elizabeth "Lizzie" Brokenhorn, her captivity and subsequent life as an Arapaho on the Wind River Reservation, is based on historical records. We know that Amanda Mary Fletcher Cook spent thirty-seven years trying to find her sister, that they were briefly reunited in 1902, and that Lizzie was deeply affected by the reunion and by learning of her background. Still she chose to remain with her husband and children and to live out the only life she had known. The records are also clear that John Brokenhorn was a good husband who cared for his wife, worried that white authorities would take her away, and tried to protect her.

But records are thin on how Lizzie might have felt about her situation—what Shannon calls "the outside of history." While actual descendants of Lizzie and John Brokenhorn no doubt exist, the descendants you meet in this story are fictional. The stories they relate about Lizzie's day-to-day life are not found in the historical records about Lizzie but are consistent with the life of a traditional Arapaho woman in Lizzie's time.

Did Lizzie Brokenhorn actually butcher cattle, make fry bread, attend to the dancers at the Sun Dance, look after the grandchildren, as the fictional descendants relate? As Shannon would say, it might not be in the historical records, but we know it is true.

Ready to find
your next great read?

Let us help.

Visit prh.com/nextread